HIGH PRAISE FOR
R.D. ZIMMERMAN
and *CLOSET*

"TIGHTLY PLOTTED AND FULL OF SURPRISES FROM THE BEGINNING." —*The FocusPoint Insider*

"*CLOSET* HAS PASSION AND POIGNANCY, POTENT PAIN AND A POWERFUL PLOT."
—*Minneapolis Star Tribune*

"The real test of a detective or mystery novel is its ability to hold the reader's interest and keep those pages turning. Zimmerman succeeds at this quite well." —*TriCity Herald*

"EXCELLENT . . . A fast-paced murder mystery."
—*The Book Report*

"ZIMMERMAN'S WRITING IS TOO BREATHLESS TO LEAVE YOU DISCONTENTED." —*Kirkus Reviews*

"R.D. ZIMMERMAN IS A WONDERFUL WRITER OF SUSPENSE and surely the most original storyteller of the genre."
—Sharyn McCrumb, author of *If I'd Killed Him When I Met Him*

R.D. Zimmerman is one of the best of the new generation of thriller writers who use the form to entertain and enlighten us on the highest level."
—Roger L. Simon, creator of the Moses Wine series

CLOSET

R.D. ZIMMERMAN

Delta
Trade Paperbacks

A Delta Book
Published by
Dell Publishing
a division of
Bantam Doubleday Dell Publishing Group, Inc.
1540 Broadway
New York, New York 10036

ISBN: 0-385-32004-3

Manufactured in the United States of America
Published simultaneously in Canada

November 1997

10 9 8 7 6 5 4 3 2 1

BVG

ACKNOWLEDGMENTS

Crossing a bridge is never easy, and I'd like to
offer my thanks to the following who helped
along the way:

My dear friend, Pat, for her encouragement, wisdom, and
gossip. Dr. Don Houge for another of his wonderful hypnosis
tapes, which helped every writing day. Special Agent Ray
DiPrima for his advice and knowledge of criminal matters.
Leslie Schnur, without whom I'd be dead in the water, and
Steve Ross with his keen editor's eye. And of course Lars,
who has been and will always be there.

1

When he saw through the windshield that the house lights
were on, his skin prickled and he started trembling in nervous anticipation. This was the night, he thought, gripping
the steering wheel so tightly that for a moment he wondered
if it would snap off. From the darkness of his car he watched
the figure move from one room to another, and he knew that
at last he would have Michael to himself. Tonight was finally
the night; there would be no interruption.

He drove his light gray car around the block and returned a
second time, slowing slightly but again not stopping. Not
there, not in front of the large stucco duplex. This was Kenwood, the fanciest neighborhood in Minneapolis. The largest
homes were here, huge old things scattered around Lake of
the Isles, which lay just two blocks west. If he stopped he
might be seen; a gossipy neighbor in this exclusive, quiet,
and protective area might be watching. So he kept moving,
his eyes trained on the building. There were just a couple of
lights on downstairs, while the upper apartment was entirely
black. Tonight was indeed the night he'd been waiting for.

He parked around the corner, carefully pulling his car into

a pool of darkness. He took a deep breath, felt his heart churning wildly, then released the steering wheel from his death grip and looked at his hands. Shit, he thought, examining his palms, noting the perspiration glistening even in this stingy light. This would be the first time, the first one. Why shouldn't he be nervous as hell? Not long ago he'd realized he had no other choice, that this was the next step in his life, as inevitable as the next breath and the one after that. But he still hadn't believed he was really going to go through with it. Not until now. There was no other step, no shirking the need, and he felt a rush of excitement meld with a rich sense of fear.

He zipped up his brown leather coat, pulled on a pair of gloves as well as a dark wool cap, and studied the street. There were no joggers coming to or from the lake, no one huffing and puffing through this mid-October air. No one walking a dog. Which was all as it should be, not a soul to see him. He climbed out of the car, gently pressing the door shut, and then hurried to the sidewalk, where he moved along, his head hung. At the alley he took a left.

And then stopped.

Quickly, he pressed himself against a mass of tall lilacs, their spindly, leafless branches spearing his side. Down by the third garage a gray-haired woman bundled up in a coat was dragging a green bin to the edge of the alley. She was putting out her recycling, he realized. She flipped back the lid, disappeared for a moment, and returned with a grocery sack of glass, which she noisily shoved into the container. She next rolled her large brown garbage container to the edge of the alley, caught her breath, and then was gone. He heard the sound of a back door opening and closing. Still he did not move, not until the woman flicked off the floodlight perched under the eaves of her garage.

When it was dark and all was quiet again, he pressed on. As he neared the woman's garage and the recycling bin, though, he did slow, checking the lights to be sure there were no motion detectors. He scurried on, realizing that, Jesus Christ, he'd never thought he'd be so . . . so excited.

He came around the back of Michael's blue Volvo sedan, glimmering starlike on the concrete pad behind the duplex. His breath steaming, the man checked the second floor apartment again, and again saw no sign of life. But there was downstairs. Yes. There was Michael in the kitchen window, tall and lanky, his short dark hair receding. That handsome face—brown eyes, slender cheeks—that could light up a room with laughter. And the dark, thick mustache, which had been his trademark for years and years. He knew him all too well.

Hurrying to the rear door, the visitor was about to press the doorbell when he saw the naked bulb affixed to the side of the house. The man reached up with his gloved hand, turned it once, twice. Then he rang. It was an old kind of doorbell, shrill and loud, the hammering kind that made you jump in fright. When it was quiet again, there was a new kind of hush. He heard a sink suddenly quieted, the rush of water cut midstream. Next, steps. But they were going away, it seemed. Was Michael going to the front door?

The man banged on the rear door, his fist thick and hard, hesitated, then hammered again. Soon he could tell Michael was rushing this way, through the kitchen. A door was pulled open, a shaft of light cutting into the back hall. Peering through a pane of glass in the door, he saw Michael's figure move down a couple of back steps, pause. Michael groped for a switch, which he flicked three times to no avail. Grumbling about that damn back-door light, Michael came right up to the door and peered out, hesitant, for although this was Minneapolis, it wasn't as safe as it had once been.

He called, "Who is it?"

"It's me, Michael."

His surprise was evident, for it took a moment to register. "What? You're kidding." He fumbled with a lock, turned it, started to yank back the heavy door, then pushed the storm.

"Why are you back here? You know, I have a very nice front door."

"I know, I know. But I . . . I was just around the corner and . . . and . . ."

Michael was still dressed in remnants of work clothes, a white shirt that was wrinkled after a day at the office, a loosened tie with the top button pulled open, the dark navy pants of a suit. The man slipped past Michael, entering through the back door that Michael graciously held open. And now that he was in, now that he was within a mere few inches of Michael, his heart seemed to be thumping so loudly that he could hear it. Standing in that dank back hall, the stairs leading down and down into some black hole of a basement, he leaned against a wall, suddenly ashamed.

"Michael, I need to talk to you."

"Of course, come on in."

"I mean, I . . ." He stared at him in the faint light of the back stairs, reached out, touched the sleeve of Michael's white shirt. "We've got a lot to talk about, obviously. No one else is home, is there?"

Michael froze as he gazed down on the hand on his arm, and clearly he sensed his guest's desperate tone, his shifting eyes, his pain, and even that pressing desire. There was a glint of panic too. Of course Michael understood.

The man continued, saying, "There's something I have to tell you. Something about me."

"Oh, God, this isn't about what I think it is, is it?" asked Michael, his voice quivering a tad.

He nodded.

"No shit," said Michael, his discomfort obvious. "I thought you were looking at me a little strange last week. Come on in. You want to tell me all about it?"

"Sure."

The man followed Michael up the short steps, through the back door, into the kitchen, a boxy room with old cabinets covered in thick, dingy yellow paint. A bright fluorescent bulb hung in the middle of the room, and the man squinted, kept moving. Not toward the living room, he thought. Too open. So he kept going, moving toward the second door, the one that opened into the dark hallway, which in turn led to the bedrooms.

Still wearing his leather coat, the man stopped there, in that hallway, and slumped dramatically against the wall, muttering, "I'm upset. My life's a mess. Totally. And this is especially hard for me."

Michael hesitated in the doorway, his tall frame outlined by the stark kitchen light behind him. "You know what? I think I'm shocked. I've heard a lot of dirt in my life but . . . but I'm still shocked. Has the whole world gone queer?"

"Will you come here?" He took a deep breath, struggling to add, "Will you hold me?"

Michael's guest held out his right hand, which was still gloved, and Michael came forward. They hesitated, both of the men in that hallway, and then Michael, the taller of the two as well as the vastly more experienced in these matters, reached forward, wrapped his arms around the other, and took him slowly, warmly in his arms. But Michael's tight embrace was a friendly one, a hug that was meant to soothe and comfort, for Michael had always had a generous soul. He'd been through this a number of times, had helped any number of men out of that closet of shame.

"Michael, I . . . I . . . ." The man reached up between them, felt the thickness of Michael's chest now pressing against him, and shuddered. "Let me take off my coat."

"Sure." Michael patted him gently and pulled away. "You want a glass of wine? Let's go in the living room. You can just start talking. Trust me, you can tell me everything. I have no judgments. Like I said, I've heard it all. Come on."

"No." Desperately, the man clutched Michael by the arm, held him right there in that back hall. "I want . . . want you."

Michael couldn't hide his surprise, and his eyes opened wide. "Now, just think about it. I don't think we really—"

"You don't understand."

And to make things absolutely clear, the man reached into his leather jacket, felt for a long hard object, and quickly pulled it from his pocket. It was a knife, quite long, quite thick. An altogether sharp tool used for carving meat.

"Holy shit," exclaimed Michael at the sight of the glinting weapon. "You don't have to get kinky on me."

"Just take off your clothes."

"You've got to be kidding," he said, a scared, nervous laugh bursting from his mouth. And then, when he realized how dangerous the situation really was, he blurted, "What the fuck are you talking about?"

Michael tried to pull away, but the man grabbed him and pressed the knife much too hard against Michael's belly, ordering, "First the tie, then the shirt."

2

In a dimly lit parking lot along Highway 494—the Strip, as it had been known since its heyday back in the disco seventies—Todd Mills stood next to his dark green Grand Cherokee. Frozen in place, he stared up at the bright lights of a billboard. It was a faceless area, well beyond the edge of Minneapolis, with fast-food restaurants and car dealerships and strip malls lined up along the broad ribbon of concrete. Yet the face that Todd Mills was focused on, the one blown up to superhuman size and pictured in the spotlighted billboard above the highway, was extraordinarily familiar. It was a photo of a man, early forties, light brown hair, with a handsome smile and a noticeably square jaw. A face Todd saw not only on billboards but in print ads, on television, and even in the bathroom mirror as he shaved each morning.

He should have been beaming with smug pride. He was famous, at least in the Upper Midwest, and in town it seemed that everyone knew his name and face. Particularly now, not even a month after the awards, as reiterated by the words beneath the enormous photo: CHANNEL 7 SALUTES OUR GUY, INVESTIGATIVE REPORTER TODD MILLS, WINNER OF TWO EMMYS!

This was his time in the stars, yet now that he had attained what he'd worked so hard for, he feared the old maxim was proving true—be careful of what you wish for—because this was going to make his life infinitely more complicated. If he could have gone back and done his career all over again, he would have done it quite differently. Why hadn't he seen until now how much he was screwing up along the way? Why hadn't he understood how difficult winning the Emmys was going to make things?

He took his beeper from the pocket of his dark blue wool sport coat and flicked it off, which was decidedly against policy—but he didn't care, not tonight. He was the lead re-porter on the CrimeEye team, and the whole angle was to not report on a crime that had already taken place, but if at all possible to get there while the crime was actually taking place. The idea had caught on, too, in a big way. Angry citizens, frustrated that the police and the law just couldn't do enough, had begun to call the CrimeEye number—WIT-NESS—in the hopes that a theft or a murder could be cap-tured live by Channel 7's cameras. It was a good idea that proved more than just interesting or shocking: People were finding the show not only titillating but empowering. It was providing them with a means to do something about the crime that was rampaging through their neighborhoods. While Todd and his crew had gone on many wild goose chases, they had also provided footage of crimes that had led to nine convictions, two of which had earned Todd his Em-mys.

So he should have had the beeper on, but he just couldn't do it this evening, couldn't go to some suburban apartment complex or some inner-city corner and try to dig up some dirt. Right now his own life was fucked up enough. As he stuffed the deactivated pager back into his pocket, he won-dered if he hadn't lost it, that compulsive hunger to scoop a story. This past week it had felt as if it were gone forever. He shook his head, knowing in his gut that winning the Emmys was forcing him to confront a decision he'd dreaded, a decision that could mean the end of his career on television. But if he couldn't do any broadcast work, what would he do with his life?

He strolled across the parking lot, his breath steaming in the night air. The weight of so many years of deceit hung on his back, and he made his way into a chain restaurant where a syrupy hostess greeted him.

"Good evening, sir. And how are you this evening?"

"I'll take the booth in the far corner," he replied.

"Oh, sure."

She looked at him strangely, as if she couldn't quite place how or where she knew him, and led him through the crowded restaurant to the distant end. With a broad, white smile, she handed him a plastic-coated menu and sweetly told him his server would be with him in a moment.

"Enjoy your meal," she said, her gaze lingering a moment too long.

As was happening more and more, Todd noted a few heads turned his way, so he sat with his back to the main part of the restaurant. He had way too much on his mind to be civil.

Except when he was sent out here to do a story, he avoided this part of town, which distinguished itself from the freeways of Chicago or Dallas only by the intensity of the winter cold. Tonight, though, he'd finished a story hours ahead of schedule, yet couldn't bear to go home. He was so confused that he just couldn't make himself return to the empty place, so he kept going and going, driving on and wanting to get away, to flee from himself and this world he'd so carefully constructed over the past twenty-plus years. He'd cranked up the radio, gotten on some freeway, and somehow ended up out here, an impersonal land of concrete and mindless shopping malls.

Turning around, he scanned the restaurant in search of a waitress. Beyond the red vinyl booths he saw the hostess and a couple of waitresses huddled and talking. One of them looked at him, said something to the others, and started in his direction. Todd glanced quickly at his menu, wondering at the same time if they'd been back there talking about him.

"Good evening, sir," said the waitress, a young blond woman with too much enthusiasm.

"Hi. I'd like—"

"How are you this evening?"

"Fine, thank you."

"Tonight's special is—"

"Just a bowl of chili and coffee, please."

"Regular or decaf?"

If he were a born-and-bred Minnesotan he would have had the real stuff, but he wasn't. "Decaf."

"Oh, sure." She hesitated, seemed as if she were about to say something else, then scurried off.

Todd leaned forward, bowed his head into his hands, and contemplated not only what he'd been doing all his life but what had gotten him into this predicament in the first place. Ever since he'd gone into broadcast journalism—he'd taken his first job at a public television station in Peoria, Illinois, just two weeks after getting his degree from Northwestern University—he'd had but one agenda: the top. And all along he'd done everything that it took to get there, from going to the gym three times a week to recently dyeing his graying hair to being there, front and ready, for any story at any time of day, no matter if it was only a cat in distress. His former wife had said his ambition was what caused their divorce, but of course that hadn't been the case.

The waitress reappeared, placing a cup and a Thermos pitcher in front of him. She smiled, took a couple of creamers from a pouch tied around her waist, and slid them across the table.

"Say," she started, "aren't you . . ."

Her words trailed off as she nodded out the window. He glanced to his left, looked past the parking lot at that frigging billboard.

"Yeah, that's me."

She giggled, blushed, and said, "Oh, that's what we thought, the other girls and me. Gee, I've seen you on the TV too. Cool. I don't think there's ever been a celebrity in here before."

"Oh."

Such notoriety and adoration was all he'd wanted before, but now he understood what one worn-out television personality had once told him. Buddy, he'd said, the difference between being famous and not is the difference between making a conversation and having one. And he'd been totally right, Todd realized, for there was no way he could tell this young woman to hush up and get him his food.

The waitress hovered, asking, "Like, are you out here to do some exposé or something?" She glanced around nervously. "Wow, like, the television crew isn't going to burst through the doors and start filming a crime or something, is it? There really isn't much going on here. Our kitchen's really clean too. The health inspector was just here. I mean, he even ate here. And he paid. I took his money." Her eyes opened wide. "Oh, my God, like, you don't think we're about to be robbed or anything, do you?"

"No, not at all. I'm not here to do a story." He caught his breath, clenched his jaw, and as politely as he could at this particular time said, "I'm just here to have a nice, quiet meal."

"Well, then, did you just come from something? You do a lot of the murder stuff, don't you? Was there another murder? Someone said there was a shooting out at the megamall again."

"No, not that I know of." Unable to keep up any pretense, his smile vanished.

"God, it's so cool that you're here and I'm waiting on you."

"You don't suppose my order's ready, do you?"

"What?"

"Would you get my chili?"

"Oh, your chili. Oh, sure," she said, turning and practically bouncing off.

He turned away, gazed outside at the huge image of himself. What had he been hoping? What had he wanted out of life? He'd been in therapy for over a year now, discussing every aspect of his childhood in a Polish neighborhood in Chicago, and his shrink was right. He didn't seek simply mass appeal, but mass approval. That was his secret fuel, the one that kept him going when things looked beyond hopeless. Then again, hadn't his father, a one-time medical student who'd emigrated to America after World War II and ended up a laborer in an automobile parts plant, also sought such a thing? Of course, that was where Todd had learned it. It was his father, after all, who'd changed the family name from Milkowski to Mills. It was his dad who had pushed Todd as well. Pushed and pushed, criticizing Todd when his grades weren't at the top, chastising him when he flubbed on the football team, and telling Todd whenever he simply wasn't good enough, for he'd been certain his boy Todd was to be the family hero, soaring to the highest heights in the New World.

Well, even though his dad had died four years ago, Todd had made it to those heights. Yesterday Stella, his agent, had called, informing him of what Todd already knew: Channel 7 was not just thrilled with Todd Mills, they were in love with him. And Todd Mills wasn't going merely to the top of Channel 7, he was going all the way. Big time. The nationals would take notice of him now, said Stella with complete conviction. The snowball had started rolling when Todd was nominated for the Emmys, then barreled along when he'd won them both, one for the report on the cop killing, the other for the story on that murdered kid. So now Channel 7 was about to offer him the anchor position, the one that would be opening up on the 6:00 P.M. news. He'd already filled in several times, proved that he could handle it with aplomb, so when the fabled Dave Ness, who'd already been anchor for a generation, retired, Todd Mills would step in and fill the legend. An announcement was to be made by the end of the week, and a publicity party was already in the works. A year or two there, Stella said, and then he'd be on his way. No CNN for you, she had said. Doll, you're going all the way—CBS, NBC, ABC, what's the diff.

Shit, thought Todd as he waited for that bowl of chili, how could he be so dumb? How could they? He'd hidden so long behind the word *divorced,* played up that image of the dashing jock reporter, his beautiful friend Janice Gray, a high-powered attorney, always on his arm, that he'd caught himself in a trap of his own making. He had to tell them now, blurt it out to his boss at the station. It wasn't too late. Not in the grand scheme of things.

Todd eyed the waitress, who was coming toward him with a beaming grin and a steaming bowl. Suddenly he knew he wouldn't be able to eat. In a burst of resolution he scooted out of the booth, took ten bucks, and slapped it down on the table. For the first time in his life he knew what he had to do, saw it before him with astonishing clarity. There it was, right in front of him, the cloud of fear finally lifting and exposing the answer.

There was still time to fix things. Absolutely. Last night they'd had a terrible fight. Last night he'd been certain that there was no other recourse but to break it off. But that wasn't right. Of course not. Love was love. And full of a giddy kind of excitement, he rushed out of the restaurant, surprisingly eager not only to apologize to Michael Carter, his secret lover of four years now, but to let Michael know that he was ready to come out of the closet. There was no other choice, none at all. Tonight he'd make up with Michael, and tomorrow he was going to tell Channel 7 that he, Todd Mills, was queer, queer, queer.

3

Just past nine that night one of the phones in the control room at Channel 7 started ringing, its shrill sound going on for nearly a minute. Finally, Brad Lewis, a young, red-haired technician who worked as the switcher, gave a good solid push with his feet and his four-wheeled chair went flying across the room.

Scooping up the receiver, Brad said, "Yo, control room."

The line was quiet until a low voice said, "Go to 1603 West 23rd Street."

Brad, who was gearing up for the 10:00 P.M. news, set down his Mountain Dew, which he'd been drinking nonstop for several hours. Immediately he started searching around the control panel for a pen. He found an old Bic, but there wasn't any paper, and he started mumbling, for he hated it when outside calls were somehow routed through the control room. What was he, a receptionist?

He gave up on finding something to write on, and said, "Say what?"

"Go to 1603 West 23rd Street." The voice paused. "Someone's been killed."

Something within him tightened, sensing this was no prankster. He caught his breath. Damn it, what had they said at that meeting? In a saving moment, it all came back. Yes, he thought, his heart shot with an exhilarating fear. He knew what to do, for with the success of CrimeEye they'd all been warned. He hesitated as he wondered why anyone at the front desk hadn't caught this one.

Finally he scribbled the address on the palm of his hand and blurted, "I'm going to connect you to the CrimeEye line." When there was only heavy breathing in reply, Brad added, "Don't hang up."

He punched the hold button, dropped the receiver. Oh, shit, he thought, staring at the phone. Holy shit. He was a consummate switcher—he operated the control panel and would follow the news director's every command, switching from camera one to camera two to camera three, doing dissolves and fade-ups. But he regularly fucked up on the phone. Just last week he disconnected the phone twice. And something told him this time that he couldn't screw up. Pushing back his chair, he leapt to his feet, bolted out of the newsroom, and ran across the set of the 10:00 P.M. news.

Cindy Wilson was sitting in the CrimeEye office, quite bored and thinking about Todd Mills, hoping his time had come. She'd recently heard the rumor that he was to be promoted to the evening news, which would be fantastic, for that could only mean great things for her. Todd was the lead reporter on the CrimeEye team, and he always made sure he got the best stories. So if he was gone, didn't she have a reasonable shot at promotion? Hell, yes. In fact, they almost *had* to move her up into the lead position; otherwise she'd cry foul, loud and clear. Todd had been in on the initial planning of the show and he'd launched it, but after the first four months she'd been brought in for political reasons.

Although it was never stated forthrightly, the producers and management at Channel 7 needed a woman—not to mention an attractive, blond woman such as Cindy—on the CrimeEye team to present a more balanced and up-to-date approach in the male-dominated world of crime reporting. It wouldn't do to have cries of sexism. Absolutely not. So she was hired with a due amount of fanfare and was used often enough, although rarely on any of the violent, gory stories. She knew she was being used to rope in female viewership— or had she yet again been cast as the bimbo to lure the male audience?—but she was using the situation as well, reporting fairly and making a good living. And now that Todd was moving up, so would she, Cindy assumed. She'd have to work like hell, which she most certainly could, and as lead reporter on the CrimeEye team she hoped to God she'd earn herself at least one Emmy. Then her career would blast off just like Todd's.

She glanced at the clock, yawned, and stared at the phone, willing it to ring. Either Todd or she was always at the station until midnight, because, of course, the dark hours were the witching ones. Tonight was awfully quiet, not like a Thursday, Friday, or Saturday night, especially when the bars closed. Last month when everything was shutting down for the night she'd been called to the scene of a fight in a parking lot next to a biker bar.

She reached into her desk drawer, pulled out a copy of *Vogue*. They should have an answering service for taking these calls, thought Cindy. They'd talked about that. Someone at a special switchboard twenty-four hours a day. Then one of them could be on call at home. She and Todd both lived in the city. It didn't take them long to get anywhere, particularly since they lived in different neighborhoods. Or forget that, she thought. They could be outfitted with cellular phones. That way they wouldn't have to be so tied to—

Her office door exploded open, and one of the switchers from the control room came charging in.

"Line three!" he shouted.

She saw his reddened face, heard his desperation, and

knew this was a live one. And instinctively Cindy Wilson was calm, which was her best quality as a television journalist. She didn't overreact, didn't get nervous. No, in a tense or demanding situation something else within her kicked in. Control. Her baby brother had suffered severely from Down syndrome, finally dying from an enlarged heart at age seventeen. Yet dear, sweet Eddie hadn't been the hard one to deal with. No, it had been his and Cindy's mother, who alternated between hysteria and depression, so distressed was she by the child she had borne. And with Cindy's father absent more often than not, it had been Cindy herself who had kept the household on track. So whatever this now was, whoever was calling, she'd handle it. Hell, yes. That inner strength clicked on, that one that told her she was going somewhere, right to the top.

She reached for the phone, took the receiver, and saw the tape machine automatically kick on, not only for accuracy but also for legal protection. She cleared her throat, for she'd learned long ago that whoever was calmest usually was victorious. That, and the tape of this emergency call might be used in the report. And she was damn sure going to come across as the ace reporter. A woman who could handle it all.

But when she went to press line three, there was no light. Her heart quivered with a ping of electricity, for she saw that in fact none of the lines was lit. Fearing they'd lost this one, she quickly punched the button for the third line, pressed the receiver close to her ear.

"Hello?" she demanded. "Hello? This is the CrimeEye line. Is . . ."

Nothing. Only the drone of a dial tone. Like a speed typist, she hit the next button. Then the next. Moving all across the phone, all through the lines.

"Shit," she gasped, looking up at the red-headed Brad. "There's no one there. They hung up."

"Oh, man. Oh, no."

She saw the panic in Brad's face and knew it had been a hot one.

Cindy kept her voice even and steady, and asked, "What did they say?"

"I . . . I was in there. In the control room. And the phone rang. I mean, I just thought it was a normal call for someone and—"

"Brad, what did they say?"

"Someone was killed."

A murder. They were the best, really juiced up the viewership. And he'd lost the damn call. She bit her bottom lip, clenched a fist in her lap. It wouldn't do any good to get mad at Brad. Not until she'd gotten as much out of him as possible.

"Who was it, a man or a woman?" demanded Cindy.

"A . . . a . . ." Brad jammed a hand into his hair, looked up with a sudden shot of fear. "Fuck, I don't know. It was just a deep voice. I thought it was a man, but I don't know. It could have been a woman, you know, someone with a smoky voice. But I don't know. I don't. I mean, I'm not sure."

"Well, what did they say? Think real carefully. Just calm down. You picked up the phone and . . . and . . ."

"I picked it up and . . . and they said someone was killed."

"Just like that? Did they say where? Did they say anything else, like where it happened or where they were calling from?"

Brad froze. He took his hand from his hair, dropped the hand, opened it. And stared into his palm.

Finally he looked up at Cindy and muttered, "From 1603 23rd Street."

"Perfect," she said, her face blooming into a broad smile. "What else?"

"No, nothing. Just 1603 23rd Street, someone's been

killed. Wait, I think they said west. Right, 1603 West 23rd Street.''

''No, shit. West? You're sure of that?''

''Yeah.''

That would be Kenwood. A murder in Kenwood was big time.

''This is hot, way hot.'' Quickly reaching for the phone, Cindy glanced up at Brad, who just stood there, not sure what to do, and she snapped, ''Go on, get Mark! He's still around somewhere. Tell him to get his camera. The van's in the back. Just don't stand there, we've got a murder!''

Brad bolted from the doorway. ''Right.''

Hesitantly, she added, ''And get someone to page Todd!''

''Sure.''

''Hurry, I want to try and get there before the police!''

She knew the procedure all too well. They had it all planned out. It was always tempting not to call the police until they were already at the scene. But the lawyers wouldn't have it. Nor the producers. If they obstructed anything or delayed the police even for one instant, they could get their asses sued backward and forward. So she cleared her voice. Steadied herself. Damn, but she loved this, getting a hot one before the police. And she was sure she was getting it first. Why else the odd phone call and the hang up? Maybe it was even the murderer. That would be only too great.

As she dialed 911, she looked over, saw the tape recorder click on, and knew they'd probably be using this in the report. She thought of calling in her cameraman, Mark, and getting him to film her while she was on the phone. But they could do that later, reenact her picking up the phone and calling the cops. That could be the lead-in for the story. And they could do a voice-over of the actual recording of her phoning in the murder.

When the emergency operator picked up, Cindy reported, ''Hello, this is Cindy Wilson from the Channel Seven CrimeEye team.'' She sounded professional, trustworthy, and exactly what white Middle America wanted on their late news. "We've just received an emergency call from the city's blue-heeled Kenwood area. We have a report of a murder at 1603 West 23rd Street. Are you aware of the crime?"

The operator coolly replied, "That's not information I'm allowed to give out. Let me repeat the address you gave me."

Cindy listened and replied, "That's correct." Then for drama she tossed in, "The CrimeEye team is on the way. We'll meet and assist the police at the scene of the crime."

With a big grin, she hung up. Kenwood was just to the south of downtown, not even a mile from Channel 7's studios. She and Mark could be there in just over five minutes, what with the flashing lights of their van and all. And if her luck still held out, they wouldn't be able to reach Todd.

Holy shit, thought Cindy as she grabbed her tan raincoat. West 23rd Street. That couldn't be more than a block from Walter Mondale's. She'd have to bring that up. Maybe as they sped into the neighborhood she'd have Mark get a shot of the house. Or was he off in Japan now? Well, no need to mention that. Hopefully one of his kids would be there and the place would be lit up. Murder was creeping into the Lake District.

Brad popped back into Cindy's office, all flushed and hyper, blurting, "Mark's grabbing his camera and they're paging Todd."

"Great." Cindy buttoned up her coat and coolly moved around the edge of her desk, knowing she'd have to do her hair and makeup in the van. "Now get back to the newsroom. I'll call as soon as we arrive."

"Right."

Brad darted down the hall, and Cindy quickly moved out of her office, down the long, straight hall that was flooded by stark fluorescents. The camera guy, Mark Buchanan, short and slightly heavy, popped out of another corridor, a camera in hand, an eager smile on his round face.

"No reply from Todd yet," he said. "He's supposed to be in town tonight, so he should be calling in any moment."

"Let's go. He'll have to meet us there."

Maybe he was off celebrating his promotion. She prayed he was across the Mississippi in Saint Paul, having a leisurely dinner or maybe even getting drunk. So just maybe he'd let her have this one after all. Todd was a reasonable sort, and on the eve of his promotion she needed to look good. He'd certainly understand that. Yes, she said to herself, this blond chick from the original dysfunctional family wants this story. Wants it bad. A murder in the richest part of the cities. Kenwood. The Lake District. How great.

As she and Mark darted through the maze of hallways and toward the small parking lot at the rear of the building, Cindy Wilson checked her watch. Right on. The 10:00 P.M. news was fast approaching. What incredible timing. There could be nothing better for her image and career than reporting live from the scene of a hot crime.

4

Now that he had reached a resolution, Todd was extraordinarily anxious to return to Michael's. He felt a burning need to apologize for his behavior and to share with Michael his new clarity, his resolve.

Steering his dark green Cherokee out of the parking lot of that restaurant, Todd headed down the ramp, onto the straight freeway. Jesus Christ, he had so much to say to Michael, so much to rehash and try to make sense of. Ever since his first same-sex feelings stirred—he'd been thirteen when he'd seen that grinning kid at the pool, Dan What'shisname, with the powerful body and the charming grin—there'd been a war waging in Todd's soul. But now at last the battle was over, for no matter how much he wanted to change, no matter how much he felt he should and had to be straight, he just couldn't be. The real him had won out. The truth was victorious.

Yet while the war may have ended, he knew there would be scars. Last night's decisive fight was the worst.

God, Michael and he had fought, but never like that, not physically. And Todd saw how it was all his fault. All of it.

The rage and frustration had just come barreling out of him. After work yesterday Todd had come home to Michael's— even though Todd owned a condo overlooking Lake Calhoun, he'd been staying at Michael's most nights for almost two years and it was home, their home—and told Michael about the promotion. Somewhere Todd had known that it was all wrong, but the job was a huge step forward, one that would carry him to the top, make him rich and famous, and that was fabulous, wasn't it? Todd Mills, an anchor on the evening news. The top Minneapolis station. It was only a matter of time before he went soaring to one of the national networks. His father, the Polish immigrant, would have been smug, muttering how the Milkowskis were the best and of course Todd should rise to the very highest point.

Michael was far wiser than Todd though. He immediately saw all the ramifications, knew at once what this meant for their relationship. Todd had come home, champagne bottle in hand, wearing his lucky Cubs hat—the real fitted model the pros wore, with the dark blue wool cap and red wool visor— and found Michael in that dingy kitchen, his tie still on and starting dinner, a chicken dish. Michael had been peeling carrots and had only smiled weakly at Todd's news. Setting down the peeler and a half-cleaned carrot, Michael had then drifted into the living room, where he slumped, head in hands, on the big black leather couch, the one they'd picked out just last month. Instead of beaming with pride for Todd, instead of toasting him, Michael had looked right at him and said that was all fine and well, but enough was enough.

"I just can't take it anymore," he'd said.

"What? What does that mean?"

Michael shook his head. "Shit, Todd, you just don't get it, do you? You're so fucking dense. So fucking focused on your career. Would you just once look at what's really important in the long run?"

Todd glared at him, and even though he knew what the

answer would be, he snapped, "And just what's that, Mr. Smart Ass?"

"Us. Todd, if we're going to make it, we can't go on hiding. It's making us both nuts and it's killing our relationship."

"Oh, please, spare me the psychology."

"Todd, this is too much, and you know it. If you want to stay in the closet, then you're going to have to sneak out at night and pick up boys in the park."

"Michael, what the fuck are you saying?"

"Either you tell Channel Seven management that you're gay or . . ." Michael hesitated, but the resolve was clear. "Either you tell Channel Seven the truth or our relationship is over. Finished."

Todd had stood there in shock.

"Do you get it?" Michael had asked. "It's just too much."

Todd hadn't understood at first, hadn't wanted to, and Michael spelled it out once again: time to come out of the closet. Either Todd accepted the anchor position as an openly gay man or their relationship was done. Over. Finished. Todd had stood there dumbfounded, clutching the bottle of champagne by its chilly neck.

"At least," Michael had joked weakly, "if management knew then I could come to the Christmas party."

"What?!" Todd yelled, ripping off his Cubs hat and throwing it on the floor as hard as he could. "You want me to jeopardize my entire career so you can come to some stupid ass Christmas party?"

Then he'd turned and hurled the bottle of champagne against the brick fireplace, where it exploded in a burst of bubbles and glass. Michael had jumped up, shouting his own anger, and Todd had grabbed him hard by the shoulder. He'd wanted to punch Michael as hard as he could, but by some bit of sanity he'd spun away, charged into the dining room, where he'd shoved over the pine sideboard.

Horrified at how crazy he'd gone last night, Todd shook his head as he maneuvered through the light traffic on 494. Everyone thought of him as so cool, so even-tempered, which he always tried to be. Had to be. The good son. The good boy. If he was likable enough then no one would ever doubt his sexuality. But then last night he'd arrived at this huge fork in the road, the one he'd never wanted to face and yet knew was lurking inevitably, and he just snapped. The soaring career and his sexuality were on a collision course, always had been, which was why he'd flipped into such a rage. No matter how hard he tried he couldn't control any of it, and he'd just been so angry that he'd gone kind of crazy. No, he'd gone fucking nuts.

He shook his head. Todd had grabbed Michael last night, clutched his flesh in his hands, and wanted to kill him. Instead, thankfully, he'd ruined a piece of furniture, broken a shitload of dishes. Then he'd stormed out, beating a furious retreat to his condo, where he fell asleep only after his third Scotch. This morning his head had ached as much as his soul. He made coffee, stared at the phone, hoped that Michael would phone. But of course he wouldn't, because Michael was nothing if not resolute. Todd had wanted to talk to him, needed to, and he'd picked up the phone perhaps a half-dozen times, yearning to hear the richness of Michael's voice, wanting to eke out one of his big laughs just so Todd would know everything would be all right. But Todd wasn't so sure of that, wasn't so sure that things would ever be right again, and he hadn't called Michael, not out of stubbornness, but because until just a few minutes ago he hadn't fully come to peace with . . . with all this crap.

Now if Michael would only forgive him. He had to, thought Todd as he gulped a huge nervous breath. It couldn't be too late. They'd come too far. No one had ever understood, ever accepted all the raging conflicts that Todd faced as fully as Michael had. No one had ever seen his pain and been able to soothe it so gently and completely.

"If people see you as uptight and closed, Todd, that's how they'll react to you," he'd said more than once before launching into his favorite lecture about setting the tone.

Oh, Michael, thought Todd, what would I do without you?

He shook his head, chastising himself for putting Michael through all this. He'd beg forgiveness. Yes, Todd had placed all these wretched restrictions on their lives, excluding Michael from dinner parties, choosing obscure restaurants where the chance of Todd being recognized was less, going to the theater in a mixed crowd to camouflage their relationship. But that was over now. Maybe they should take some time off. Go on a vacation. Have some big fun. Things were going to change. Absolutely. So Michael was just going to have to accept Todd's apology. And Michael would. He was that accepting. That forgiving. So sweet-natured. So . . . so wonderful. And if Channel 7 management forced him to choose between the anchor position and Michael, the choice was now clear. It was better to let the truth catch up with him, better to face reality at this point, than to let his career pull his life any further out of line.

Driving well over the speed limit, Todd sped toward downtown, then veered left, shooting briefly onto 94 before riding a ramp upward and then down and onto Hennepin Avenue. God, wondered Todd, maybe he should put his condo on the market. That would make complete sense. No use in having to maintain two households. And maybe Michael should put his duplex on the market as well. Then they could buy a place together, one of those great houses in Kenwood. Maybe between Michael's and his salary they could even afford one of the grand old ones perched right on Lake of the Isles.

Todd turned right on 24th Street, checked the digital clock on the dashboard, saw that it was just after ten. Of course Michael would be home. He was addicted to the late news, always watched it because, Todd joked, Michael was a true Minnesotan: obsessed by the weather. Michael would sit through twenty minutes of news even if the most important item was a high school marching band in desperate need of tubas, all in order to find out how cold it would be the next morning.

It was only a half-dozen short blocks from Hennepin over to West 23rd, and the closer he drew to Michael's house the faster Todd's heart began to beat. Yes, Michael had to be there, waiting, wondering, wanting to talk to Todd as much as Todd wanted to talk to him. With any luck Todd would find him camped out on the living room sofa, watching the late news, one hand stuck in a bag of microwaved popcorn.

Oh, shit, thought Todd. The 10:00 P.M. news. He reached into the left pocket of his dark blue wool coat and felt his pager. Yes, the small box was there, right where he'd put it after he'd flicked it off. Had anyone been trying to contact him? He didn't want to know, didn't want to care, but compulsively he pulled the small device from his pocket, turned it on. And sure as hell, the thing was flashing. As he drove through the dark October night, he tried to see the brief message. What was it, a robbery, a drive-by shooting, a murder? He couldn't tell, but Cindy was good, she could handle it. There just wasn't enough light, and screw it anyway, he thought, tossing the pager on the seat next to him. Michael was infinitely more important. That was what he had to focus on now, their relationship. Absolutely, he told himself as he approached the corner of 23rd and Irving, as he turned the corner and suddenly saw this brilliant display of lights and a scattered mélange of vehicles.

The surprise bowled him over, and out loud he muttered, "What the hell's going on?"

Oh, Christ. He didn't know what to think, to do, as he took in an amazing spectacle of activity. He saw bright lights focused on one house, then saw quite clearly that it was Michael's duplex, that big white thing with the stucco that glowed moonlike both day and night. And there were clumps of people gathered on the sidewalk, in the yard. Next he saw the familiar van, the white one with the big red lettering:

CHANNEL 7'S CRIMEEYE TEAM ON THE WAY! Oh, shit, thought Todd. They're all here. His heart charged ahead like a racehorse. Dear God, they'd come here to announce his promotion live on the 10:00 P.M. news. His face flushed red and he even began to tremble. What a disaster. Couldn't he be left alone, just for a while, just for tonight?

He took his foot off the gas and parked three or four houses short of Michael's. What the hell was he supposed to do, turn around and flee or walk right up to Michael's and into a celebration?

Wait a minute, he thought. A celebration at Michael's? What the hell was he thinking, how self-centered had he become? His official address was his condo, not here. No one at the office knew he was spending most of his nights at this place, in that bed, with that man.

A deep chill shot through Todd. Up there, on the flat walk that led to Michael's front door, the very walk that Todd had shoveled last winter and swept this past August, were two uniformed cops. One of them slipped on a pair of clear plastic gloves and rushed inside. The other was unrolling a yellow plastic band, tying it to Michael's mailbox, stretching it out. Oh, dear God, thought Todd. There was an ambulance too. Right past the Channel 7 van. The Channel 7 van that was parked halfway up on the sidewalk, its doors open, cables flowing like languid snakes out and onto the lawn. And there was Cindy Wilson, touching up her makeup, straightening her tan raincoat, adjusting the collar.

Electrocuted with fear, he snatched up the pager, clutched it in both his shaking hands. He was suddenly very hot and short of breath. Nearly crushing the small device in his hands, he leaned into the seeping streetlight. He saw what he feared: 1603 West 23rd Street. Next on the miniature screen he saw something totally absurd, totally ridiculous, impossible, and horrific: murder. Todd threw the pager against the passenger door, where it shattered into a handful of cheap pieces. This wasn't possible. Next his heart seized up: if not murder, then suicide.

He threw open the door. Not that. Michael couldn't have killed himself after their fight last night, could he? No. That wouldn't be like him. But then again, why hadn't Michael tried to call Todd today?

He stumbled down the sidewalk, past a neighbor swaddled in a red plaid bathrobe. Todd might be panicking needlessly. There were two renters upstairs, a young couple. The lawyers Ken and Marcy. Oh, God, if someone's dead in this house, let it be one of them. Just not Michael. Anyone but him.

Everything seemed to rush out of Todd as he climbed the short grassy knoll on Michael's front yard. He kicked through wet oak leaves. Cindy Wilson saw him, but pretended not to. Like a zombie he stumbled on, wanting nothing to do with her or television ever again. As he neared, her voice rose sharply, an entirely new set of stark lights burst on, and then Mark Buchanan's camera was rolling.

"Good evening, this is Cindy Wilson of the CrimeEye team," she began coolly, "reporting live on what appears to be a gruesome murder in the heart of Kenwood, just a block from the home of Ambassador Walter Mondale. On this dark night, a mere two weeks before Halloween, a horrible crime has taken place."

She driveled on. Said something about a phone call. Then her contacting the police. Todd pushed a short woman out of the way and zeroed in on Cindy.

Mark lifted his head from the camera, mouthed the word *Live!*

But Todd didn't stop, not even when Mark started waving at him to get back. Todd couldn't. He had to find out what happened, who was dead.

Cindy Wilson struggled to ignore Todd, but couldn't quite do it. She tripped over a couple of words. Todd pulled closer, staring at her.

Cindy reported, "The police arrived only moments after

we did, and an ambulance, as you can see, was called as well. A squad of detectives is now inside, but as of yet no body has been—''

Todd stepped forward, blurted, "Who?"

Always the professional, Cindy masked her anger at having Todd literally walk into her story, instead saying cordially, "And here we have our lead reporter on the CrimeEye team, our own Emmy Award–winning Todd Mills."

"Was it downstairs?" he demanded, raising his voice, as the camera turned on him. "Damn it all, who is it, who's dead?"

Taken aback, Cindy Wilson failed to reply at first, then stared at Todd, tried to remain ever-poised, saying, "Yes, that's right. It was the man downstairs. As of yet we don't have his name."

He felt himself scream, but no sound came out. In a vacuum of horror, Todd stood there staring up at the white house. Two medics emerged. But they weren't hurrying, nor were they pushing a gurney. They were just gabbing, making it clear there was no emergency.

With a barely audible gasp, he muttered, "Michael."

"What was that, Todd?" ventured Cindy, jumping at the situation and holding the mike right up to his mouth. "You don't know the victim, do you? You don't know his name by chance?"

There was nothing around Todd. Nothing but shock. Nothing but innocence. And horrified disbelief.

Gasping, he managed to say, "My . . . my . . ."

With one hand Todd batted the microphone from his face, and then he left a speechless Cindy Wilson standing there. He started running, unaware of everything, even the television camera that was still trained on him as he charged across the front lawn, shouting one name over and over again. Faces turned toward him. From the side he saw a figure in blue. A cop. The guy was hurrying toward Todd, but Todd leaned down, his college days never far off, and clipped him. Todd had to get inside the house. He had to reach Michael.

Todd screamed. Something came out of his mouth that he couldn't even hear. And then there were a couple more cops emerging from the dark, rushing to the front of Michael's, blocking the door. Todd charged into them. This was his place. He had to get inside. They were grabbing him though. Shouting at Todd. He started bucking, twisting. This couldn't be. It was impossible. Nothing made sense. But they were stronger than him, those cops, and within seconds his hands were pinned behind his back. He lunged forward, broke free, fury racing through him like never before. A cop grabbed at him, but Todd twisted free. Next something or someone was slamming into his back and he was hurled forward, thrown down and onto the concrete steps. And three or four guys were squashing him to the sidewalk.

Then someone, a woman, was shouting at the cops, telling them to back off.

"Take him down to my car!" she yelled.

There was a scrambling of limbs. A good amount of cursing. They lifted him, dragged him toward the street.

And this cop, a woman with short, blond hair, was by his side, saying, "You can't go in. Michael Carter has been murdered. We need to talk to you."

It all ran out of him, every bit of fight, of resistance. As if shot, Todd let himself be dragged along. He looked up. Cindy Wilson and Mark Buchanan were charging toward him, the camera trained on him. Of course all this was running live. This was America. This was real-life drama. This was good television.

Pushing for something, anything, with which to shock her viewers, Cindy Wilson shouted, "Todd, what is it? Who was killed? How do you know him?"

And as Todd Mills, star reporter, the big Emmy Award winner, was hoisted to his feet and shoved toward an unmarked cop car, he looked back, focusing on the camera. All his defenses had been blown to bits, and the naked truth that he'd hidden for so painfully long just slipped out, the words crossing his lips more easily, more naturally than he could ever have imagined.

"Michael Carter was my lover!"

5

The rest of Todd's life began that night. It was as if he'd crossed over a line, or been dragged over it. And as he was pushed from the glaring lights into the back of an unmarked car, which a few minutes later sped off, he knew deep inside there would be no coming back, no withdrawing ever again into the warmth of Michael's arms or, for that matter, into the darkness of the closet where he'd hidden for so very long.

Todd had been at the Minneapolis city hall many times. He'd cruised the halls of the huge granite structure, filming the accused, lobbing questions like grenades. Yet this time he was the one being led along, directed down this corridor, up that one. As he passed deeper and deeper into the hulking building, he was silently watching all this, observing even himself, as if he were seeing it all not in person but on television. This was too weird, too unreal, and he was docile as the blond woman and another man escorted him into an elevator, upward, and then through the homicide department.

Only an hour after he'd turned the corner onto West 23rd Street and spotted all those lights and activity—had he really

thought for a moment that they'd all gathered there to celebrate his promotion?—Todd found himself in a small room.
He was seated on a comfortable couch, and in front of him
on a Formica-clad coffee table sat a Styrofoam cup of coffee.
Todd stared at the steam rising from the cup, then looked
down at his hands. Why was he here? What did they want?

"Would you?" repeated the woman.

He looked up. There were two other people in this small
room with the gentle light and the short carpet. Detectives,
isn't that what they had said? He couldn't remember who
was who. They'd told him their names when they sat him
down in that car, a Ford Taurus, and said they needed some
help. Would he talk to them? But Todd couldn't even speak.
He'd just stared up at the house. Yes, they told him. Michael
was dead. There was a squad of detectives in there, and the
guys from the crime lab had just arrived. Todd couldn't go
in. And the body couldn't come out. Not just yet. The crime
scene was sealed indefinitely.

So they asked if he'd come downtown, which he somehow
had agreed to, and now the woman was raising a tiny packet
of something dry and asking again, "Would you like some
creamer?"

"No."

He stared at her, this woman with the round face and blue
eyes and short blond hair who was sipping her coffee. She
was tall and hefty, dressed in blue jeans and a navy blue
sweater. Todd turned from her, looked at the other one, the
guy, who was short and stocky, handsome in a clean-cut way,
face pale and serious, his brown hair cropped.

The guy said, "Mr. Mills, Detective Lewis and I want to
thank you for agreeing to come down and talk to us tonight."

His reply was a faint, "Sure."

"We're seeking information regarding the murder of Michael Carter," said the woman. "If we could just ask a few

questions. You're free to leave at any time. Do you understand?''

Todd nodded. ''Yes.''

''Did you know Michael Carter?''

''Of course.'' Todd looked at them, cleared his throat.
''Are you both detectives? The two of you?''

''That's right,'' said the woman. ''I'm Detective Lewis
and this is Detective Rawlins with the Minneapolis homicide
division. We want to find out what happened to Michael
Carter, which I'm sure you do as well.''

''Yes . . . yes, of course.''

Rawlins gently said, ''I've seen you on TV, haven't I? You
do the crime stuff, right?''

''Channel Seven.''

''Have you been in television for long?''

''Since college.''

''Are you from here?''

''No, Chicago.''

''That's a nice place. A lot of fun. How long have you
been in the Twin Cities?''

''Six . . . six years.''

''Do you live in Minneapolis or St. Paul?''

''Minneapolis.''

''Where?''

''By Lake Calhoun. In a condo.''

Rawlins smiled. ''What a great part of town. All the lakes.
Lots of fun in the summer.''

''But . . . but . . .'' Todd shook his head. ''What's this
have to do with Michael? What happened to Michael?''

''Just relax,'' said Rawlins.

''Did you know Michael Carter?'' asked Lewis, cutting in.

''Of course.''

''For how long?''

''Four years.''

She said, ''How well did you know Mr. Carter? Were you
close friends or . . . or . . .''

Todd didn't hear the rest of her question. Instead he thought of Michael. Michael who'd gone to the huge march in Washington. Todd had opted out, but Michael had gone with a handful of friends, returning somehow touched or transformed. Oddly empowered. Legitimized, that was how Michael had put it. Full of excitement, Michael had insisted that Todd absolutely had to go to New York for the Gay Games. Instead of hiding at home, watching all those queers on CNN, Todd had to experience what it was like to be surrounded by a million people that were just like him. Todd, however, had bowed out of that one too, manufacturing some lame excuse, which in turn had led to a rather vocal argument all its own.

Todd said, "Michael and I were lovers."

Rawlins raised his eyebrows, took a sip of coffee, then asked, "Michael Carter and you were gay lovers?"

"That's what I said." Todd had talked about his sexuality so seldom that he was surprised how easy it was to say "I'm gay."

"Sure. Of course." Rawlins glanced at Lewis. "We just want to understand everything. We just want to make sure everything's clear."

"How long had you two been involved?" asked Lewis.

"About four years."

"Did you have a good relationship?"

"Yes." And bit by bit they'd been getting closer. "For the past couple of years I spent most evenings and nights with him at his house."

Lewis shifted in her chair. "Have you had other homosexual relationships?"

"What?" It didn't make a difference anymore just what he revealed, did it? "A few. I was married before. But Michael . . . Michael was the first serious one with a guy."

"Any problems?"

Todd stared at her. What was her name? Lewis? She looked to be in her late thirties, strong, determined. He glanced at her left hand, saw no wedding ring. A lesbian? If so, would she understand?

Todd said, "Just the usual."

"The usual, such as?"

"It's just not easy loving another man. . . ."

Rawlins volunteered, "You find having a same-sex relationship is stressful?"

"Yeah, well you should try having a straight one," interjected Lewis, "and two kids and a career. I'll bet you ten-to-one that's harder."

Detective Lewis was married? Unlike Michael, who had a natural sense for it, Todd had always been pathetically weak at picking out who was queer and who wasn't.

"You're not open about your sexuality, are you, Todd?" asked Rawlins.

"No."

"Do they know at the station where you work?"

He looked at the floor. "No."

"That must be hard. Did that affect your relationship with Michael Carter?"

"Of course."

"How?"

"In some ways it made us closer. In other ways it made things much more stressful." Todd couldn't hide his irritation. "Do we have to talk about this?"

"We're just trying to piece things together." Lewis moved on, asking, "When did you last see him?"

"Last night."

"Did you sleep there?"

"No."

"What about tonight? When were you at his house this evening?"

"I wasn't."

She studied him. "But that's where we just came from. We just left Michael's house."

"Well, I wasn't there before that. I was just coming . . .

coming home. My car should still be out front. A green Cherokee. I saw all the cars and lights, and I just parked right there on the street and ran up to his house.''

''I see,'' she said, nodding. ''So when did you last see him? Sometime earlier tonight?''

''No.'' Todd shook his head, cursed himself for leaving. ''I haven't seen Michael since last night.'' He fell into thought. ''What's going to happen now? I mean, to Michael's body?''

''When the guys from the crime lab are done, the coroner will bring the body downtown,'' explained Lewis. ''There there will be an autopsy.''

Todd bowed his head into his hands. ''Oh, God.''

Rawlins leaned forward, said, ''Todd, you said you slept most nights at Michael's. Why didn't you stay there last night?''

''What?''

''Why didn't you stay with Michael last night?''

''Because . . .''

''Because?''

''Because we had a fight.''

Todd didn't care how it sounded. That was the truth. And Todd hadn't spoken to Michael since that horrendous argument. Nor would he ever again. Those were their last moments together, all that shouting, all that cursing. The last memory.

After a long moment Lewis said, ''What did you and Michael fight about?''

''My job. Us. Where we were going. Or weren't.'' He looked at Lewis, then Rawlins. ''It's kind of complicated.''

Todd took a sip of the coffee, which had grown cold, and then he told them about the pending promotion at Channel 7, how he'd gone to tell Michael the good news. Michael hadn't taken it as such, though, and when Michael had asked about the stupid Christmas party, Todd had burst into a rage. Todd told them in detail, holding nothing back because he wanted to talk about it, make someone understand why he hadn't been with Michael since yesterday. If only he had been. Maybe Michael would still be alive.

"At first I just threw my Cubs hat on the floor—it's still over there somewhere, I think—but then I really lost it. There's a broken bottle of champagne in the living room. Maybe Michael already cleaned up, but I was so pissed I hurled it against the fireplace. And I tipped over a piece of furniture. I'm sure you'll find some broken dishes. A lot of them, actually."

"This was some sort of frustrated outburst?" Rawlins paused, then said, "So you've had a hard time being gay?"

"Yeah." Todd looked at the floor, seeing how complicated he'd made everything. "And I've made it harder than necessary."

"Would you say Michael was forcing you to be gay?"

"What?" Todd stared at him, couldn't hide his surprise. "No, he was forcing me to be honest."

"Where were the broken dishes?" asked Lewis.

"In the dining room."

"So you dumped over some furniture, and then what?"

"I left. I don't know, maybe I shouted something too."

"Did you strike Michael Carter?"

"No."

"You didn't hit him before leaving?"

"I said no."

"Where was he when you left?"

"In the living room."

She asked, "Alive?"

"Of course he was."

"What was he doing? Did he threaten you at all?"

"Michael? Absolutely not. Michael would never have hurt anyone. He was much too . . . too gentle."

"So it was you who lost your temper?"

"Yes, that's what I said."

Rawlins cleared his throat and asked, "Do you own a knife?"

Todd glared at him. "Of course I do. I've got a half-dozen in my kitchen."

"Do you hunt?"

"No."

"Fish?"

"No."

"Where were you earlier this evening?" demanded Lewis.

"At the station. Channel Seven's right here, right downtown on Marquette."

"You were there until what time?"

"About six or six thirty."

"And then?"

"Then I just started driving."

"Where?"

"I don't know. I was still upset about our fight."

Rawlins jumped in. "When was that?"

"Last night, damn it all. And I was upset about it all day today too."

"Why?"

"Because I didn't know what to do about the job offer at the station. And I didn't know what to do about Michael and me. So I just got in my car and started driving. I headed south on Thirty-five W. I just needed to get away. To think."

"Was anyone with you?" said Lewis.

"No."

"Did you visit or see anyone?"

"No." As an afterthought he added, "Wait, I did stop at a restaurant out on the Strip."

"Did you speak to anyone?"

"Barely."

"Did you hurt Michael Carter?"

"No!" Todd was suddenly on his feet, pacing to the side. "I was mad at Michael. I was mad at the situation I was in. The promotion and all. But, hell, no, I didn't hurt or kill

Michael! Do you hear me? No, no, no! I most certainly did not hurt Michael Carter!''

Rawlins said quietly, ''But you did break a bottle and some furniture. Did you damage anything else?''

''Nothing!''

He grabbed at his head with both hands, pulled at his hair. He'd hated his father's temper, which his mother had dismissed as his Polish nature coming through. Todd had more rightly suspected it was the vodka. In any case, for whatever reason, Todd had inherited it.

''Yes,'' he said, sitting back down. ''I was angry as hell, and I guess I smashed all that so I wouldn't hurt Michael.''

''When was that?''

''Last night.''

''Not tonight? You weren't over there tonight?'' demanded Lewis, continuing to press him. ''You didn't break that bottle and then hit Michael?''

''No! It was last night. Just ask the upstairs neighbors. They must have heard something.''

''We did. The couple upstairs heard a large fight. And they heard you yelling.''

''Right. That was yesterday evening,'' said Todd as if he were vindicating himself. ''About eight thirty, I think.''

''You have a key to Michael's, don't you, Todd?'' Lewis asked, moving on.

''Of course.''

''And you were over there earlier this evening, right?''

Todd was suddenly quiet. He understood where this was going. What they were trying to construct. And he understood what this and some of the earlier questions implied.

''Is that how it happened?'' Todd asked. ''Michael was stabbed? Earlier this evening?''

''Yes.'' Rawlins nodded. ''There were multiple wounds in the stomach and chest.''

''Oh, Christ . . .''

''You didn't know?''

Todd looked up at him. "Of course not."

"Todd, I'm sorry, I'm just trying to get all this straight. I'm a little confused here," began Lewis, shifting in her seat. "So the last time you saw Michael Carter was in the back hallway? Is that what you said?"

"What?"

"The last time you saw Michael Carter alive was in the hallway by the bedrooms?"

Todd shook his head. "No, he was out in the living room. We were both there. I dumped over that sideboard . . . and then I left. I went out the front door. The place was a mess— I trashed it." He took a deep breath. "Did Michael clean any of it up?"

"A bit, but everything's pretty much like you described it."

Todd was rubbing his eyes. What were they trying to imply?

Lewis leaned forward, pointed at him, and said, "You've got something on your neck."

Todd reached up. "I do?"

"Is that a bruise?" she asked. "Here, why don't you take off your coat and let me take a look."

Why did this sound so familiar? Where had he heard a line like that before? Oh, crap, he thought. This was almost straight out of a story he'd done about a twenty-year-old punk who'd been picked up for a shooting. The detectives had proudly told Todd how they'd gotten the kid to lift his shirt, show them some rather incriminating bruises from an all-too-recent fight. He'd shown the detectives the bruises and that had been the basis for his arrest.

Dear God. Todd fully realized that he was downtown at police headquarters and in a soft room. He looked around quickly. Yes, that's what they called these chambers. And he knew what they were for too. A pleasant, intimate place for interviews, equipped with a couch, coffee table, a couple of squishy chairs. And a microphone. Probably a video camera too. His heart started pounding. In one of these walls there was most certainly a pinhole, and they were most likely videotaping him. He'd played right into them too. From the beginning they'd made it perfectly clear that he was noncustodial. Sure, they'd even said it, told him he was free to leave at any time. And Todd, in all his confusion, had just been blabbing on and on, giving them everything they wanted.

Oh, shit.

Lewis pressed on, dialing up the feigned concern and saying, "Here, let me take a look at that. You might need a bandage."

"I know what the fuck you two are trying to do," said Todd, sitting firm.

"I beg your pardon?" replied Lewis, feigning naïveté.

"I need my lawyer. Her name is Janice Gray."

"Really?" said Lewis.

"Yes, really. I won't say anything further until I've spoken to her." He repeated, "Her name is Janice Gray."

Rawlins shrugged and glanced over at Lewis, and said, "I guess that takes us into the next phase."

"Guess so," replied Lewis. "Would you care to do the duties?"

"Sure."

Then Rawlins took a sip of coffee, cleared his throat, and read Todd his Miranda rights. There were no more questions after that. They pressed him no further, of course. They only conferred with one another, whispering a few words, then nodding in agreement.

Detective Lewis rose and said, "I'm sorry, Mr. Mills, but we're going to have to hold you overnight for further questioning."

6

"What the fuck's this all about?" barked Roger Locker, the managing director of Channel 7, as he stormed into the conference room. "Our own Todd Mills in shit up to his neck? This is too fucking unbelievable. I mean, I just can't believe it."

Cindy Wilson couldn't either. Not even this morning. There she'd been, just doing her job, taking a hot tip and reporting on a murder. It was going to be the perfect CrimeEye segment. Live too. Right on the late news. And then Todd comes darting in, screaming this and that, making it perfectly clear to the entire universe that he was gay. And the police haul him off and keep him for questioning. Way, way weird, she thought, lifting a paper cup of coffee to her lips.

She glanced across the broad table and saw the two others—Mark Buchanan, who'd caught it all on camera, and Brad Lewis, who'd taken the original call—looking equally lost, equally worried. And with good reason. Shit was going to be flying over this one for a long, long time.

Locker, who was overweight and bald, always shouting

about something, always angry at someone, now dropped into a chair and threw the morning's paper onto the table. "I mean, look at this!"

Of course they'd all seen today's *Tribune.* Right there on the front page. It wasn't the main headline—this week's turmoil in Russia continued to be top news—but it was still plenty big: AWARD-WINNING REPORTER ARRESTED IN GAY MURDER. As if that weren't enough to ruin anyone's career, there was the photo. No longer the hunk smiling down from the freeway billboards, this morning the Twin Cities were greeted with a big front-and-center photo of the Twin Cities' own favorite guy, Todd Mills, being dragged toward a cop car. And the quote. Dear God, the quote: "Michael Carter was my lover!" That certainly was enough to derail Todd's stellar career, everyone understood that automatically, and the fallout was definitely enough to damage all of Channel 7.

"What I want to know is, where the hell did the paper get this picture?" demanded Locker, surveying the group gathered around the table. "Well?" When he failed to receive the desired confession, he prompted, "Did one of you give it to them?"

There was a grumbling, some shifting. But no reply.

Cindy looked right at him. "I really doubt that anyone here at Channel Seven would do something like that."

But the others were looking down, each in his own way looking guilty as hell. Or, she wondered, ashamed? Could someone have sold the photo to the *Tribune?* Sure, she thought, either to spite Channel 7 or as an affront to Todd.

"Well, I suppose it doesn't make any difference," began Locker, shaking his head. "But it's a disaster for Todd. As some of you are aware, we were just concluding negotiations with his agent regarding the anchor position on the evening news. At this point, however, that's obviously on hold. My main concern at this point is damage control for Channel Seven."

Locker took a deep breath, held it, and then exhaled

loudly. Then he started laughing. He quickly ran his right hand over his bald head.

"What the hell am I saying?" he continued. "This is already a catastrophe. An incredible one. Oh, my God, I wish I could say I've never heard of anything like this, but it's almost as good as O.J. Except, of course, Todd isn't as famous." He shook his head. "I've been talking with our lawyer this morning, and he's been talking with Todd's lawyer. As of this morning Todd Mills has been suspended with pay. I don't understand what happened, who did what, or what any of this is about, but our official position is that we're a hundred percent behind Todd. Depending on what the police and their investigation turn up, however, that could change any minute. Is there anything else any of you can add?"

Cindy cleared her throat, volunteered, "It happened just as I told you on the phone last night. Brad got a call in the control room and came charging into the CrimeEye office, but the caller had already hung up. After calling the police—that part's on tape, by the way—and paging Todd, Mark and I headed out at once. Todd didn't answer his page and didn't show up, so I started the segment. The rest is pretty much all there on videotape."

"Right. I was at home, watching the news like everyone else. I saw it." Locker shook his head. "It was pretty incredible. In fact, if this had happened to Channel Five, I'd be laughing my ass off." He leaned forward, lowered his voice, and asked, "So Todd's really a homo, is that right? What about him and that lawyer, the one he always brings to the Christmas party? What was her name? Janice . . . Janice Something. I thought those two were an item. So did anyone know about this; I mean, did he tell any of you? Was I the only one in the dark?"

The room was painfully quiet, and Cindy sat back. No way did she want to get into this one.

Locker turned to her and demanded, "Didn't he ever talk to you about who he was dating?"

"No. Actually he never said anything to me about his personal life," she replied. "And I never asked."

"Mark, did he ever say anything to you?"

"Nope."

"But you worked the most with him. Hell, you were probably the closest to him of anyone here. Didn't you just have him look at that house you put a bid on?"

"Yeah, but . . . but . . ."

"Come on, Mark, you must have known he was gay."

"Frankly, it never crossed my mind. There were always women after him."

"Brad?"

"I . . . I just work the control panel and switch the cameras. I don't think about those things." He was quick to add "Sir."

Locker pounded the table. "Well, his agent is in deep shit. His private life is his own, but this is the kind of thing management has to know about. A scandal like this can sink a station."

He was silent for much too long, and Cindy thought, here it comes. The other shoe. Dear Lord, she wondered, why hadn't she just been a nice weather girl on that station in Detroit?

"Well, I met with the president of the station this morning, and for now the CrimeEye segment is postponed. All of you will be assigned to different projects for the time being," said Locker bluntly. "Depending on what happens with Todd, depending on what kind of publicity there is, well . . . well, we'll just have to see where we go from here. If you think of anything else, know anything else, come to me right away. And remember, no talking to any of the other media. Clear?"

"Gotcha, chief," replied Mark Buchanan.

"Brad?"

"Not a word, sir."

"Cindy?"

"Sure." Cindy cleared her throat and ventured, "But you know, we could have record viewership tonight."

He looked at her. "What?"

"This is pretty juicy stuff, isn't it?"

"Of course it is."

"Well, you were the one who said this was like O. J.'s case, so . . ." She looked at the others, tried to ascertain if they were behind her too. "A lot of people are going to be turning on the evening news for the latest. Either they're going to get it from us or—"

"The other guys," added Mark Buchanan with a grin.

"Exactly," said Cindy, nodding. "I mean, we're all curious as hell as to what this is all about."

Locker rolled his eyes. "I know I am."

"People want dirt and they're going to get it somewhere, so they might as well get it from us."

"I hear what you're saying, Cindy," said Locker, nodding slowly. "And you're absolutely right. Any ideas?"

"A few," Cindy replied, even though she had none.

"Okay, then. You were in on this whole thing right from the start. Meet me in my office in thirty minutes."

With that decree, Roger Locker blew out of the room. Well, shit, thought Cindy, as she and the others began to get up. Todd Mills might have sunk his own career, but she certainly wasn't going down with him.

7

"This is good, very good," she said.

Todd looked up, stared at her as she sat across from him in some dingy room, jotting everything and anything he managed to blurt out on a legal pad. None of this made any sense. Janice Gray was really his friend, not his attorney. Tall, attractive, with dark hair and a slim face that tapered to a narrow chin, Janice had been his beard. With this striking, beautifully dressed woman on his arm at two or three official functions throughout the year, no one ever suspected he was gay and he didn't have to fend off any interested women, of whom there tended to be a fair number. He performed a similar function for her as well. Although Janice was out as a lesbian to everyone in her firm, there were times when a fortyish woman needed an escort, be it female or male, in the corporate world. Which was to say that ever since Janice's partner had died of breast cancer eight years earlier, she'd been single.

"You believe me, don't you?" Todd asked.

Janice, wearing a navy suit and white blouse, stopped writing. "Never a doubt."

"I loved him."

"I know."

"I mean, I can't say I never lost my temper. And I can't say we never fought, but I'd never . . . never . . ." Todd, who hadn't slept—just tossed and turned in that dank cell—bit his lip. "I can't believe it. I can't believe he's dead."

"Neither can I."

"They're not going to charge me with murder, are they?"

"I doubt it."

"Oh, God."

Janice looked nearly as exhausted and distraught as Todd, for she'd come down last night and spent several hours arguing with the police. She hadn't been able to get him out, just as she hadn't been able to stop Rawlins and Lewis from getting a search warrant. So there Todd was at two in the morning, standing naked in a cell while he was inspected for bruises, cuts, and/or blood. None of which they had found.

Janice rubbed her dark eyes and returned to the task of the morning, saying, "Let's keep in focus here. Now, you've admitted to arguing with Michael the night before his death. The upstairs neighbors have already substantiated that. Actually, they did so last night when the police first arrived. When Michael didn't answer the door, the police rang upstairs, asked if they'd heard any commotion and so on. They replied yes, they'd heard a horrible fight the previous night and seen you leaving. That's when the police decided to break into Michael's."

"But he was alive when I left that night."

"Of course he was. He was alive all day yesterday too. Don't forget he was at work first thing yesterday morning. About two hundred people can substantiate that fact." Janice looked up and asked, "When did he usually get home?"

Theirs was a typical life. Michael left for work about eight, worked all day as an accountant, was usually home by dinner. Dinner. Todd had gotten to be a pretty good cook. With his varied work schedule, he usually had a meal at least under way by the time Michael returned home. A pasta dish loaded with vegetables was a favorite of theirs. Then Michael would clean up, Todd would often head back to the station, and—

"Todd?"

He turned to her. "What?"

"When did Michael usually return home?"

"About six."

"We'll have to check with his office, see if anyone saw him leave, but if that's right it means he was killed somewhere between six and ten last night. The coroner's report isn't back yet, but they'll be able to be more specific. They're doing the autopsy this morning and the report should be in by noon. So the period of interest, obviously, is yesterday, specifically the evening. We just have to prove where you were during that time."

"Christ, I don't know."

"Yes, you do. You already told me," said Janice, calm and direct.

Always so steady, he thought, gazing at Janice. He'd always been a bit in awe of her, even when they'd first met in college at Northwestern University. She was just so attractive, so assured, so intelligent. They'd actually dated back in those days, then had totally lost touch until three years ago. They bumped into each other while walking around Lake of the Isles—Janice had been on a date with a doctor, Todd had been with Michael—and suddenly Todd and Janice started roaring with laughter, because for the first time it was perfectly clear just what they did and did not have in common. The following night Todd and Janice had a long, emotional conversation over an expensive dinner that neither of them noticed. And ever since they'd been best friends.

"Yoo-hoo, Todd, are you listening? Let's just go back over it one more time. I want to make sure I've got everything before I go to the judge and ask for your release. Try to be a little more concrete. We're only talking about a few hours last night.''

Yes, but just yesterday Michael was alive. A mere twelve or fourteen or sixteen hours ago he was still here, still on this planet.

Todd bowed his head, ran his hands through his hair, and said, "I left the station sometime after six. I wanted to talk to Michael, but I remember thinking I wanted to let him get home first. I usually was home before him and I hated that, being there alone and turning the lights on and starting dinner. I don't know why, but I wanted him to walk into a dark house instead. Plus, I was still so confused. I just wasn't sure what I was going to do.''

"Did anyone see you leave work?"

"I . . . I don't know."

"Think, Todd. Go back over every step."

He shut his eyes, studied that memory. Looked at it as if it were a photo. His life had seemed a mess. He'd been depressed all day, really hadn't gotten much of anything done. All he wanted was to sort things out. Where had he been as the day faded and it had gotten dark? His office? No, getting another cup of coffee. That was right. He remembered pouring himself a cup, then checking the huge wall clock. He'd seen what time it was, dumped the coffee down the drain, returned to his office, and headed out the back door. He'd passed someone. But who?

"It was about ten after six when I left," began Todd, picturing the clock in his mind. "I went out the back door to the parking lot. The janitor was there. What's his name? He's Hmong. Xhua. I think that's it. He said hi."

"Good. And then?"

"I got in my car, started it up. And then I just sat there. It was dark and I just sat there with the engine running."

"Why?"

Todd shrugged. "I don't know. I didn't know what to do,

where to go. I just sat there and then finally I picked up my car phone and called Michael. It just rang and rang.''

''But he wasn't home?''

''No.''

''Okay. So by then it was about six-fifteen and Michael wasn't back yet. Either that or he was already . . .''

Already dead, thought Todd. Already knifed.

''Did they find the weapon?''

''No, I don't think so.''

''But they're sure he was cut?''

''Apparently. I'm sure they're checking for drugs. There were no bullet wounds though. I do know that.''

Todd volunteered, ''They won't find any drugs in him. Michael was much too straight for that.''

''Did he ever use anything?''

''Maybe he smoked a joint or two in college, but he didn't like to be out of control.'' In his mind Todd saw the image of Michael tasting a sampling from a local microbrewery. ''He liked beer, that was about it.''

''Okay.'' Janice jotted all this down, then steered the conversation back, saying, ''So you went out to your car and called Michael, but he wasn't there. Then what?''

''His answering machine picked up. I was going to leave a message, just say hi or something, but . . . but I didn't know what to say, so I just hung up.''

''But you listened to the message, maybe even got all the way to the beep?''

''Yeah, right. I didn't hang up until after the beep.''

''Excellent.''

''But I didn't say anything.''

''That's okay. If you listened to the message then the connection was completed. For billing purposes the cellular phone company should have a record of your call. And if we can prove Michael was still at work, that's good.'' Janice said, ''Okay, what did you do then? Did you go somewhere?''

"I didn't want to go home. Home to Michael's, I mean. So I just started driving."

"Where?" she asked.

"I don't know. I got on the freeway and—"

"Which freeway?"

"Thirty-five W."

"Going which way?"

"South."

"Good. You were heading south on Thirty-five W. How far did you go?"

He remembered cranking up the radio. A song by U2 had played. Yes, full blast. He wanted the voices, the guitars to blast everything from his mind, clean it all away. Like a zombie, he'd just driven and driven.

"How far, Todd?"

"I don't know. Until I stopped for gas."

"Where was that? What did you do then?"

"Past Burnsville. I remember going by the mall. And that ski place, you know, the one that's on the right. I might have gone another ten miles. Then I looked at the gas gauge, saw the fuel light was lit up, and so I pulled off."

"Where? Do you remember what town?"

The vision of that glowing sign poked out of the night and into his memory. "No. It was just some gas station on the edge of a cornfield."

"Did you pay cash or charge it?"

"I don't know. Probably charged it." Wasn't that what he always did? "That's what I always do."

"Where'd you put the charge receipt?"

"I don't know."

"Do you keep them?" she asked, trying to coax the answer out of him.

"I usually stuff them in the glove compartment."

"Okay. Good. We'll have to see if we can dig that up." She jotted more down, making an arrow up to something else, some other little point that could be tied in. "Did you talk with anyone?"

"Not really."

"What do you mean, not really?"

"I just went in and paid."

"Do you think the cashier would remember you?"

"Shit, I don't know."

"Was it a man or a woman? Did he or she say anything?"

It had been a chilly night, particularly down there, out of the city and on the plains. There'd been a breeze rustling the browned cornstalks. And the smell of earth. Except for the streaking of the cars, it had been so quiet. He'd gone in, picked up a pack of Trident, then paid.

"I handed the cashier my credit card, and she looked at me, my name." Yes, thought Todd, they did exchange a few words. "She said she knew she'd seen me before. I was the guy on the crime thing on TV. I didn't say much, just signed the receipt. I just wanted to be left alone, but she did push a piece of paper forward and ask for my autograph."

"Which you gave her, right?"

"Automatically." Todd looked at her, shrugged. "I always have to be on. Always the nice guy. You know, presentable, pleasant. And I always do signatures. Stella, my agent, is always beating it into me: 'Your fans are gold, doll, pure gold. Once you lose them, your career is kaput.' "

"Excellent, Todd. This is excellent." Janice hastily added a couple of things. "And then you started back to the city?"

"Exactly. I was going to go home, but then I realized I still didn't know what I wanted to say to Michael. I wasn't completely clear about everything. When I got to Four ninety-four I just sort of veered right, and I kept going until I saw my picture up there on a billboard. That's when I stopped at that restaurant."

"Right." Janice flipped back a couple of pages. "I've already got all that. Was it two or three girls who saw you?"

"The hostess, my waitress. There might have been another

waitress too. I think they were all talking." He recalled looking over, seeing them huddled together, glancing at him.
"Talking about me, I mean. That happens sometimes. You go
in a place, and then people huddle and point at you. It kind
of drives me crazy. I've always been worried that they're
looking at me, saying, he's a fag, isn't he?"

"Oh, Todd." Janice reached across the table, placed a
hand over his. "It's time to let go of all that. Otherwise
you're going to get an ulcer or go crazy. Or both."

He managed a small laugh. "I suppose I don't have to
worry anymore, because from now on everyone'll know what
I do when the lights are off. Did it make this morning's
paper?"

"Front page."

"Oh, shit. Stella's not going to like this." He asked,
"What about the station? What are they saying?"

"They're concerned about you."

"Bullshit. They're concerned about their fucking ratings.
Locker must be quaking. Could you—"

"Todd, we'll worry about them later. Let's just finish up.
The most important thing is to get you out of here." She
studied her notes, said, "How long were you at that restaurant?"

"I don't know. A while."

"What did you have?"

"Uh, a cup of coffee." There was something else too,
wasn't there? "A cup of coffee and some chili."

"Good," she said, scribbling.

"But I didn't eat the chili. She was bringing it over and all
of a sudden I knew I had to get back to Michael's. So I threw
ten dollars on the table and left." He'd been so sure he finally had it all figured out and he'd been so excited to tell
Michael. "Why do you want to know?"

"If need be, we might have to go through the checks, that
is, if they still have them. I don't think we'll need to, but

there's probably a time on it. Which would be very convenient in proving just when and where you were.''

"Oh.''

"You're sure it was just coffee and chili? Nothing else?''

"No. But I didn't eat the chili.''

"Right, I've got that.''

"I just went out to my car and drove to Michael's.'' He added, "I would have been there sooner, I suppose, but I'd turned off my pager. In case they ask why I didn't call when they paged me, you can tell them I was in life crisis and had flicked that fucking thing off.''

"And then you got there, and . . . and . . .''

"Right.'' Todd rubbed his eyes. "It was really on the front page?''

"Russia got the headline, but you got the photo.''

"No shit?''

"No shit. Front and center.''

"Well, was it a good picture, at least? I hope it wasn't that stock one that the paper keeps using, the one of me at the fishing opener. I mean, I look like a real geek with that hat on and that rod.'' Notwithstanding that it made him look exactly like what he wasn't: straight. "I hate to fish. You just sit there. It wasn't that picture, was it?''

"Definitely not. You'll see soon enough—it was a photo taken last night—but trust me, Todd, you've gone way beyond being famous. I'd say infamous was more like it. This is going to be big.''

"Oh.'' Quietly he asked what he knew was a dumb question. "So people'll know that I'm gay?''

"Uh, no doubt about that.''

He rose to his feet, started pacing around the little box of a room. It didn't matter, not now. Who cared if the entire world knew his deepest secret? Suddenly it just seemed so . . . so unimportant.

"You know what, Janice?'' he said, turning toward her. "I don't care anymore. In fact, I'm kind of relieved. I'm tired of all that, tired of worrying what people are going to think of me.''

"Good. You're going to need every bit of strength you can muster.''

"Do you think they'll release me today?''

"With all this,'' said Janice, touching her pad of yellow paper, "there shouldn't be any problem. You're lucky you're so famous—it's going to work in your favor. People will remember seeing you.''

"Will I have to post bail? I can. I've got lots of money.''

"Todd, you haven't even been charged with anything, so there won't be any bail posted. I think you're going to be fine, but I wouldn't count on going back to work right away.''

"Of course not. In fact, I don't know if and when I'll ever want to.'' His career, which had always been the first and foremost thing in his life, had overnight tumbled to the bottom of the list. "Michael just had such a great heart.''

"I know. Nobody could make me laugh like him.''

That was what had drawn Todd to Michael. That laugh. He was this straight-looking, straight-acting guy—gays that were too queenly had always made Todd uncomfortable, as if by association people might realize he himself was queer—an accountant who was a real whiz with numbers and anything digital, yet who could look at something totally odd and just start to laugh. A deep, hearty laugh that turned high-pitched right at the end. When he really got going he even snorted, which was the one surefire way to crack up Todd as well. Anything could set Michael off too. If Michael broke something, he'd look at it and then just burst out cackling. And Todd loved that about him. Loved the irreverence beneath the businesslike sheen. It was so unlike the atmosphere in which Todd had been raised, where everything was either good or bad, right or wrong. Michael had found joy in life, and it was that characteristic that had captured Todd's heart right from the start and had even steadily chipped away at Todd's own homophobia and self-hate.

Todd closed his eyes, couldn't imagine that this was really his life. "You don't think he was killed because he was gay, do you?"

"I don't know, I really don't." The thought had obviously occurred to her and frightened her, and for a moment or two she couldn't speak. "A hate crime is a real possibility though."

Todd had never talked to anyone about this, but he'd been frightened for so long. All his life, really. He'd known he was different, sensed it first when he was eight or ten, but didn't know what it was, why he wasn't like all the other boys. He didn't know specifically until he'd seen that Dan guy at the pool. Or was it the next year? Like all the other boys, he'd done a little sexual experimenting. Nothing major. But one of the kids had been threatened by Todd's eager, even aggressive exploration and had accused him outright of being a homo. Three or four other kids had joined in, taunting and pushing Todd, until Todd had fought them off, punching them all, even giving one kid a gusher of a nose-bleed. After that there was never a problem, but ever since Todd had been standing against a wall, guarding his back, fearful of letting people see the other side of him. And fearful of exactly this, that someone would find out that he was a homo and extract the ultimate punishment: death. Is that what had happened to poor Michael?

Todd muttered, "Why, Janice?"

"I have no idea why anyone would kill him, but I'm sure the police will do their best to figure it out."

"No." He cleared his throat. "No, I mean why are we queer—you, me, Michael?"

"Oh, Todd, why's the sky blue?"

"It's just so much. I mean, who could think that you'd ever choose to be gay? I wouldn't, would you?"

"The wisest thing my shrink ever said was stay away from

rhetorical questions. And that one definitely has no answer, not until they find the gene or something, so I won't touch it with a ten-foot pole.'' She quickly added, ''My only choice has been whether to be honest or not, and I must say I've been forthright from day two or three.''

''I admire you for that, believe me.''

''Well, I'm very happy in my life. Probably much happier than if I were straight, because I haven't been able to walk blindly through life. I've had to confront and accept so much within myself, and because of that I've found some kind of inner peace, which is also my strength.''

Todd turned away, stared at the wall. ''We dated for, what, two or three months? Four? And then you went to Europe for a semester and came back with a girlfriend. It freaked me out, it really did. Have I ever told you that? It freaked me out because I didn't know what it meant about me, if anything.''

''We were young.''

''But you were strong, even then. And courageous.'' He shook his head. ''Oh, Christ, I knew life wasn't going to be easy, I just never expected it would be this hard. I'd just like to get to the point where I walk into a room and I don't worry about . . . about how people perceive me.''

''You'll get there, honey. And when you do, you'll realize how wonderful it is because you've earned every blessed step.''

''And Michael was helping me! He'd been there for years, you know. And for some wonderful reason he was waiting for me, helping me along.''

''That's because he knew you were worth it.''

''Shit!''

Todd made a tight fist, held it to his mouth, and clenched his eyes shut. If only he could block it all out.

Janice stared at him, knowing Todd was not one to leave stones unturned, and said, ''Todd, I have to advise you this is best left to them, to the police. Michael's murder isn't something for you to go poking around in.''

If he heard what she said it didn't register, and he plugged
on, saying, "It's just that I had this wonderful person and
this wonderful life, and now it's gone. Vanished. Just like
that."

"Of course, but don't—"

"Do you realize, Janice, I didn't even stop to look at how
good my life was? I mean, I complicated the hell out of it
and my work complicated the hell out of it too, but there was
something really wonderful there. In fact, it was almost great.
Michael and I were just about to that point too." He went to
a wall, leaned against it. "This is just so fucking unbelievable."

"Todd, stay out of it."

"What?" he said, looking up.

"You're already in enough trouble. Let the police take
care of it. Just keep clear."

"Good God, how am I supposed to do that?"

"Todd, listen to what I'm saying." She paused, looked
him up and down. "Don't be a pigheaded guy about this.
Heed my words, alright, mister?"

"Yeah, yeah."

"I couldn't be more serious. You're in deep enough shit as
it is." She hesitated, then asked, "So, when are you going to
. . . to . . ."

"To what?"

She studied him long and hard. "You know, when are you
going to stop being so butch about all this?"

"What do you mean?"

"Jesus Christ, Todd, when are you going to cry?"

"I don't know." He turned away, rubbed his face, sensing
only this tremendous emptiness. "I was wondering that myself."

8

Detective Steve Rawlins sat at his desk in the bull room, a large space filled with about eight other desks, and stared at an intimidating pile of unfiled papers. He was trying to ascertain just how and where he was supposed to begin filing all this, when suddenly someone pushed the pile to the side. He lunged forward and wrapped his arms around the stack as he tried to keep his precious mess from dumping all over.

"Hey, watch it," snapped Rawlins as several pieces of paper slid off his desk and floated down to the linoleum floor. "This is important crap. All my cases for the last month."

"We're letting him go."

Rawlins reached down, grabbed the papers, and slapped them back on top of the heap, then looked over at Donna Lewis, who'd perched on the corner of his desk. He always had trouble reading her, this woman with the short hair and pale skin. She was just so steady. Or so cold. So Minnesotan. And now as she sat there, rolling a pencil back and forth in her hand, he couldn't read her, couldn't tell exactly what was on her mind. Nor, for that matter, did he have any idea who she was talking about.

"Who's that?" asked Rawlins, grabbing a file out of the middle of the pile and placing it to the side. "We're a tad buried under these days."

"The TV dude, our Mr. Mills."

"What?" snapped Rawlins, unable to hide his disbelief.

Lewis shrugged. "His lawyer was in again this morning. She spent a couple of hours with Mills and then went to see the judge. Apparently she came up with a series of alibis."

"Series?" said Rawlins, sliding the entire stack of papers over to the other side of his desk. "What the hell does that mean?"

"It means his lawyer couldn't pinpoint any one alibi to cover him for the entire time frame, so instead she patched together two or three." Lewis shrugged. "And apparently the judge bought it."

"Oh, come on, you're shitting me."

"Nope," replied Lewis, jabbing her short, sharp fingernail into the pencil's eraser.

"That fucker should be locked up."

"Sorry, he'll be out within the hour."

"That's crap. You know as well as I do that he's getting off because he's famous." Rawlins shook his head. "If we're really letting him go, then I'm going to personally check out each and every one of those alibis."

With a sly grin Lewis asked, "So what's the matter with you and Todd Mills?"

"His type bothers me, you know that." Rawlins leaned back in his chair. "Besides, you heard Mills yourself. Those two guys had a fight and Mills got violent. Real violent. Shit, you saw all that broken crap too. Mills said he didn't hit Carter, but who's to say? We should check with Carter's employer, see if Carter said anything at work. Or maybe someone noticed he was limping or something. Maybe he told a fellow worker he'd been threatened. Who knows? We've got to talk with them. Is the coroner's report in yet?''

''As of about twenty minutes ago all they could be certain of was that Michael Carter had suffered multiple stab wounds. It appeared that his heart was penetrated by a ten-inch knife.'' She added, ''The coroner did say that so far there wasn't any trace of semen on or in Carter. No anal penetration either. Carter's pants were down when his body was found, but so far they've detected no sign of any sexual contact or activity.''

''Well, maybe they'll find something else. Like I said, how do we know Mills didn't take a couple of swipes at Carter before he busted all those fucking dishes?''

''We don't. Not yet anyway.''

''Exactly. Trust me, something's wrong here. Among other things, there's still no sign of that Cubs hat.'' Rawlins thought for a moment and then added, ''But even if Mills didn't do anything the night before last, he could have come back last night. You know, like maybe he was still pissed and so he came back and lit into him. I mean, shit, there wasn't a forced entry at Carter's house—all the windows and doors are still secure—so either it was someone Carter knew or someone who—''

''Had a key.''

''Right.''

''Okay, okay. So we have to find out who has a key besides Todd Mills. Maybe the upstairs tenants. Maybe a neighbor. Speaking of which, be sure and get copies of all of Mills's keys before we let him go.''

''Already did,'' replied Rawlins, searching his desk. ''Two sets. They're here somewhere. Yep.'' He pulled the shiny keys from beneath a pad of paper. ''Oh, and what about family? Doesn't he have a sister here in town? Or what about a cleaning service? They'd probably have a key too.''

''Right.'' Lewis rubbed her forehead, bit her bottom lip. ''We have a complete search warrant, so we still have to get

him over to Hennepin County Medical. I'd like that done
before he leaves this morning."

"Meaning I'm the one to maintain the so-called chain of
evidence?"

"If you wouldn't mind."

"But why me?"

"Because you're a guy." Lewis went over to her desk,
which was only a few feet away, and picked up a sexual-
assault kit. "Here you go, buddy. Have fun."

"Oh, brother," said Rawlins, shaking his head. "Do you
think I should get a gay nurse to help me? Someone flaming
perhaps?"

"Actually, I don't think you want to intimidate him, not
right now, and I bet anyone gay, let alone a queen, would
make someone like him squirm." She stared at Rawlins,
looking him right in the eye as she said, "So what's your gut
tell you on this one?"

Not missing a beat, Rawlins replied, "Most crimes are
crimes of passion, right? So I'll bet it was a love fight between two homos, one of them horribly closeted and paranoid. A fight Todd Mills won."

"Maybe. Time will tell." She pointed to the stack of papers on his desk and said, "Rawlins, you're a mess, you
know it? You really got to clean all this up. I mean, how can
you find anything?"

"I got my own system."

"You're hopeless."

"I ain't no interior decorator, if you know what I mean."

"No shit. Listen, I'll go get Mills, and then you can take
him over to the hospital. We'll continue with the search as
soon as you're done." Lewis advised, "Just remember, be
real friendly. No matter how guilty you think he is, be real
nice to him, keep him talking."

"I love dirt."

"I'm serious. You're his new best friend."

"Don't worry, I'm good at this shit."

"I know."

He chuckled, briefly so, but as soon as she turned away Steve Rawlins's smile vanished. He watched Lewis disappear, eyeing her anxiously until she slipped out of the room and down the hall. He sat there for a few minutes, the thoughts rushing and sliding through his mind. Screw these papers. Fuck the filing. He just prayed she didn't know. There was no way she could, was there? No, he thought, replaying not only this conversation, but every moment, every word since last night. He thought back on it all, from the time they arrived at the scene of the crime to the interrogation of Todd Mills. No, no fucking way she could have picked up on it. He'd played it perfectly. Oh, but if she or anyone else here on the force ever suspected, even hinted . . .

Right, he thought, reaching around and grabbing his dark leather jacket from the back of his chair. He was going to have to forget about everything else that lay buried in this stack of papers, all the cases that were begging for attention, even the ones on the way to court. Screw them all, he thought. Nothing was more important than making sure no one found out about his connection to Michael Carter.

9

"So when did you first do it?"

Todd Mills climbed in and pulled shut the passenger door of the Taurus sedan. Glancing out the windshield, he squinted at the bright sunshine. Had he heard Detective Rawlins correctly? No, that couldn't be what he was asking. Todd, who hadn't been released more than five minutes ago, who was exhausted and dazed, had to be imagining it.

"What did you say?" Todd asked.

"When was the first time?" Rawlins started up the car, glanced over with a sly grin. "You know, with another guy."

"What?"

As they pulled away from the looming city hall, Todd shook his head. He couldn't believe this. Any of it. Wasn't the body search last night humiliation enough? Or the news reports?

Todd said, "I'm only doing this because my lawyer said I had to."

"Correction, you're only doing this because of a court order." Rawlins patted the sexual-assault kit next to him and added, "Don't worry, pal, it's painless and it won't take long. Kind of a formality. We're not looking for anything, really. It's just stuff for the record."

"How nice."

"Don't worry. I'll have you over at your lawyer's in forty-five minutes. Where's she taking you to lunch?"

"I don't know and I don't care." Todd thought for a second, then asked, "What do they want this stuff for? Where's it go? What record?"

"No big deal, the results just go to the crime lab. It's not public."

He slumped in his seat. "You know, I don't care what people know about me anymore. Not that I have a choice, but I really don't. I'm just too tired." He'd finally seen today's paper, and even he had been surprised at how open and vulnerable he appeared in the photo.

"You worried about the hospital?"

"No. Well, yeah, a bit. I just don't want to have to talk to anyone."

Rawlins quickly said, "Don't worry. I know a back entrance. We'll go in that way. We'll keep it quiet. No one will see you."

As they passed around a corner, Todd looked up at the towering red granite walls of the building he'd just exited. He saw a series of smaller windows. Was that where he'd been last night, way up there in a cell?

"Me?" began Rawlins, driving through the light traffic. "I wasn't a real early bloomer, if you know what I mean. I was a virgin until I was twenty. And that first time was the absolute best. I was really in love too. I was the star hitter on the college baseball team, the girls were all over me, and I could have had anyone. I mean it, almost any one of those chicks would've loved me like there was no tomorrow. Instead, I fall for someone who dumps me, and almost twenty years later I'm still not over it. Man, imagine falling in—"

Todd eyed him suspiciously and interrupted, asking, "Why the hell are you telling me this? You think I care?"

"Maybe not, but I think you're wound up about as tight as they come. And trust me, man, everyone's going to be asking about your sex life. You're in the hot seat, buddy, and you just got to relax a bit. Do you have anyone you can talk to? Any other gay friends?"

"Well . . ." He'd almost mentioned Janice, but he stopped short, unsure just what was okay to divulge. "No, not really."

"I'd recommend you find some fast. You've just come exploding out of the closet, and it's no time to be alone. Even I know that. The pressure's not going to let up on you for weeks, maybe months. You're going to need some good support."

"So you're a therapist? And here I thought that you were just a detec—"

"Please, my duties are endless. I went into this field just so people could call me a real dick." Rawlins laughed. "Which reminds me, have you heard what they call a lesbian detective?"

Todd wasn't sure he wanted to know. In any case, why the hell was Rawlins talking about this?

He said, "No."

"A dyke dick."

Todd shook his head, and stared out the window as they headed over to Washington Avenue, then headed east. The Mississippi River and the St. Anthony Falls lay to the left, just beyond a series of grain mills. Straight ahead, a mile at most, was the West Bank of the University of Minnesota. It all seemed so simple. For the first time Todd saw clearly how he'd taken so many false steps in life and how suddenly everything had caught up with him.

"You're one of those guys who'd change to being straight, aren't you? I mean, if it were possible you'd turn hetero, wouldn't you?" asked Rawlins. "I'm right, aren't I?"

"At one point that's all I wanted, yeah." So, thought Todd, am I really that uptight, that transparent? "I even got married."

"Yeah, you mentioned that last night. Were you happy?"

"She was very pretty, very nice. I was nice. We were nice together. Besides the fact that we stopped having sex after the first year, it just didn't work." Todd shrugged. "What about you?"

"I almost got married a couple of times, but . . . but . . ." He shrugged and laughed. "Like I said, that first time was really the best. Unfortunately nothing's come close since."

Todd saw how Rawlins was going toward the hospital, swinging wide past the Metrodome, then cutting back in. Why the circuitous route? This had to be twice as far as just cutting across town. Was Rawlins merely heading for the promised back door? Or was there another reason—namely, was he trying to prolong this conversation?

A few blocks later he saw it, the Hennepin County Medical Center, a massive beige and brown building, very long and low. Todd had been here a number of times as well. The best trauma center in the region was here, and Todd had charged in after a half-dozen crime victims. Frequently he'd cornered a hassled doctor for a comment too. And once he'd even been there filming when an old guy who'd been mugged went into cardiac arrest. A great segment. Quite intense.

"So when did you meet Michael?" asked Rawlins, as he turned another corner and started hunting for a parking place.

"Four years ago."

"Where?"

"At the lake."

"What'd you do, pick him up at the gay beach?"

"No."

"In the bushes? There's a gay pickup place there, isn't there?"

"If you really want to know, I was jogging and twisted my ankle in a hole. He was out for a run too, and he stopped, asked if he could help."

"Love at first sight?"

"Kind of."

Todd recalled how Michael had helped him over to a bench, then stood there, quite concerned, as Todd loosened his shoe. Todd wasn't all that lame, but Michael insisted on walking him the three or four blocks to his condo. Nothing had happened then, but they saw each other out running the next week and pretty soon they were jogging regularly together. Then Todd had invited Michael up for a beer. And then . . .

"So were you two committed right from the beginning?" asked Rawlins.

"Yeah."

"You didn't date anyone else?"

"No. It felt that strong right from the start."

"You were lucky." With a grin, Rawlins pressed, "Really, totally monogamous? No fun on the side?"

"Nope." Todd eyed Rawlins, wondered what his situation was. "What about you? Are you in a relationship?"

"I was last year. Or was it the year before?" he said with a laugh.

"What happened?"

He shrugged. "Someone started screwing around, if you know what I mean."

Todd waited for the rest of the story, but there was none. He saw the change in Rawlins's mood—the still eyes, the flat mouth—as if he were recalling something not at all pleasant. Todd assumed that Rawlins had been dumped, his girlfriend probably left him for another guy. Everyone had a story, but he wasn't particularly interested in this detective's.

Rawlins, lost in thought, silently pulled the car into an empty spot and shut off the engine, then climbed out.

"Wait a minute," said Todd, pointing to the box on the seat. "Don't we need this?"

"Right."

As Rawlins scooped up the sexual-assault kit, Todd climbed out. He then followed the detective toward a side entrance, one that was off the main street and hardly used. Passing through a series of long white corridors, Todd kept his head down. He wished he had a hat. Or some big sunglasses. When a couple of nurses looked their way, Todd scratched his head and looked at the floor. They hadn't recognized him, had they?

Finally Rawlins ushered Todd into a small room, saying, "Wait in here."

Todd entered the small chamber, saw a sink, an examination table, a chair. He stood there realizing he'd never felt so humble. Nor so lost. He just wanted to get this over with and go home. The details of Michael's funeral loomed before him like a dark cloud.

Less than a minute later Rawlins came back in, going over to the examination table and placing the kit on it. He opened the box and withdrew a small comb and several plastic bags. Jesus Christ, thought Todd, watching all this. What was going on?

"Okay," explained Rawlins. "This bag is for pubic and the other for head."

"What?"

"You know, hair samples."

"Wait a minute, my lawyer didn't say anything about this."

"Trust me, this is all standard."

"But she told me," protested Todd, "I was just coming over here to have some blood drawn."

"That too. That's what those vials are for," said Rawlins, nodding toward the inside of the kit. "But besides that I need fifty plucked pubic hairs and fifty plucked hairs from your head. They gotta be plucked, too, so you get the follicles or whatever.''

"No way.''

"I can show you the search warrant. Do you want to see that again? Or maybe you'd like to just go back to the jail?''

Todd shook his head. "I can't believe this.''

"No need to panic, bud,'' said Rawlins. "Now, either you do it—you just put the samples in these little bags—or I can get a nurse. Would you like him to do the plucking?'' He held up the comb. "Or would you like me?''

Todd shook his head, reached for the comb and bags. "No, thanks. You can leave.''

"Remember, fifty.''

"Yeah, yeah. But this is ridiculous. It's not going to prove a thing.''

"I'm just following rules.''

As Rawlins was shutting the door, it just popped out of Todd: "I was fourteen.''

Rawlins pushed the door back a bit. "What?''

"You know, the first time.''

"No shit, you were that young? Were you just experimenting or was it the real thing?''

"Well, frankly I'm not as straight as I've been pretending.''

"What was his name?''

Todd thought for a moment. "Tommy. He lived down the street.''

"And who was your best lover?''

"My last.''

"Meaning?''

"Michael, of course.''

"Yeah,'' mused Rawlins, "there really are lovers who just pass through your life and others who change your path. Don't you think?''

Todd nodded. "That's the kind of guy Michael was.''

Then, before Rawlins could ask anything else, Todd pressed the door shut. He stood still in that small white room, wondering why? Why on earth would he confess any of his sexual history to Rawlins? And more important, why the hell would Rawlins want to know?

10

So they thought Todd Mills had done it. How fucking unbelievable. Incredible, really.

The little things in life offered the biggest rewards. Or something like that. His grandmother had had all sorts of little wisdoms, most of which he'd dismissed. But the old lady had been right on this one, by God. The one about the little stuff in life was absolutely true.

The man who'd most definitely been the last person to see Michael Carter alive now sat behind the locked door of his apartment, staring at the front page of the *Tribune*. It was early afternoon as he sat reading the paper over and over. He still couldn't believe it. It had been on the radio and television as well, a little feeding frenzy of guess-who's-fucking-who. He'd been so worried, had taken every precaution he could imagine so that no one would spot him and the police wouldn't be able to trace him. Obviously he'd done it all right. It was good, too, that he'd made Michael undress before doing him, for it made it look like a passionate crime. But Todd Mills? They thought Todd Mills had knifed Michael Carter? Holy shit, it was too good to be true. Why hadn't he had the brains to set it up that way? Then again, if he had tried, he probably would have blown it and been caught. So it was better this way. Totally unexpected. A surprise reward for a job well-done. He dropped the paper in his lap, felt another wave of smug pride.

It had also never occurred to him that he would be this exhausted after doing Michael. It was the release, he supposed. Even now, not even twenty-four hours later, he felt so relieved, so spent. For weeks he'd been anticipating last night. The sheer inevitability of it had loomed before him each day. The suspense of when and how had been unbearable, but now that it was over he felt like celebrating.

And he felt like having a cigarette too.

Still chuckling to himself, he pushed himself out of his chair and passed into his kitchen. It was a little box of an apartment, identical to all the other ones in the building, a two-and-a-half story walk-up built in the early seventies. It was comfortable enough, particularly given how little time he actually spent there.

He reached the dark-wood cabinets, pulled open a drawer. There it was: the knife. Just lying there with the big ladle, the grater, the can opener. Of course he'd never use it again for carving meat, not after last night. He wasn't some sicko after all. He'd come home and washed the blade thoroughly, then put on a spaghetti pot of water, brought it to a boil, and dropped the knife into it and let it cook for a minute or two. He guessed he should eventually get rid of it, but there certainly weren't any traces of Michael or his clothing left on it after all that. And what better place to hide it than with the ladle and grater and can opener?

He always knew he was smart, and this proved it, he thought, reaching past the knife for a half-empty pack of cigarettes that languished at the back of the drawer. He'd quit smoking—what was it?—five years ago, but he still allowed himself two cigarettes a month. That was nothing, really. Down from a pack a day. And he allowed himself two smokes a month not merely for the carnal pleasure but to show that he had real control. He wasn't like those wimps in all those stop-smoking groups, the ones who needed to be babied along. Nope. Not him. Just like everything else, he did it all alone. Grandma would be proud, so very proud.

He dragged a match over a burner on the stove, lit up a cig, and took a deep, soulful drag. The rich, hot smoke filled his lungs. He held it, let it burn his lungs, and strolled out of the kitchen, through the living room, and to the sliding glass door that opened onto the balcony. He pulled the door back a bit, leaned forward, let the smoke spew and steam out into the cool afternoon air. No sense in smoking up the joint.

There was at least one more guy he wanted to do. And if there were others who knew too much, he'd do them too.

Just as he'd done with Michael, he'd been studying the next one, a fat, lonely guy, for weeks. He knew where Mr. Number Two lived, where he worked, even when he went to sleep. He knew that and so much more. Once, right in the middle of the day, he'd even stopped over at the guy's house and thumbed through his mail. That had been dumb, one of the neighbors could have seen him, but he couldn't resist. Anyway, that was almost a month ago, and he had to know everything. Now that he did, it was time to whack him. So to speak. Yes, he had to do it. Had to. It was an obsession, he understood that much. But an obsession born of necessity. And he had to take care of this next man.

He sucked on the cigarette until his head grew light. That was a real plus about smoking rarely. When you did have a cig it made you kind of high. Oh, blessed life, he said to himself, loving every bit of this. Last night had gone better than he'd ever imagined.

He'd tried to anticipate it all, tried to make a plan or a schedule, but now that he'd finished with Michael everything was different. Not at all as he'd expected. This side of murder was entirely different than he'd ever thought. Beforehand, he was sure he'd have to wait a few months, maybe even six, before he could get up the nerve to start after his next target. He'd even considered the possibility that after he'd killed for the first time he wouldn't be able to do it again. But that wasn't the case. Not at all. He was actually eager.

Cigarette in his mouth, he turned from the sliding glass door and headed over to his chair. The picture, now where was it? He lifted up a couple of books, pushed aside a coaster. Yes, there it was on the side table. It didn't mean much, not at all. All he had was this one photograph, a small one, and even if the police raided his apartment and found this snapshot it certainly wasn't going to prove anything. Nevertheless, what had Grandma always said when she'd measured and remeasured flour for her cakes? You can't be too careful, no sirree. It was an adage that had served her well. And him too.

Photo in hand, he returned to the kitchen, struck another match, and held it to the picture. The flame took to the paper, crawling up and around the image of a very heavy man in his late thirties and capturing it with fire. He turned to the sink, held the burning thing over the drain. Of course this man knew Michael. They'd been good friends for a long time, actually.

Pinching the burning photograph by the very edge, he held it until the very last minute. Mr. Number Two was going to be easy. He worked hard, lived alone, was in terrible shape. There had been no lover in his life for a long time, perhaps years. He might even beg for it. Yes, this target would be that excited, so delighted that another living and breathing soul had taken an interest in him. Christ, he'd probably be down on his knees, screaming: Give it to me, oh God, give it to me! And he was going to get it, no doubt about that.

Only one problem. This one was a real talker. A gabber who loved to expound on everything and anything. He'd tell the world all of his joys and woes as loudly as he could. So now the man resolved he'd have to sneak over after the bars had closed. Nothing said beforehand. Absolutely not. And no seeing him beforehand whatsoever. No way.

Yes, that was the way it would be. Only with one twist. God, this was great. Okay, okay, so he didn't have the idea at first, but at least he was smart enough to pick up on a terrific thing. Namely, if Todd Mills had taken the fall so easily for the first murder, why not the second? He'd just happen to drop a little something of Todd's at the murder site, a little something that he so happened to have in his possession. Even if the police didn't jump on it, the media most certainly would. Then it would turn into a real circus.

With that in mind, he glanced at his watch. Oh, shit. It was almost time. He dropped the photo into the sink, turned on the water as well as the disposal, then flushed the remains of the picture down the roaring drain. He dropped his cigarette butt down too, and turned and hurried into the living room, where he switched on his small color TV.

It was almost time for the midday news, and the talk of Todd Mills was sure to be juicy.

11

"Listen, lunch was enough," Todd said as they rode the elevator downward. "You don't have to take me home."

"Like hell I don't," replied Janice. "Are you still mad?"

"About the fifty plucked pubic hairs? No, just a tad sore."

"I'm sorry I forgot to tell you."

They'd eaten in an empty corner of a cafeteria, Todd not finishing the small tuna sandwich. And now the elevator halted three levels beneath the street, and the doors eased open into the small lobby of a vast underground parking garage. Janice stepped out first, briefcase in hand, her high heels clipping along.

Todd hurried after her, suggesting, "I could just grab a cab and go over and pick up my car."

"Think again, sweetheart. You ain't got no vehicle."

Todd stopped, put his hand to his forehead. What the hell was she saying?

"Todd," said Janice over her shoulder as she led the way out of the small lobby and between two cars, "you're out of the slammer, but your car isn't. For the time being the police have your Cherokee. It's nothing serious, you don't have anything to worry about, they just want to check it out. No big deal. You don't have a second car, do you?''

"I used Michael's when mine was in the shop.''

"Well, you can forget that for right now. You have to stay away from Michael's place and his things—including his car—for a while. His apartment is still a sealed crime scene.'' She thought for a second and added, ''Remind me to check on this, but you might even have to get permission from his next of kin to go into his place.''

"Isn't that me? Aren't I next of kin?''

"Not legally.''

"But we were pretty much living together. And I have a lot of stuff over there. Clothes, books. I think I even left my checkbook in the bedroom.''

"Sorry, you weren't married. Not that you could have been, that being against the law for two people of the same sex in this great nation of ours.'' She turned down a row of cars, headed for hers, and, her voice thick with judgment, said, ''Of course if you and Michael had bothered to register as domestic partners, the legal status between the two of you would be much better. But we didn't bother to do that, now did we?''

"No.''

Michael had wanted to register when the city made it legally possible several years ago. But to do so would have meant an open public process, and how could Todd do that? That gossip columnist over at the *Tribune* could have picked up on it, and then what about his career? So Todd had nixed that one. But Michael had kept pressing, suggesting another symbol, say, the exchange of rings. Todd had tripped on that idea as well, asking what kind of ring, a gold wedding band or something totally different? Michael said it didn't matter, just something, a symbol of their commitment. Then Todd had stalled over the design.

Bullshit, thought Todd. He'd stalled because he'd been worried what people at the station would think about him wearing a new ring and what it might imply if it had even slightly looked like a wedding band. He'd hesitated on any public symbol of their relationship, and now Michael was gone forever.

What an absolute fool Todd had been. He now saw that so completely. Obsessed by what others would think, when all that mattered in the end was how deeply he cared for someone and how that someone had reached into his heart and said, yes, we are good. Together the two of us are good. Well, Michael had been better than Todd. Far wiser. And infinitely less uptight.

"Janice, you go back to your office. You've got work to do. I'll just take your car."

Janice stopped next to a van and turned, studying him out of the corner of her eye. He glanced away, wondering if Janice, the purveyor of truth, might see through him. Would she approve?

"Pardon me, Todd," she began, one hand on her slender hip, "but you look like shit. Your hair's shooting this way and that, your eyes are red and puffy. Your clothes are wrinkled. You need to go home and get some rest, and that's where I'm taking you. Home. And I want to escort you all the way there, just so that I know you make it."

"Janice, I can—"

"Have you realized that there might be some journalists waiting at your building, hoping to get a word or a photo of you?" She paused. "Well, have you? You're good bait, and this makes a great story. I wouldn't rule out *Newsweek* or *Time* going after this story. Don't forget how the media swarmed over O. J."

"What?" None of this had even occurred to him.

"That's why it would be good to have your lawyer with you. Let me remind you, this is big, juicy stuff to Middle America. A queer TV journalist arrested for killing his secret lover. Sounds like a movie of the week, doesn't it?" She shook her head. "Dear God, don't I sound ridiculous? Middle America. I mean, what is it? And who are they? A coffee klatsch consisting of all our mothers waiting to pass moral judgment? Lookit, Todd, here we are, the two of us, in an underground garage, smack dab in the middle of the Midwest. If this isn't Middle America, where is it? Better yet, if we aren't part of it, who is?''

''Janice, really, there's no need for—''

''Okay, out with it.''

''With what?''

''Listen, I'm not some dumb old dyke. You're not planning on going home just yet, are you?''

''No.''

''You don't want to go to the station, do you? That's not where you're going, is it? As your lawyer and your friend, I'd advise against that right now. You've been suspended with pay, don't forget. It really would be best if you let me contact them.''

''No, I—''

She stared right at him, fear whisking across her face. ''My God, you're going to see someone else, aren't you?''

''Well, actually, yes.''

''Oh, shit, Todd, you shouldn't have told me that,'' she said, putting her left hand to her forehead.

He watched as she spun on a heel and stormed off toward her car, then stopped, turned again, and started toward the elevator. Her face was flushed red with fury.

''Janice, please.''

''As your lawyer I've got to hear everything, but as your friend this is exactly what I didn't want to know.''

He jogged after her, caught her gently by the elbow. She stopped, bowed her head, couldn't even bear to look at him.

''What the hell's going on?'' he asked.

Finally she said, ''You've got another boyfriend and you're going to go see him, aren't you? Did you spend the night with this other guy after you and Michael fought? Oh, Christ, wait until the police find out about this. No, wait until the paper gets ahold of it. My God, you're dead meat. They'll make you out to be just another pervert fag. Shit, why did Michael ever put up with you, what did—"

"Janice, there was only Michael," Todd said softly. "Only him. I was a jerk about a lot of things, but I knew right from the start that I never needed anyone else."

She looked up at him, her own exhaustion showing through, and asked, "But . . . but then where are you going?"

"I need to see Maggie."

Janice gasped and put a hand to her thin lips. "Oh, Todd . . ."

"I won't be able to rest or sleep until I see her."

"No, of course not."

"It's not a problem, my going there, is it? Legally, I mean. That's why I didn't want to tell you. I've got to see her."

Her voice was faint. "No, no, it's okay."

She closed her eyes, tried unsuccessfully to hold back several tears. Michael's murder was going to shake up the entire gay community of Minneapolis and St. Paul, Todd knew. For Michael's close friends like Janice, however, the tremors would resonate much deeper and much longer.

"I'm sorry," began Janice. "This is too much, all of it. I'm really sorry. Maybe I'm too close to you. And I adored Michael. Maybe I shouldn't be handling this case."

"Nonsense." He bent forward, kissed her on the cheek.

"I hate it when people die. I hate being left."

"Yeah," he said, understanding she was referring to her own tragedy. "Thanks for liberating me this morning."

"Yeah, right," she said as she fumbled through her briefcase, searching for her keys.

"I can pick you up later this afternoon."

"No, don't. I'll take the bus." She was quick to add, "And keep the car. Don't forget, I still have Julie's Beetle. I'm pretty sure I can get it going."

"That old orange thing?"

What was it, twenty-five years old? Janice's partner, Julie, had had it from her college days right up until her death. And yet, even eight years after Julie's death, Todd knew Janice couldn't sell the Volkswagen with its convertible top. The little thing with the rattly engine just seemed so much like Julie, free-spirited and fun, particularly on a hot summer day with the top folded down. And so it remained in Janice's garage, covered by a couple of old dingy sheets, started up not more than three or four times a year.

Janice plucked the car key from her key ring, stuffed it into Todd's palm, and said, "I'll call later, see if you need anything like a pizza or ice cream." She kissed him on the cheek. "Give my love to her."

It was a straight shot out of the city to Lake Minnetonka. The state had recently spent a ridiculous amount of money— nearly a half-billion dollars on not quite fifteen miles of concrete—to make it as easy as possible for white folk to flee the city to the wealthiest and most exclusive western suburbs. Todd had never understood that one, why the state would work not to slow the hemorrhage of tax dollars out of the core city but instead to encourage it. In any case, that afternoon the smooth, straight highway made Todd's drive simple, even thoughtless. Whisking along in Janice's red Honda Prelude, Todd found himself squinting, for he couldn't take it all in, particularly after the darkness of the jail. The clear, crisp day was just so bright, so beautiful, the fall colors still at their peak of bright gold and orange. It looked so disturbingly heavenly.

Just over twenty minutes after he left Janice in the underground garage, Todd pulled off the highway and passed along the edge of Lake Minnetonka, a huge lake that never seemed to quit, only twist and turn. He followed a winding and hilly road lined with trees in multicolored splendor and then turned down a small lane. Soon he was maneuvering down a familiar narrow drive strewn with fallen leaves. Then he saw it, the Cape Cod house perched right on the edge of the lake. Through the collection of shedding oaks and maples he spotted a number of cars as well. It all appeared so perfect, but of course it wasn't, not today of all days. A moment later a frisky golden retriever bounded out of the woods, barking his announcement. When Todd parked and climbed out, the dog came rushing up.

"Hi, Pronto," he said, patting the exuberant creature, which had been a gift from Michael two years ago. They'd been at the state fair and Michael was talking about the kids, how upset they were about their parents' separation. And as Michael chowed on a Pronto Pup—that peculiar corn dog on a stick—he resolved to get them a golden retriever, just like he'd had as a boy, in the hopes that it would bring them the same joy.

"And I'll recommend they call it Pronto," he'd said with a big laugh. "Absolutely. It's got to be a golden retriever too. They're such happy dogs."

The dog, like Michael, had indeed brought joy to this house, for the parents had gotten back together. The magic hadn't lasted forever though. The parents had split again, and now they'd been apart for three or four months. Todd glanced to his left, saw the silver Oldsmobile. At least Rick was here today.

He pressed the doorbell, heard small, quick steps, and the door was pulled back by an eight-year-old boy with curly brown hair. As the dog went shooting past them both into the house, the child stared up at Todd and his eyes quickly grew huge with fright.

In an instant he was running back into the living room, shouting, "Mom!"

"Wait, Jason!" Todd called, reaching fruitlessly after him.

He hadn't thought about it before, he'd been too tired, but now that he'd seen the fear in Jason's eyes, Todd worried how the others would react. They couldn't possibly think that he'd been involved in any way, could they? Dear God. Todd stood on the threshold, switching his weight from his left foot to his right and back again. Should he have called first? Or maybe not come at all? He put his hand to his forehead. Perhaps he should just turn around, race away. Was this how everyone was going to react to him, assume he was a killer?

A weak voice said, "Todd?"

He looked up. Michael's sister Maggie stood there, her hair dark brown and curly like Michael's. She was pretty, with brown eyes, a handful of freckles set high on her wide cheeks. Outside of their own homes, there were very few places Todd felt comfortable being openly gay, and this was definitely one of them. Michael and his sister were extremely close—her rock, she called him—and Todd and he had come here at least several times a month for dinner, a swim, a long talk. Yes, the long talks. While Michael had been out playing catch with his two nephews, Todd had often sat on their deck, beer in hand, discussing with Maggie and Rick the traumas of the world. Lately, of course, it had just been Maggie, and lately the subject had been marital bliss, or the lack thereof.

Now Michael's little sister stood at the far end of the hall, staring at Todd with red, swollen eyes, and for a long moment he thought she was going to scream at him. He bit his lip, couldn't move, didn't know what to say. How was this going to go?

"Oh, God, Todd!" she finally said, and started rushing toward him, her hands lifting upward.

He hurried forward, embraced her, one hand wrapping around her back, the other up into her hair. All at once he could feel her crying, the sob racking her body, bursting out of her mouth. He bit his lip, clenched his eyes shut, held his pain as deeply and tightly as he could.

"I loved him, Maggie," he managed to whisper. "I didn't hurt him."

"Of course you didn't."

"We had a fight the night before last. I broke some

dishes,'' he said, clutching her and compulsively confessing, wanting her to know, understand everything. ''I think they were your grandmother's. I'm sorry, but the station was going to offer me an anchor position and . . . and Michael said I had to come out to them or he was going to leave me. He said he wanted to come to the Channel Seven Christmas party, and I just lost it. All the pressure, you know. Them and him. And me. And those fucking Emmys. I couldn't handle it. I just didn't know what people expected of me. But I loved him. I didn't hurt Michael.''

''I never thought you did.'' She pulled away, wiped her eyes, kissed him once on the cheek. ''Come on in. Some friends are here.'' She raised her eyebrows. ''Rick's here too. Actually, he's been a big help. The kids are real upset.''

He sucked it in. All the pain, the fear, the horror. He didn't want to see anyone else besides Maggie. He didn't want to have to put on any pretense, have to hold it all together for anyone. Yet when Maggie wrapped one arm around him and nudged him on, he didn't resist. He let her escort him down the hall and to the edge of the sunken living room, a large space lined on the far side with sliding glass doors that overlooked the lake.

As they stood three steps above the gathered friends, Maggie whispered into Todd's ear, ''Trust me, Todd, everyone knows now.''

As they should, he thought, his stomach wrenching tighter. As they must. Maggie and Rick had been asked not to talk about it before, but suddenly those dark days of secrecy were over, finished forever.

''Everyone,'' said Maggie, sniffling, ''this is Todd, Michael's partner.''

It was so easy. No one cared. They were Maggie's neighbors and friends, four or five of them gathered for her support. As they rose and expressed their sorrow and shook his hand, all Todd could think was that he'd been crazy to hide like that, so deeply in the closet. Good God, what had he put

Michael through anyway? Who cared about the ratings or career or any of that crap? As these people swarmed around him, as he replied with all the perfunctory remarks, he suddenly wished he'd never gone into television. So much was so clear now. Television had enlarged and broadcast all of his fears, placing all of him out there for judgment.

"Uncle Michael was going to teach Jason and me to drive the boat next summer."

Todd looked down. What was he, six or seven? Josh was all boy, with an impy twinkle in his eye, just like Michael.

Todd knelt down, roughed the boy's hair, tried to speak but had to clear his throat, finally saying, "Well, he won't be able to. But I'd sure like to. Can I come back when it's warm and I'll teach you everything that Michael taught me about boats?"

The child glanced away and nodded.

"Thanks," said Todd.

No sooner had Todd risen than he was faced with his most frequent daytime drink, a glass of mineral water sporting a wedge of lime. Rick handed it to him and embraced Todd awkwardly, the glass somewhere between the two.

"I'm so sorry. He was such a great guy. I . . . I . . ."

What was Todd supposed to say? He looked at Rick, Michael's brother-in-law, a handsome man with a round face and reddish hair that was receding. He was a burly guy, a jock's jock, always energetic, though now Rick looked exhausted as he stared at the ground, shaking his head. In spite of the trouble Maggie and he were having, Rick and Michael had been close and for years had had a standing monthly racquetball date. Michael was proud of Rick too, calling his brother-in-law the least homophobic het he knew.

"I just don't get it," said Rick, staring out the window and at the lake. "It just doesn't make any sense."

Todd took a sip of the water. No, it sure doesn't.

Rick led Todd away from the others, lowered his voice,

and volunteered, "We saw the papers. I'm sorry it all came out like this. You and Michael, I mean. I'm sure the police have been hard on you. It's just so awful. Do you have a good lawyer? Is there anything I can do?"

"I think I'm all set for now, thanks. My friend Janice is handling the case for the time being."

"Well, I'm sure it's going to be rough, particularly for a few weeks." He reached into his pocket, pulled out a card. "You know Maggie and I are still having troubles. We talk every day and I've been over here a lot, but . . . well, don't forget you can always reach me at the office. Things are busy, but I'm around."

"The business is still going well?"

"Gangbusters. Finally. It sure as hell took long enough."

"You've been working at it for a long time," said Todd.

"Over ten years, night and day, can you believe it?" Rick shook his head. "Then something like this happens and you realize what's really important. Good God, where's this country going? So much violence. Are any of us safe?"

"No," replied Todd. "I suppose we're not."

Maggie came up next to him, quietly said, "Todd, we need to start making the arrangements. You know, the funeral."

"Of course."

He stared out the windows at the flat blue waters of the lake. His mind flashed on Michael's body. What was the coroner doing to poor Michael this very moment? Todd turned away, felt a wave of nausea tightening his throat. No, he couldn't think about that.

"I already contacted one place," continued Maggie. "The funeral home we used for Mom and Dad. But it's your decision, really. Are you up to it, or would you like me to take care of it all?"

If in many ways Todd had not given himself fully to Michael in life, if he'd held back out of any one of his myriad of fears, then he wouldn't now, not in the end. Nothing else mattered, and his pride in Michael rallied and began to surge forward. Of course he knew better than anyone what Michael would want.

Maggie pressed again, asking, "Can you handle it?"

Todd nodded. "Yes, absolutely."

12

Todd stayed at Maggie's much too long. It was after four thirty by the time he made it back into town, and he could feel the exhaustion creeping like a numbing drug up his arms and legs. He knew he needed to sleep, yet he couldn't imagine closing his eyes or finding any kind of tranquility, because the closer he drew to home, the more he feared what he was about to find.

As he turned Janice's Prelude onto the wooded Dean Parkway, he scanned the area in front of his building, and there it was, just as he'd pictured it: the next in this string of nightmares. A group of eight, maybe ten, people was gathered on the sidewalk like a band of union picketers. Todd clenched the steering wheel, but focused on his destination. Drawing close and turning into the drive, he took a deep breath, steeling himself, just as a thin, older man in a white shirt and tie turned his way, pointing at the small red car with an accusatory finger.

"All homosexuals will go to hell!" he shouted, waving a Bible in his other hand.

Todd quickly closed his window, and it was soon apparent

that the group was by no means united. Two men in short plaid kilts and crowns of flowers—obviously from the fringe gay group Radical Faeries—jumped forward and blew Todd kisses. Next a woman in a long, billowy dress lifted up a sign that read I LOVE YOU, TODD MILLS! MARRY ME!

Todd's entire body tightened like a single muscle, and he headed up the drive, stomping on the gas and speeding past them all. As he left them shouting in his wake he wondered, was this just the beginning? Oh, Christ, he thought, his head pounding. While before he'd hidden his sexuality so well, now it was being rubbed and smeared in his face.

As he passed the lobby he saw the security guard, Bob, a beefy, handsome blond man, stepping out the front door. Todd had always had a crush on this young man, and Bob had always been—until recently anyway—exceedingly friendly toward Todd, either because Todd was famous or because Bob was queer and he sensed Todd was too. That still wasn't clear, especially since one night last month when Bob had delivered a UPS parcel to Todd's apartment; when gorgeous Bob had lingered and wanted to talk, Todd had nearly panicked, saying he was working on a story and didn't have a moment. So was Bob stepping out now to make sure Todd had safe entry to his home, or had he come to gawk and stare with disdain at Todd, the homo killer?

Todd stopped by the door and opened the car window. He looked at Bob and cleared his throat.

"Have . . . have they been out there long?" asked Todd, referring to the demonstrators.

Bob didn't even look at Todd as he muttered, "All afternoon."

"Anyone from the media around?"

Bob shrugged, then stepped back, retreating into the lobby.

Great, thought Todd. He continued up the ramp and into the garage, where he parked Janice's car. He glanced around the vast dark space before climbing out, eyed no one, and then caught the elevator up to the fifteenth floor. As the doors opened he was pleased that there hadn't been any journalists lurking about. Now at least he'd be able to retreat to the confines of his two-bedroom condo, where he could barricade himself behind a locked door. Maybe he'd even unplug the phone, something he usually hated doing for fear of missing something, anything.

Thinking of the phone as he walked down the long corridor, he reached into the pocket of his sport coat and felt nothing. Then he touched his shirt pocket. It, too, was empty. So where was it? Had he left his beeper down at the police station? Wait, no. He recalled checking it last night just after he pulled up in front of Michael's. Had he tossed it aside, broken it? Right, he'd thrown it across the car. But that didn't matter now. He'd probably be fired from Channel 7 anyway, and he most certainly wouldn't get the promotion.

Nearing his place, he reached into his pants pocket and pulled out a key. As he went to unlock his door though, he froze. What was that? He heard a mumbled voice, some rustling. Todd turned, glanced down the hall. Was someone coming out of another apartment? Or was he merely hearing something from one of his neighbors?

No, it was coming from his own place.

His heart flushed with concern and he was very still. It sure as hell was coming from within his apartment. He heard talking. Yes, there were at least two people in there, conferring about something. As quietly and carefully as he could, he leaned forward, pressed his ear against the thick wooden door. He couldn't discern what was being said and he moved over, tried peering through the peephole. A black blob of a figure crossed the room, temporarily blocking the light.

This couldn't be anyone from the station, could it? Dear God, had he given his key to anyone at Channel 7? Sure, not long ago he'd given a complete extra set to Mark Buchanan so he could drop by and pick up a videotape. So was this some sort of cheap stunt, were they now in there filming his place?

He slowly twisted the knob, found the door unlocked. Carefully he eased open the door. Where were they? Who were they? He took a half-step in, paused, moved a little bit farther. The door to the kitchen was on the right, and he hesitated, peered around the corner. Although the kitchen was dark and empty, several drawers were pulled all the way open and a couple of things were spread out on the counter. Fuck, thought Todd, this wasn't the television crew. He was being robbed.

"Found something," called an amused voice down the hall. "Sock drawer syndrome!"

Todd froze in disbelief, for he most surely recognized the voice. The next instant he exploded with rage and charged down the narrow hall, past the first bedroom, which he used as an office, and to the second, his bedroom. He tore through the doorway, saw a woman with short blond hair reaching into his sock drawer and pulling out a plastic container of lubricant, some condoms, and a glossy magazine full of naked men. An hysterical burst of panic overwhelmed him.

"What the hell are you doing?" screamed Todd.

His left hand was out, ready to grab her. He plowed forward, an out-of-control anger surging through him. But just as the woman spun around and before she could even raise her hands in defense, another figure came barreling out of the walk-in closet. Todd didn't see him until it was too late, until the guy smashed into his side, which sent Todd hurtling through the air onto the bed. Every bit of wind was knocked out of him, and he doubled over, gasped for breath. And then they were upon him, both of them pinning him down. Todd caught some air, bucked and screamed, but within a matter of a few short moments he couldn't even move.

"Get out of here!" gasped Todd. "You have no goddamn right!"

"Take it easy!" yelled Detective Lewis, her knee on his left shoulder.

"You can't do this! You can't be in here! You can't go through my things!"

"We've got a search warrant, asshole!" hollered Rawlins, who was on top of Todd's other shoulder and arm. "You know what a fucking search warrant is, don't you?"

"But—"

"We showed it to you last night," said Lewis. "We told you it was for everything—body, house, work."

Towering over Todd, Rawlins added, "It's a court order, there's nothing you can do. Nothing! We're just doing our jobs. So cool it! Cool it, man! We've got to do this. There's nothing you can do."

Gradually it sunk in. Of course there wasn't. Not a blessed thing. And when they finally let go of him, Todd could barely move. He rolled onto his side, just lay there on top of his down comforter, wanting nothing more than to fall into a screaming, crying fit. But he didn't.

"Don't worry," said Lewis, catching her breath. "This is nothing unusual."

Todd eyed the magazine of naked guys, lying there across the bed, and he lifted an arm to take it. Rawlins grabbed the magazine and threw it aside.

"Forget it, man," snapped Rawlins. "We can take whatever we like. Now go on, get out of here."

It was all too much, and like a beaten dog Todd disappeared, retreating to the living room where he pulled an overstuffed chair up to the window. He sat there, lost in shock and staring at Lake Calhoun while Detectives Lewis and Rawlins went through the drawers of his dresser, his closet, his medicine cabinet. His desk. His files and bills. Sure, they'd told him about this. It just hadn't registered. He knew what a search warrant was, of course. He just hadn't realized it would mean this . . . this humiliation.

Todd sat in the fading light, staring out over the oval lake for another half hour or so. He watched as a ring of park lights around the lake was illuminated and as car lights came on too. Finally he heard their voices behind him, heard them zipping up their jackets. Todd glanced back briefly and saw that they had gathered three large plastic bags of stuff.

"We're going to be on our way," called Rawlins from the entry hall. "I'm sorry about this. We thought you were going to be home all afternoon. We thought you'd be here. We didn't mean to surprise you, but we had to do it today."

Todd didn't move and his voice was faint. "Oh."

"Well, we have a few things," Rawlins continued. "Don't worry, we'll take good care of it all. You'll get it back. We're going to have to go down to your office too. Oh, by the way, do you have a computer there?"

"Yes."

"Well, we'll have to print out all of your files."

"Sure. Go right ahead. Take the whole fucking thing." Staring out at the car lights as they moved around the lake, Todd asked, "How did you get in here? Did the security guard let you in with his passkey?"

"No, actually, I had copies of your keys made."

"How convenient."

Rawlins asked, "Say, where were you this afternoon?"

"At Michael's sister's." Todd saw the lights of a plane heading toward the airport. "Anything else you want to know, like when I arrived there and when I left or when I last took a leak?"

"Yeah, actually I do have one more question," said Rawlins, lowering his voice. "Are you going to be all right?"

"Eat shit."

The door shut a minute later, and Todd sat motionless. He'd always expected that he or Michael would die of AIDS. He'd feared the disease so much that he was sure that that was their fate. He'd confessed that worry to Michael once, and Michael had said don't be silly, it was primarily a heterosexual disease, they had nothing to fear, for they were healthy and their relationship secure.

"Come on, you idiot, chin up. If people see you as full of shame, then that's what you'll get in return," Michael had begun, launching into his favorite lecture about how others perceive you. "And just remember, you don't die of AIDS just because you're gay, right?"

Apparently, thought Todd. AIDS hadn't killed Michael. A knife had.

A knife wielded by whom?

The phone rang and the sound cleared away his thoughts. He didn't budge though. The answering machine would get it. The phone rang on and on, however, before the caller finally hung up.

Todd twisted around, saw some dangling wires, and understood. He had a digital answering machine, so Lewis and Rawlins hadn't been able to remove a tape. They'd simply taken the entire machine. He shrugged and slowly pushed himself up. The phone, he thought. That reminded him that there was one person in particular he had to call. A call he'd put off for a long time, but which could wait no longer.

He had no idea of the time. It was dark outside, dark in his apartment. He stepped into the kitchen, turned on the small light over the stove, then went to the refrigerator, poured himself a glass of chilled water. Taking a sip, he felt the icy water slide down his throat and slither around the massive knot in his stomach.

He reached for the cordless phone, but on second thought he placed it back in its stand, for he needed this call to be absolutely private. He'd once done a piece where the details of a drug ring had been picked up from a cordless phone. Anyone might be listening in now, from the cops to reporters to amateur sleuths. Instead, he dragged the old phone from the kitchen counter and into the dining area, the cord trailing the entire way. Sitting down at his glass dinner table, he cradled his stomach with one hand, took a deep breath, and stared across the dark living room, out into the night. At last he punched in a long-distance number.

On the third ring someone picked up on the other end and said, "Hello?"

Todd tried to speak, but nothing emerged. It was partly because he was so exhausted. And it was partly out of fear.

The voice demanded, "Hello, who's calling? Anyone there?"

Finally he managed to say, "Hi, Mom. It's me, Todd."

"Oh, hello, dear. How are you?"

"Not . . ." He coughed, clearing his throat. "Not so good."

"Why, what's the matter?" Always the mother, she knew immediately this was serious. "What is it? What's happened?"

Mom. He pictured her down in Florida, just north of Miami, a gray-haired widow in a bright white mobile home. After his dad's death some five years ago, she'd picked up and moved south. Sold most of the furniture and just took off. Never too late for a change, she'd said. And besides, I'm sick of this cold weather. Jiminy, I could slip on some ice and break my hip, do you know that, Toddy? So she'd moved to a little mobile-home park, an enclave of Chicago Poles, and in an odd way had seemed to blossom. Todd and his younger brother had talked about it, tried to figure out why she'd mellowed, even gotten nicer, and wondered if there weren't a new man in her life. After all, it couldn't just be shuffleboard, could it?

"Todd, talk to me. What is it, dear?" she said, the concern coming over the lines.

"There's . . . there's something I need to tell you." He hoped she was alone. "Do you have a minute?"

"Of course."

"It's about my personal life."

He'd imagined this moment. He'd pictured telling her. Seen her falling apart in tears. Heard her deep, Polish moans.

Maybe even screams. He'd pictured the scene any number of ways. But he had to tell her now. With his name in the papers like this she was bound to find out anyway. Better from him. And he'd stay on the phone as long as she needed, as long as it took to comfort her, to settle her down. God, he didn't want to make her cry. He hated it when his mom cried. He should be doing this in person, of course. Or by letter. But there just wasn't time. At least, he thought, his father was dead. At least he didn't have to tell the old man. He would have had a screaming shit fit, maybe taken a swing at Todd.

He heard her silence and thought the words. Thought them over and over in his head.

He clenched his eyes shut, opened his mouth, and finally blurted, "Mom, I'm gay."

He cringed, waited for the tears, the explosion of anger. Instead, there was silence, and then his mother's voice.

Softly she said, "I know."

"Wh-what?" But how? Oh, shit, he thought, bristling. "Did a reporter call you? Someone from the station?"

"What, dear?"

"How do you know, Mom?" he demanded. "Who told you?"

"No one. I just figured it out a few years ago."

"You're kidding."

So it was just as Michael had said. Mothers were the first to know and the last to find out.

"No," replied his mother. "Remember when I came up that summer? You and Michael took me out to dinner. I guess that's when I knew for sure. I saw you two together and I just knew you were a couple."

This other pain, the one he'd been carrying all his life, suddenly cut itself out of his body. She knew? Jesus Christ, she knew? And then it wasn't Todd's mother who broke down in tears, but Todd. He clenched his eyes, but there was no stopping the pained relief.

"Todd, dear, it's okay," called his mother. "Not to worry, I love you."

"But . . . but . . ."

He couldn't believe it. He was crying. He wasn't supposed to. It was supposed to be her, his mom. She was the one who was supposed to be crying. She was the one who was supposed to need help and comforting.

Instead she became the pillar, saying, "Not to worry, dear. I've seen *Oprah*. I understand."

"What?" The oddness of her words made him smile despite himself, and he wiped the tears from his cheeks.

"Really, I understand." Like any good mother—although right then, as far as Todd was concerned, she was a great one—she added, "Todd, I love you."

"Thanks, Mom I . . . I love you too."

He choked on his tears, couldn't believe how easy it had been. In a flash he wondered why the hell he hadn't done this years ago. Or was the time only right now? No, that wasn't it. He'd been horribly afraid of hurting and losing her.

"What about Dad?" Was there any way to answer that one? "Did he know? Did you two ever talk about it?"

"No, we never did, but in his own way he probably knew." She was quick to say, "He was awfully hard on you. You were the oldest and he came down so hard on you. I know that. I did what I could. He was just so . . . so frustrated, and unfortunately he took it out on us all. But, Todd, we've talked about that. And you've got to move past it. It sounds odd—God knows, your father was no prince, him and his temper and his vodka—but he was so hard on you only because he loved you so much. He wanted you to be the best you could be. There's only one thing you need to know: He loved you very much." Trying to sound cheery, she said, "So you see, everything's all right in the end, isn't it? You have Michael and—"

"Mom . . ." He caught his breath as another flow of

tears began. "Th-there's something else. Something horrible's happened."

"Oh, God. What?"

"Mom, Michael's dead."

She was so stunned she couldn't speak. "I . . . I . . . what?"

"He was killed. Murdered."

"Oh, no! When?"

"Last night."

"But . . . but . . ." she mumbled, now bursting into tears. "Why? He . . . he was such a nice man."

In a flash of realization, Todd saw that all his life he'd been like this dam. Sure. In that way he was just like his dad. This big solid wall, holding back the weight of the world. But he couldn't do it anymore. Not by any means. Michael was dead. Everything was crumbling. The dam was forever shattered. And clutching the phone with his mom on the other end, he sobbed like a baby. Swell after swell of tears poured out of him, and he muttered Michael was dead, what was he going to do, they thought he'd done it but he hadn't, he hadn't, did she understand? Did she? Of course, she replied. He rambled on and on, not making any sense, telling her how they'd arrested him, that it was in the papers and everything. Michael was dead, and he'd never cried so hard, not even at his father's funeral, and the more he sobbed, the harder he felt it, nearly writhing with pain and frustration.

Finally he told her, "Mom, I gotta . . . I gotta go."

"But are you alone, dear? Is there anyone with you?"

"Janice. Remember her? She's coming over soon."

"Oh, Todd, I'm so sorry. Should I come up?"

"No. Listen, Mom, I'll call you later."

He quickly hung up, dropping the phone into the cradle. He couldn't get up from the chair though. Instead, he wrapped his arms around himself, clutching himself around the waist. His head fell forward, landing with a thump on the glass tabletop. The tears spilled out of him, and in a way he thought this was it, he was dying too.

And over and over he muttered, "Michael . . . Michael . . ."

Sometime later he woke up because of the knocking. Todd opened his eyes, peered around in the darkness, and ascertained that he was at home, not in some prison cell. He blinked, lifted his head from the cold glass table. His eyes felt swollen and achy, his nose wet. Quite obviously he'd fallen asleep, an extraordinarily deep one at that. So how long had he slept? Only a matter of minutes, or was it in fact hours?

Someone pounded on the door and called, "Todd?"

Who was it, Janice? Was Bob still on duty, could he have let her in downstairs, and was she now out there, the threatened pizza in hand?

"Just a minute," he called.

He stumbled into the kitchen, grabbed the roll of paper towels from atop the refrigerator, ripped off a couple of sheets, and blew his nose. Then he turned on the cold water, let it run, and splashed his face. He was exhausted. What he needed were days of sleep. He should just crawl into bed and not emerge for a week.

He was about to open the door when he hesitated, wondering if it was indeed Janice out there. Or was this how Michael had been killed; had someone knocked and he'd just opened the door and let in a murderer? Or, God, was it Rawlins and Lewis again? They weren't coming back to continue the search, were they?

"Who's there?" called Todd.

"It's me."

It struck him as odd. Sure, he knew the voice, and he leaned forward, looked through the peephole, saw the familiar face. What in the hell did she want?

"Cindy?"

Was this day never going to end? Obviously it was something about work. Probably Lewis and Rawlins had already made it down there, already gone through his office and carted off his calendar, notes, whatever. So was there a problem? If so, why hadn't she just called? And how had she found out where he lived? Cindy Wilson had never been here before, but perhaps she had retrieved a few of his things or was coming to see how he was.

He twisted the bolt, opened the door, and suddenly was assaulted with a glaring white light. He squinted, raised his right hand over his eyes.

"Jesus Christ, what's going on?" he demanded.

Clutching a microphone, she turned her back to him, facing the light.

"What the fuck is going on? How the hell did you get in?" He looked at the lights, saw the camera aimed at him. "Mark, is that you?"

"Yeah. Sorry, buddy."

"But . . ."

Todd couldn't believe it. Mark was his pal. Just two weeks ago he'd taken Todd out for a steak dinner; Mark wanted to celebrate that his AIDS test had come back negative. Some eight years earlier, Mark finally explained as he drank his third martini, he'd done some dope, gone to a very hip, very swinging party in San Francisco, and . . . and . . .

Mark's voice counted, "Three, two, one."

"Good evening, this is Cindy Wilson, here at the home of Emmy Award–winning reporter Todd Mills, who last night was arrested for the murder of his gay lover, Michael Carter. Good evening, Todd. How are you?"

"What the hell kind of stunt is this?"

"Todd, can you tell us how long you were involved with Mr. Carter?" she asked in her best reporter voice. "You were his homosexual lover, were you not?"

"My God, what kind of cheap trick is this?" he shouted.

"Was there a history of violence in your relationship? We

understand that the two of you fought the night before Mr.
Carter was so brutally knifed to death. Is this true?''

''Wh-what?''

''And why did you deceive the management of Channel
Seven, your coworkers, and all of your loyal viewers?'' she
pressed. ''Todd, why didn't you tell any of us that you're
gay?''

Unbelievable. He stared at Cindy Wilson, with whom he'd
worked for over a year. And he stared at Mark, the cameraman, whom he'd known for years. Fucking unbelievable.

''Good night,'' he gasped, backing away.

''But, Todd, why did the police arrest you?'' called Cindy.
''What happened? Did you kill Michael Carter?''

''Absolutely not!'' he yelled. ''Now get the hell out of
here!''

As he slammed the door his heart was thumping so hard
that he thought he might collapse. He twisted the lock shut,
realized he couldn't breathe. Clutching his throat, he gasped
for air. Then he heard her voice outside, and he quickly
squinted into the peephole and saw the bright lights still
burning. Shit. She was still out there. The camera was still
running live right outside his very own door.

''And there you have it, ladies and gentlemen, the first
glimpse of star reporter Todd Mills since his arrest last night.
Stay tuned to Channel Seven for the inside scoop on this
tragic story of gay love and gay murder.''

Trembling, he collapsed to the floor. He knew this trick:
ramming a mike into a suspect's face and letting the cameras
roll live. It was a CrimeEye trademark. And he had started it.
Only now Todd was the fodder, and the public was going to
love every second, eat it up, gobble him alive.

13

Todd bought a plot for them both. It was on a gentle hillside, close to several towering oaks and a pond, in the depths of Gracewood Cemetery, the priciest place to be buried in the Twin Cities. He'd already ordered a headstone too. Minnesota granite from Cold Spring. Michael would have like that. And there was a space for Todd as well, though Janice had balked a bit at that one.

"Don't box yourself in just yet," she'd advised. "After all, you're barely forty."

"And already I'm so tired," he replied. "Here I've been married and divorced, and now in a gay relationship and widowed. It's just more than I wanted, more than I expected."

"I'm sure, but there are plenty of other fish in the sea, don't forget."

"How about stallions? I like that image better."

"Okay, then let me put it this way: Wouldn't you like another horse in your herd?"

"As long as he's not a gelding."

"Way funny, Todd. Way funny."

Just one more, he hoped. That would be plenty. But regardless of who Todd might meet and form a relationship with, he wanted to be there in Gracewood, right next to Michael, in the end of ends. Michael had never liked being alone; in fact, he'd been afraid of growing old with no one else in his life. Well, he hadn't had the chance to get old, and Todd felt the least he could do was to make sure he wasn't lying alone forever. Todd owed Michael that much. If, by chance, that meant bringing along someone else, Todd's next partner perhaps, then that's where they'd all go, right there in the fertile soil of Gracewood Cemetery. He laughed at the thought of it. A threesome. Michael would finally get his fantasy, for all of eternity no less.

The funeral took place four days after the murder, not long after the police released the body and just as soon as the undertaker could prepare it. It had threatened to rain, but the wind came up and the skies cleared, and so Michael Carter was laid to rest on one of the last warm, sunny days of the year. Fifteen minutes before the service began, Todd, Michael's sister, Maggie, her kids, and Rick, her estranged husband, all gathered in a small, private room at the rear of the cemetery's chapel.

"Is my tie all the way up, Maggie?"

He always asked that question right before he went on the air. Is my tie up? He hated having a small bit of shirt showing above the knot of a tie, but the question was more like a ritual before a performance. A final check-in with his ego. And this felt like a performance. How many people were out there? Hundreds? He'd peeked through the heavy oak doors. Who were all these people, and where had they all come from? If they were all Michael's friends why were there so many he'd never seen before?

Maggie was smoothing down the hair on one of her son's head. She glanced over at Todd and said, "What? Oh, sure."

Rick crossed over to him, gave a closer inspection. "But it's not quite straight." Reaching forward, he said, "Here, let me, buddy."

"Thanks," said Todd, standing still in his charcoal-gray suit as Rick fixed the errant tie.

"You hanging in there?"

"More or less."

"This is going to be tough."

"Yeah." Todd nodded his head toward Maggie, Joshua, and Jason, and in a hushed voice asked, "How about you? How's your family unit doing?"

"Maggie's having a really hard time, of course. She and Michael were so close, you know." Rick hesitated, then added, "But it's nice for me to be needed. I'm glad there's something I can do for her. Actually, Maggie and I haven't spent this much time together for months, and I think she's appreciating it as much as I am. I know the kids are. I just wish the circumstances were different."

The service began a few minutes later with the voices of a gay men's choir filling the chapel and seeping back to the waiting room. Todd heard the deep, soothing voices, went over to Maggie, and kissed her on the cheek. The minister, who was waiting out there, had told them this was their cue.

"Ready?" he asked.

She reached out, hugged Todd, held on to him, bit her bottom lip. He embraced her, and they stood for a few seconds locked on the memory of Michael. This was awful for her, he knew. Her parents had died five years ago, and now her only sibling. And her marriage was hovering on the brink of divorce. She was as strong as Michael, but could she pull through all this?

"I hope I'll still be invited for Sunday night dinners," he said.

She wiped her eyes, kissed him briefly on the cheek, saying, "You'd better. We're going to need you, the boys and I."

He took her hand and the two of them started out, followed by Rick and Jason and Joshua. They passed through the door, into the chapel, into the music. The place was so

packed that there were fifteen or twenty people standing at
the rear of the chapel, and suddenly all eyes were upon Maggie and him. Todd glanced over this sea of faces, saw that
about two-thirds of them were men, but recognized hardly
anyone. There was Janice in a simple black dress, seated in
the second row. A few people from Michael's office. A handful of other friends. It shocked Todd, though, to see so many
unfamiliar faces. Certainly some were Maggie's friends, but
he had no idea Michael had known this many people. Or
were they mostly well-wishers, gay men who'd read about
the service and wanted to be supportive?

Todd's eyes beaded with tears, and he slowed, almost
stopped before they reached the front pew. At the cemetery
gates he'd caught sight of the Channel 7 van and Cindy Wilson, not to mention a handful of newspaper reporters lingering just outside the chapel. It had been like this all week, the
media hounding him, calling, wanting interviews, anything
they could mask as news. They and a handful of others had
been hanging out in front of his building, wanting a sighting
at least. But in here there was none of that. Sure, all the eyes
were upon him. And he wanted them to see him, Todd Mills,
as he really was. He'd been wrong, for this wasn't a performance. This was reality, not to mention the first time Todd
had been in public since Michael's murder. Yes, everyone
was looking at him, and everyone knew he was gay and they
knew about his relationship. Dear God, here he was, coming
out at Michael's funeral. Without Michael.

A surge of grief and guilt passed over Todd. Maggie, Rick,
and the boys sat down, but Todd didn't. As the choir sang, he
looked at Michael's dark coffin. He was in there. Alone, his
eyes shut forever. Suddenly Todd was crossing the empty
space between him and the coffin. And then he was placing
both his hands upon it. He stood there, his palms warming
the wood, trying to imagine Michael. Michael. Michael.

He bent down, kissed the coffin, and returned to the pew
and sat down. His mother had been right. She'd wanted to

come up for the service, insisted Todd needed her. But he'd said no, don't, there was too much going on. He was afraid he'd have to take care of her, couldn't imagine entertaining her, so to speak. But now he was sitting on the pew between Maggie and Rick, and he wished his mom were there. Placing his left hand to his face, he started to cry again and for only the second time in his adult life he didn't hold himself in check.

The voices of the men's choir rolled over him, and he looked over at the dozen men, saw one of them staring back at him. It was Jeff Barnes, a heavyset man, bald, small eyes, and probably Michael's oldest friend. The two had not only gone to elementary school together, they'd been inseparable, for along with one other boy they'd made up the Banditos, a group of three once infamous in Linden Hills. And Jeff, who'd had nothing but disdain for Todd and his insistence on a closeted relationship, now gave Todd a cold glare.

The service began, led by a woman minister, a lesbian neither Michael nor Todd had known but who was well-respected within the gay community. Todd had asked her to preside because she was sure to understand all the nuances of Michael's life, their relationship, what had happened. She spoke, this woman with the plain face and short dark hair and black robe, for some five minutes about love knowing no boundaries, about love everlasting. Todd heard it but didn't hear it. He stared at the coffin. Why had they fought about that stupid promotion? Why hadn't he been home the following night? If he had, none of this would have happened, right? If only he could do it over. Not merely that night. But the last four years. With the absence of Michael looming right in front of him, Todd realized the emptiness he now faced.

The minister asked everyone to rise and join in song. A slow, solemn hymn filled the place. Maggie started crying, and Todd clutched her hand. Then the music stopped, and everyone was seated once again. After a minute of silent prayer the minister asked if anyone had a few words.

One woman, a friend from work, was the first to stand up, saying, "Michael was such a source of joy. We had so much fun together."

"I knew Michael for ten years," said an unknown man, rising next. "He was such a great friend."

"I always looked forward to seeing him," volunteered another.

"I loved his laugh."

"He was so wise."

"Sometimes he said he peaked during the disco days, but I never thought so. What energy."

"He gave so much."

"He could always make me feel good."

They went on and on, rising one after another. People who Todd didn't know spoke about Michael in the most intimate ways. They were people from work. People he knew from the gay bars. Todd had known Michael so intimately, so closely, yet at the same time he saw how much he'd forced Michael to shut off and give up. All these people who cared so much for him. Good God, what had Todd done to Michael's life?

The service concluded, and Todd and Maggie proceeded to the main doors, where they stood and thanked each person individually. Maggie and he shook hands with nearly everyone, mumbled gratitude over and over again. People Todd had never seen before kissed him. Two women, obviously a couple, whom Todd had never heard of, stopped and told Todd how much he'd changed Michael's life. A guy embraced Todd, said how lucky Todd had been to have a guy like Michael. Another guy said he'd always had a crush on Michael.

Who were these people?

They went out, one at a time, slowly and patiently. As the crowd began to thin, Todd glanced to his left, saw two familiar faces. The detectives Lewis and Rawlins were waiting to offer their condolences.

"I'm surprised to see you here," said Todd, extending his hand first to Rawlins. "Thank you for coming."

"It's part of our job, but I'm glad we came," replied Rawlins. "How are you? Hanging in there?"

"Kind of."

Lewis shook his hand, said, "Nothing new to report just yet. We'll be in touch."

The two greeted Maggie, whom they'd already met and interviewed for almost three hours in the hopes of learning something new about Michael. As they now talked to Maggie, Todd stared at them. Doing their job? Nothing new to report? Of course he knew what they were inferring. The detectives had come to the funeral not simply to observe Todd and what emotions he might or might not be displaying. No, they'd come to note who was at the funeral. Certainly. Todd hadn't thought about it, but Michael's killer could very well have just been there, and that thought frightened him, reverberated in his mind. There was so much of Michael that Todd didn't know, simply because Todd hadn't wanted to socialize too openly, too outwardly. But what did that really mean?

Suddenly washed with a new fear, Todd turned away from the crowd, left them outside, and went back into the chapel. He stood in the large empty space, stared down the main aisle at the coffin. It wasn't possible, was it? Todd had assumed they'd had a devoted relationship. Todd had thought he'd known Michael so well. He'd been so sure he had. Yet today, seeing all these unfamiliar faces, he saw how wrong he might be.

Specifically, thought Todd to himself, could there have been another man in Michael's life, and was that who he'd let into his home that fateful night?

14

Todd couldn't let go of it. The idea lodged in his mind and he could think of nothing else.

The actual interment was limited to the family and took place an hour after the chapel service had concluded. Todd and Maggie and her family stood at Michael's grave, his coffin hovering over the open pit, while the minister spoke still more prayers and thoughts. But Todd heard precious little. Instead, he stood there, the late-autumn sun on his shoulders, wanting Michael back. Just for a minute. There was just one thing he wanted to tell Michael: I love you. And one thing he wanted to ask: Was there someone else?

The grass was clipped short, fading from its summer brightness to an autumnal dullness, and Todd's eyes drifted away from the grave, down the hill, past all the other gravestones and to the pond below. He watched a handful of ducks skim the surface of the water, settle down, float there. And then Maggie was pulling on Todd's sleeve. It was over.

"I'll be right there," he told her. "You all go ahead."

Maggie, Rick, and their kids followed the minister down the slope toward the narrow paved road, where they started walking back to the chapel. Todd watched them, then turned back to the coffin, which seemed to float magically above the open hole. He'd been so obsessed by his own secret—that of his sexuality—that Todd hadn't seen how self-centered it had made him. Certainly there could have been something or someone in Michael's life that Todd didn't know about. An old boyfriend. Someone from the past. Or some new guy. Someone Michael had flirted with at work or the gym. Sure, it was possible. Maybe Michael had wanted to tell Todd about this person. Or maybe Todd had driven Michael away, forced him into a secret of his own, a closet of a different kind. Yeah, that was possible. Perhaps likely. But why, thought Todd, didn't that feel right?

Their closest moments emotionally were when the lights were out and they were in bed, side by side. It was only then that everyone and everything was blocked out. Or rather, it was only then that the entire world seemed to spark from their love and passion. When Todd held Michael in his arms, when he was assured that no one was watching and judging and that the expectations of the world were blind to them both, he knew this was right, the two of them. There was no paranoid doublethink, no wondering if others were looking, staring, hating. There was just the purity of the moment, the honesty of their emotions.

"Here," Michael had said sometime last winter when the temperature had plummeted to twenty below and they had slipped naked beneath the down comforter. "Put your forehead against mine. There. Now I can't tell where you stop and I begin."

Todd had held him tighter, pressed him closer, for all that Todd had known was what he'd said: "I love you."

He'd told Michael that, hadn't he? Yes. Absolutely. Then and any number of other times. In spite of that horrible fight just a few nights ago, even though Todd had smashed that champagne and broken all those dishes, Michael had to have known how much Todd cared. God, he hoped so. As wretched as these past days had been, Todd only prayed that in the end Michael never doubted Todd's love for him.

Todd now shook his head. He'd screwed it all up, their relationship and so much more. Yes, he'd told Michael how much he cared for him, but at the same time Todd kept throwing up barricades, thereby preventing things from becoming truly great. Not long ago Michael and he had gone downtown to Dayton's, that massive department store on the Nicollet Mall, and instead of perusing the clothes and enjoying just being out with Michael, Todd had worried what the clerks were thinking. Sure, they were looking at Todd. Sure, they recognized him as the star reporter. And yes, they were closely watching how intimately he was talking with Michael, how Todd was asking for Michael's opinions on this shirt, that color. So what were the clerks thinking, that he was queer? Were they recognizing the truth? Would someone find out?

So what if they had, Todd thought now. It wouldn't have made any difference then or any other time, he thought, shaking his head, understanding how much he'd twisted things. If anything, most of the male clerks had to be gay, and yet Todd denied his sexuality to them and thereby denied them a potentially positive role model.

"You know," Michael had said more than once, "a queer like you—responsible, intelligent, masculine, not to mention on TV all the time—would be a very positive thing to a lot of people. A lot of gays would look up to you, and a lot of straights would be amazed because the only gays they see are the visible ones, you know, the swishy kind."

Perhaps it was simply that ever since he was a child, Todd had been equally fearful of rejection and approval, fears that over the years had manifested in his own homophobia. But now, just as he had to let go of the man he loved, he had to let go of all that self-hatred.

Todd reached over, touched the edge of the coffin. And just stood there. Five blank minutes passed.

And then, with tears once again in his eyes, he softly said, "Sleep tight, dear friend. I'll always love you."

He turned and walked away from the suspended coffin, back toward the chapel. Glancing toward a distant street he saw someone peering through the wrought iron fence. And he saw that someone holding something. A camera? Shit, he realized. Always people watching him, judging. That was a photographer with a telephoto taking Todd's picture. Had he gotten the whole thing, Todd and Maggie and all gathered around the grave site?

They piled into two cars, Rick's Oldsmobile and Todd's Cherokee, which the police had just returned, and then they drove the six blocks to Uptown, the small, trendy neighborhood packed with shops and cafés. As planned, they met Janice at a small restaurant, Café Laurie, where she'd already commandeered a large corner table for a late lunch. It was a simple establishment, the walls tall and white, the food simple but elegant, and Todd sat with his back toward the main part of the room. He didn't want to be recognized. He didn't want to be disturbed. And they weren't.

When they were done, Todd pleaded exhaustion. Janice wanted to come back to his apartment, sit with him for a while. Maggie couldn't hide her concern, wanted him to come out to her place for the night so he wouldn't be alone. But Todd declined.

"I'll be okay," he assured them all.

"I can't believe it, you're turning into a Minnesota martyr," Janice said, referring to the staunch and inexpressive Scandinavian types that were so prevalent in the area.

"No, I just need some downtime."

So by sunset he was home and out on his fifteenth-floor balcony, wrapped in a jacket and watching the last of the joggers and walkers make their way around Lake Calhoun. He sat there, the evening chill whooshing into the city, the sky fading from blue to orange to red, then back to a deep, dark blue, and still he couldn't let go of that thought.

It wasn't so much that he feared there had been someone else in Michael's life. He didn't feel betrayed or jealous. He just wanted to know. To put things in perspective. Todd saw how much of the world he'd blocked out by being so closeted, how distant he'd kept so much and so many, but now he wondered, feared, that he'd blocked out a good deal of Michael as well. And, of course, he had to know if this other person, if indeed there was one, might have been the one who'd visited death upon Michael.

Todd knew who he had to talk to. It was dark out now and cold, and he left the balcony and went to the kitchen, where he looked up a phone number that had been scribbled on a list. He then went to the dining room, sat at the glass table, and picked up the phone. The line was answered on the fourth ring.

"Hey, there," said the big voice on the answering machine. "This is indeed Jeff. And I don't know where I am, but you know where you can find me Wednesday through Sunday, rain or shine!"

It was late in the week and Todd did in fact know where he could find Jeff. But not yet. If he remembered correctly, Jeff didn't begin performing at the Gay Times until nine. But would he go onstage tonight? Did rain or shine include the funeral of your oldest and closest friend?

Todd had only been down to the Gay Times once, about three years ago. At Michael's insistence they'd gone down one Saturday night to see Jeff's show. But it had been risky for Todd. The new segment at Channel 7 was just starting up, his career was just gaining some momentum, and he didn't want to jeopardize anything by prancing into a gay bar with only Michael. So instead they'd made an evening of it, inviting Maggie and Rick and Janice. They'd all gone out to dinner beforehand, then arrived in mixed couples at the Gay Times and taken a front and center table. Sure, some people recognized him, but the gay bar was straight-friendly, as Michael always said, and no one knew what to make of Todd's presence. God, how stupid, Todd now thought. How really queer.

He didn't hesitate tonight, however, and as it approached nine Todd got into his car and headed downtown. He drove down Hennepin Avenue, that lively and somewhat tawdry street of entertainment, and parked in a lot less than a block away from the Gay Times. As he approached the building he saw the flashing lights and the other men heading toward the place and heard the muffled thumping music as it filtered onto the street.

The Gay Times was the biggest gay bar in the area. And it was always growing, gobbling up more space, annexing neighboring buildings. When Todd had been here before, there were just a couple of bars and only two dance floors. But it had mushroomed in recent years, or so Michael had reported, claiming that it was now a complex of ten or more bars, and as soon as Todd walked in the front door he saw what Michael had been talking about. Though it was still early and the place wouldn't fill up until eleven or twelve, the huge main room was filled with tables of guys eating dinner. To the left he saw another room with a long bar, and to his right he heard the pumping and throbbing of dance music coming from a distant room.

Todd stood on the edge of the main room, and more than a couple of tables turned his way. Sure, they recognized him, if not from television then from the recent scandal. Feeling as if he were going live on the air, the alter-egolike voice of his agent, Stella, popped out of nowhere. If you ever want to make it big in broadcast, she had advised shrewdly, don't ever let your waist get bigger than your chest. I'm talking about if you want to go to the top, doll, and I know you do and I know you can. In fact, if you can make sure your waist is about a third smaller than your chest—any more than that and you'll look artificial, like a squeezed toothpaste tube, and people will think you're dumb and cheap—then I can guarantee I can get you on the nationals. I think you'd fit in at

CBS. Connie would love you. And don't forget about the dental bleaching. Get that set up right away.

Todd shook his head, tried to block Stella out. It was time for his public and private lives to merge; it didn't matter how people perceived him anymore. And with a sense of relief, Todd realized that coming in here didn't make him feel nervous. He didn't feel threatened as he used to whenever he went into a gay bar, which was usually in some distant city like Dallas or New York.

He turned right and headed up a staircase, passing a mezzanine where a guy in a baseball jacket stood with a bowl of condoms and a big admonishing smile, saying, "Don't forget to dress up tonight, boys!"

Todd continued to the top of the stairs, where he turned to the right and stepped into a long pool hall with a motorcycle on the wall. Butch-looking guys in plaid shirts and jeans were standing around, shooting pool, drinking beer, laughing. One handsome, thickly built guy who looked like a construction worker—then again, thought Todd, maybe he was a lawyer by day and a pretend construction worker by night— walked past Todd, gave him a friendly smile and a deep stare. Maybe some other time, thought Todd, but not this week, not this month.

He passed through the room, turned again to the right, and entered the piano lounge, a small, intimate room with a baby grand in the middle. A striking black woman with short hair and a rich, melodic voice sang and played, and Todd looked around. There were a dozen or so couches with couples seated about, men and men, women and women, black and black, white and white, black and white, cocktails in hand. Except for the diversity, it reminded Todd of a Polish piano bar in Chicago.

He continued on, passing through a coffee bar, where two women were laughing over cappuccinos in one corner and three guys were deep in conversation by the window. He came to another dance hall, a huge, dark room with raucous music. He saw guys in black leather pants, leather vests, leather shirts. And chains, lots of them, draping from waists, over crotches. Some were dancing next to a beat-up old wire fence. No, thought Todd, Jeff wouldn't be here. Definitely not his scene.

It wasn't Michael's either. Michael had been encouraging Todd to relax, to be himself. Just because you're gay, he'd told Todd, doesn't mean you fit neatly into a stereotype. It doesn't mean you like bouquets of pink flowers and little dogs. It doesn't mean you like to watch figure skating and have a museum-size collection of cologne. It doesn't mean you have to be supermacho either. Look at me, Michael had said, I'm gay and I'm an excellent accountant and . . . and I read the sports page every day! We're a whole spectrum of people, Todd. Just look at you. You're a great journalist, you work incredibly hard, you're too serious, and you love to change the oil in your car. The only thing that might tip someone off that you're queer is that your socks always match your shirt. Either that or those deep, penetrating blue eyes of yours that tend to linger a millisecond too long on one half of the population.

Oh, Michael, thought Todd, who's going to balance my checkbook now?

Todd turned and headed down another hallway, following the arrows to the Show Room. He glanced up at the wall, and immediately everything drained out of him. He froze, leaned against a door frame. Oh, Christ. A small poster was taped on the wall opposite him. On the poster was Michael's face. Todd started reading. And started shaking.

WANTED!
Information on the murder of our dear friend,
Michael Carter.
The night before he was killed
Michael was seen at the Gay Times.

If you saw Michael leave with anyone
please notify . . .

Todd couldn't focus on the words. He closed his eyes,
breathed deeply and slowly, then opened his eyes, stared
again at the poster. A grinning picture of Michael was staring
back at him. How was any of this possible? And is that what
you did, Michael? Did you come down here after we fought?

Quite obviously so, thought Todd. Michael hadn't curled
up with a book. He hadn't gone to the gym and worked off
the tension of their argument. They'd had that horrible fight,
Todd had rushed out, and then Michael had left the house as
well. To do what? Have a drink with Jeff? Hang out with
some other friends? Or meet a replacement for Todd Mills?

A voice behind him said, "We haven't had any calls yet."

Todd turned, saw someone standing there, a bottle of beer
in hand, and couldn't quite manage a reply.

"But I'm hoping we're going to get some," said Detective
Steve Rawlins, in black jeans and a T-shirt.

Todd was so stunned to see him in this crowd of men that
he didn't know what to say, and only managed to mutter,
"What the hell are you doing here?"

"Guys, guys, guys."

Todd looked around. Detective Rawlins? Here?

"What?" replied Todd.

"Come on, dude, your head's not stuck that deep in the
sand, is it? You knew I was gay, didn't you?"

"Well . . . actually, no. I mean, what was all that about
your first lover?"

"I was talking about a guy, you dumb shit," laughed
Rawlins, who then took a slug of beer. "I thought you'd
already figured me out."

"Oh . . ." Confused and overwhelmed, Todd didn't
know what to say, and he turned back to the poster. "I'm
surprised to see this."

"Well, don't be. The entire gay community is afraid this is

a hate crime, and everyone's up in arms. I think five hundred of these things were photocopied and plastered around town. Haven't you seen them? They're everywhere.''

''I haven't really been out. I haven't seen it before.'' Todd quickly studied Rawlins—really, queer?—then hesitantly asked, ''So Michael was down here?''

''Didn't you know?''

''No, how would I?''

''Michael. Didn't he mention it?''

''Of course not,'' said Todd defensively. ''I didn't talk to him after our fight. I told you that.''

''Oh, yeah, right. Right.''

''So what . . . what was Michael doing here?''

''Having a good time, I guess.''

''But . . . but . . . what did . . .'' Todd didn't want to ask, but he had to know. ''Did he go home with anyone? Do you know that for a fact?''

Rawlins looked away. ''Nope.''

Theirs had been a monogamous relationship. Or so Todd had always thought. But had the fight changed all that? Could Todd's loss of temper have convinced Michael that the relationship was no good and it was time to move on?

A frightening scene passed through Todd's imagination. What if Todd had returned to Michael's that night, what if he'd found Michael in bed with some other guy? Todd would have gone truly ballistic. Or would he have just cracked, dropped into tears and utter confusion? He hoped the latter. He feared the former. He wouldn't have hurt Michael, would he? Could he have? Exactly what were his limits?

''What do you think?'' asked Rawlins. ''Did he usually pick up guys? Was he into cruising?''

''What? Michael? No. Hell, no.''

''Well, you never know. Some guys cheat all the time on their wives, some guys cheat all the time on their boy-friends.''

But not Michael. We talked, Todd wanted to say. We

talked about our desires, our fantasies. How Joe Blow was incredibly hunky, what a great body he had. Who we wanted to sleep with. Why we wouldn't. How important we were to each other. We talked. And we had a great sex life. No, if Michael had been sleeping with someone else he wouldn't have been able not to tell me. Right?

Rawlins grinned and glanced around. "So what are you doing here? Out for a good time? Actually, I don't think I've ever seen you down here before."

"What?"

"You got your eye on anyone?"

"No, I . . ." He shook his head quickly. "Not at all."

How could Rawlins even think that? They'd just buried Michael this afternoon.

"I'm looking for Michael's friend Jeff," Todd said quickly. "I wanted to talk to him."

"I see." Rawlins took a swig of beer, gazed down at the floor, and then looked up with a grin. "Can I buy you a drink?"

Stunned, Todd saw no other way than to be direct. He asked, "What are you doing, hitting on me?"

"A good-looking guy like you, what would make you think that?" He gave Todd a firm pat on the shoulder, said, "Take care of yourself, buddy. And be safe, there's an epidemic out there."

Rawlins then turned and cut into a crowd of men, his broad shoulders and trim waist not going unnoticed by a handful of guys. Todd stared after him as well, then turned back to the poster, looked into Michael's frozen eyes. What the hell had all that been about?

Moving on, pushing down the hall and toward the show lounge, Todd just had this sense. Of course Rawlins wasn't being forthright. From being so closeted for so long Todd knew how to recognize that screening technique, the way you make people look at the surface of you and let them think they're seeing every sincere inch. It was like a one-way mirror. While the real you was lurking back there unseen, people saw what they wanted to see.

So had Rawlins purposely bumped into Todd in a deliberate effort to pick him up? Or had he followed him to the Gay Times in an attempt to squeeze as much information out of Todd as possible?

15

She was a big gal, maybe six feet tall and fifty pounds over-weight, and her long, pink-sequined dress flowed from her broad shoulders down every ripple and fold of her body, all the way to her wide ankles. Her round face was thick with makeup, the eye shadow too heavy, the false eyelashes much, much too long. Her light brown hair, obviously an expensive wig, was huge and perfectly coiffed, and the silver earrings were massive, a collection of glittery balls that drooped almost to her shoulders. Lush, overly voluptuous, she strolled onto the stage of the Show Room in red high heels. And that was the only thing that surprised Todd. The height of the heels, so tall, so sharp, and the ease with which she moved in them.

The emcee called, "And here she is, ladies and gentlemen, our own, our favorite, our delightful Miss Tiffany Crystal! Give it up for this charming and talented creature! And, I should add, Miss Crystal is dedicating this one to the memory of her dear friend—our dear friend—the late Michael Carter."

As the audience burst into applause, Todd felt like he was

being haunted by a ghost. Michael was everywhere in the Gay Times tonight, and Todd sipped at his bourbon and soda, gazed around the dark room. He sat at a cocktail table off to the side, a candle flickering in front of him. He looked about the small room. Were they clapping for Tiffany or for Michael?

Sure, Jeff Barnes would want to sing to his longtime friend Michael on the day of his funeral. They'd known each other since the fourth grade, way before they knew what sex was. Later, during high school, they hadn't spoken about their raging desires, or so Michael had claimed. While the other kids had been dating and playing football, Michael and Jeff had just hung out together. They hadn't spoken about guys, guys, guys until one boring Saturday evening when they'd snitched some beer from Jeff's father, gotten tipsy, and put on Aretha Franklin. Jeff had started strutting and lip-synching, they started laughing, and the truth came pouring out at last.

Thus was born the future Tiffany Crystal, trusted bank teller by day, glamorous drag queen by night.

The recorded music started, stopped. Was quickly started over again. Through the speakers came the sound of a piano, simple and melodic. Todd recognized the song. Tiffany closed her eyes, lifted the wireless—and forever silent—mike to her glossy lips, and began lip-synching the Mariah Carey song "Hero." Her mouth and throat moved with such realism that Todd couldn't tell she wasn't actually singing. Oh, Christ, he thought, watching that big body sway, hearing the music build. A huge swell of emotion rose from his stomach and lodged in his throat.

As if she were on a stage in front of a thousand clamoring fans, Tiffany raised her right hand, clutched the mike, and crooned about a hero in your heart. She sang about not being afraid of who you are, of reaching into your soul, of finding an answer. Yes, she sang, let the sorrow melt away, let it disappear, look within, and see the truth.

Todd was surprised to find his eyes misting up; since when could a drag queen do this to him? He picked up his cocktail napkin, blotted the light tears, and for the first time understood why he'd always hated drag queens. They so strongly symbolized homosexuality and for that reason were so very threatening. But of course being gay was not synonymous with being a queen.

Oh, shit, thought Todd. It just didn't matter. Nothing did, not anymore. As the music rose emotionally, Todd felt himself swept along, propelled by the memories of Michael, the wisdom of Michael.

"Hey, buddy, you gotta unwind," Michael had urged not long ago as they jogged around Lake of the Isles. "The world's this big broad state of mind, a rainbow of colors rather than the little black and white boxes you're always trying to arrange in just the right order. Just remember that—"

"Okay, okay, I know the lecture about cues," Todd had interrupted.

"You may know it, but I don't think you're willing to accept it."

"Michael, all I can say is I'm doing the best I can."

"That's right. You are. And you're going to make it too."

And now he had, he understood as he watched Tiffany swirl around on the stage, her lips and chin quivering as if she really were belting it out. He stared at her exquisite shimmering gown, and right then and there, deep in his heart, Todd felt an unbearable sense of joy dance with an unbearable sorrow. All along Michael had been nudging Todd toward a kind of greater truth. He'd been nurturing him every step of the way. He'd gotten Todd right up to the edge of the cliff. And Todd had finally, stubbornly, yet in the end gladly jumped off. Only to wake up in this new world of acceptance and find it was a world without Michael.

Tiffany sang on about casting fears aside, being strong, and finally seeing that the real hero was within yourself. Yes, you find the truth and the hero, and you know you can survive.

Oh, brother, thought Todd, I can't believe I'm crying. It wasn't as if these were the most profound words of the world. It wasn't as if this was enduring music. Nevertheless, the whole spectacle was speaking to his soul in a way Todd had never thought possible.

With a big rustle and whoosh, someone sat down next to Todd. He looked over and saw an old queen in a ruffly black gown batting her lashes at him. Her hair was big and dark and stiff-looking, her dark foundation cracking in her deep wrinkles. And the lipstick ran all along her broad lips, which formed a huge smile. Todd couldn't help but grin back.

"What's a matter, gorgeous?" she asked, her voice deep and breathy. "Got a broken heart?"

"Yeah."

She looked down at herself and touched her cleavage, which was as pronounced as Elizabeth Taylor's. "Are you laughing at me?"

"What?"

"Or is it my dress? You know, this dress cost me eight hundred bucks. I bought it at the Oval Room at Dayton's. It's beautiful, isn't it? The material's just so smooth and nummy." She smoothed it over her knees. "Don't worry, tiger. I don't bite. No hickeys either. Promise. Girl Scout's honor," she said, raising several fingers and batting her eyes furiously. "My name's Limoge. What's yours?"

"Todd."

"Well, you know what, Todd, dear? This old queen's seen a lot of pain in her life. I've seen it all, really. Truly, I have. And you know what?"

Limoge reached for Todd's hand, which she took in both of hers.

"What?" said Todd, not sure he wanted to hear this but knowing he had to.

"I understand all about broken hearts. We see a whole hell

of a lot of that in here. And you know what I feel in my heart?''

''No.''

''This guy of yours, the one who left you—and trust me, I know it pained him terribly to go because no man on this earth would freely leave a doll like you—he loved you too. With all his heart, he did. And he still loves you.''

Todd could barely speak, but managed to say, ''Thanks, Limoge.''

Todd wondered, did she know? Had she seen Todd on TV or read about what had happened in the papers? Or did the Oval Room and the Show Room constitute her entire world?

Todd glanced up at the stage, where Tiffany was approaching a soft, emotional climax. Several guys were lined up at the base of the stage, each in turn passing dollar bills to Tiffany, which she graciously accepted as she sang.

''Oh, isn't Tiffany beautiful?'' said Limoge. ''God, she has such beautiful clothes. And the presentation. Just look at her sing. It's perfect. That gal's presentation is just perfect.''

They sat there, Todd and Limoge, as Tiffany's song ended and the audience broke into a raucous applause. Tiffany curtsied, accepted a bunch of roses, then exited, her sparkly pink gown billowing as she flew off the stage.

The emcee came back on, saying, ''Isn't that Tiffany a delight? Yes, of course she is. And now for one of our most popular stars, the one you've all been waiting to hear, our very own, the very delightful Limoge!''

''Oh, fuck!'' said a man's deep voice right next to Todd. ''I mean,'' she said, clearing her throat and speaking with ever so much breath, ''I mean, oh, dear, that's *moi.*''

An image of fashion and grace, Limoge rose from the table and began making her way toward the stage. A spotlight searched for and caught her, and she waved to her fans, blowing each and every one a big, bountiful kiss. Someone came out, handed her the mike, helped her onstage. And then she started belting it out, a big Broadway tune made famous by Ethel Merman: "Everything's Coming Up Roses." The boisterous, showy song filled the entire Show Room, and Limoge used the entire stage, strutting back and forth, broadcasting her song, her personality, just like the very best, the very biggest Broadway star.

But Todd only smiled briefly. He wasn't transported to some rosier place, because, of course, everything hadn't come up roses. No matter how hard he had tried, he wasn't living the life he was led to believe would be his. There was no beautiful wife, no kids, no dog, no warm, wonderful house. And now there was no Michael either. A wave of melancholy rose within him, and the song sucked him back to Chicago. His parents had had a dinner party in their small brick house. That song was blaring. All the adults were singing along with the powerful Ethel Merman. What fun. What joy. Life was so great.

Yet none of it turned out like that. Not even his parents' life, his father having died a curmudgeonly, vodka-sodden death, his mother now having a rebirth in some Florida trailer court.

Overwhelmed by memories of those days and of Michael, Todd rose and pushed through the seated crowd. He glanced up at the stage, and Limoge waved bye-bye as she blasted the audience with that big song. Todd lifted a hand in return as he headed for a side door. He'd come down to talk to one person, and he had to find him.

Exiting, Todd found himself in a side corridor. He looked to the right, saw an open door, heard some voices back there, lots of cackling. He went to the doorway, peered in, and saw her there. Tiffany, a cocktail in hand, was surrounded by three others: a black queen in a purple gown, a white queen in a pants suit, and a much younger one in a miniskirt. Todd rapped twice on the door frame, and the conversation dropped away as all eyes fell upon him.

"Oh," said Tiffany flatly.

"Well, look what the cat dragged in," said one.

"I don't believe it."

"My, my, my."

"Someone hurry up and dial four-one-one. We desperately need some info on why this dude is here."

Of course they knew who Todd was. That much was perfectly clear. And from the bitchy, judgmental tones of their voices and their dismissive, glaring eyes, Todd assumed they had some strong opinions about the whole affair.

"Do you have a minute, Jeff?" asked Todd.

"This is our place," said the black queen politely, "and in here she's known as Tiffany."

"Sorry." He tried again, saying, "Can we talk in private, Tiffany?"

She glared at him for a long moment. Then she shrugged, put her drink down on a table, and started out.

"Excuse me, girls, time for some serious chitchat," Tiffany said, turning. "Come on, Toad, I mean, Todd."

He followed her through another door, down a narrow hall, and into a tiny dressing room that was packed with a collage of show things. One entire wall was taken up by a rack of glittering gowns, the other by a large makeup table that was strewn with cosmetics. Three or four wigs were carefully perched here and there, and Todd spotted a half-filled ashtray and two Styrofoam cups with huge lipstick marks on them.

Shutting the door behind them, Tiffany nodded to a folding chair off to one side and said, "Have a seat."

Todd sat as Tiffany took her place at the makeup table. She flicked on the lights surrounding the mirror, looked at herself, smoothed her eyebrows, and groaned. Then she took a cigarette, lit it, and dramatically spewed out a big cloud of smoke.

In his male voice, Jeff Barnes's dislike of Todd was clear as he asked, "Why the hell are you here?"

"I wanted to ask you a couple of questions about Michael."

"Like what?"

"If you saw him when he was down here that last time."

"Oh, God," he mumbled, rolling his eyes.

"Listen, Jeff," began Todd, "I know you've never liked me. And I know you didn't care for my relationship with Michael."

"The word *bogus* comes to mind."

"I won't say that I didn't complicate things, but I loved Michael more than you can—"

"Oh, please spare me," Jeff said, reaching up to his scalp and pulling off his wig and revealing a mostly bald head. "Yeah, he was down here, we talked, if that's what you want to know."

"When?"

"That night. It must have been an hour or two after you played the madman and busted all of his grandmother's dishes."

"What about the next night? It would have been early, right after work. He would have stopped by for a drink."

"I don't know. I wasn't here and I haven't heard anything."

"Well, when he was down here," asked Todd, "when you saw him, was he with anyone?"

Jeff took a long, pensive drag on his cigarette, stared at Todd with his huge eyes that were further highlighted by all the makeup, and said, "Jesus Christ, is that all you care about?"

"What do you mean?"

"You just want to know if Michael had a fuck buddy, don't you?"

"Jeff, no, that's not why I . . . I . . ." Todd shook his head, bent forward, and covered his face with his hands. "I really screwed things up. I can't believe what a jerk I was. But now Michael's dead, and I've got to try and understand what happened. So, yeah, I guess I want to know if he was seeing anyone else. Did I drive him that far away? Had our relationship come to that?" Todd looked up. "And the other side of the same coin is that, yes, I need to know—the police need to know—if he was seeing anyone else, because perhaps, just perhaps, that was the person who killed him.''

Jeff, sitting there in the gown, ran a hand over his bald scalp, puffed on the cigarette, stared at the top of the vanity, and said, ''Yeah, he came down here. He came in just like you did, right after I finished singing. And he sat right there, right where you are. He'd been crying and he looked like shit.''

''Oh, God.''

''He didn't want to leave you, but your little outburst scared the shit out of him. He didn't know what to do.''

''I was just under so much pressure,'' pleaded Todd.

''I told him he didn't have to take that crap.''

''I loved him.''

''Well, there's good love and there's bad love,'' said Jeff. ''I told him exactly that—that there's good and there's bad love—and if your man is getting violent on you, then it's time to change things. I told him he should leave you, absolutely. Frankly, I thought you two were wrong from the beginning.''

''What did Michael . . . what did he say?''

''Not much. He just started crying again.'' Jeff shook his head as his eyes started reddening with tears. ''Poor, poor Michael. Do you know we'd been friends for over thirty years?''

''They were getting ready to offer me an anchor position at Channel Seven,'' launched Todd, wanting, almost begging Jeff to understand. ''These two worlds were colliding, my private life and my public. I couldn't handle it. You don't know what it's like being on television, what it's like to be rated on a daily basis. It's so sickening being judged on how you appear. If someone doesn't like your tie they call the station and say you're a dork of a journalist.''

''Todd, you know what I think?'' said Jeff, looking right at him. ''I think my dearest friend Michael was too good for you, that's what I think. He was an innocent, always had been, and he gave and gave and gave to you. On the other hand, you, the original closet case, took and took and took from him. All you were focused on was your career and your Emmys. No, that's not right. All you were focused on was your fucking image. How people saw you, you know, if you looked good on that little bitty screen and if your fucking tie looked good with your fucking shirt. It just wasn't an equitable relationship. Michael, the accountant, kept coming up with a negative net worth.''

"Jeff . . . don't," said Todd. "Don't say that. Don't talk like that. I loved Michael. He changed my life in ways you'll never know. That night that he was killed I was coming over to tell him that he was right, I had to come out. I was going to tell Channel Seven about Michael and me. I was going to make things right.''

"Well, you were a little late, weren't you?''

Not willing to let go of the one shining kernel of truth, Todd pleaded, "I was late, but . . . but I did make it. Doesn't that count for something?''

"Todd, don't you get it? This isn't *Sleeping Beauty.* Nothing's going to bring back my dear Michael.'' Dismissing him with a dramatic wave of her hand, she said, "Now go on, get out of here. I've got to change gowns.''

In preparation for her second song, Tiffany reached across her vanity, took another wig—the hair on this one was long and curled—and began tugging it on. Then she looked at herself in the mirror, saw how dreadfully sad her face had fallen, and immediately burst into tears. How in God's name could any of this be happening? Why had that Todd Mills come down here and asked so much? She only hoped she'd bowled him over with her version of the truth.

Tiffany pulled a couple of tissues from a box and dabbed daintily at her eyes and blew her nose. Though she'd never liked Todd Mills and had nothing but disdain for what he'd put Michael through, tonight she almost felt sorry for him. But, no. She couldn't let herself get sucked in. Oh, she saw how Michael had. A guy like Todd, so butch, such a rugged, handsome face. And that dazzling smile. Sure, Todd could be charming, but he knew how to turn it on and off as easily as a television. Cheap. He was cheap.

Regardless, this wasn't good, Todd's coming down here, wondering this and that. Not good at all, thought Tiffany, as she opened the top drawer of her vanity and pulled out a small telephone, her treasured pink Princess phone. Taking a pen so that she wouldn't break her long nails, she dialed a number that she had called all too frequently in the last week.

A few rings later the phone on the other end was answered by a machine, into which Tiffany angrily shouted, "Are you there? If you are, you sure as hell better pick up. Pick up the fucking phone, would you, you bitch? Hello? Hello?" But when no one came on Tiffany said, "Well, we've got a big problem. Todd Mills was just here. He came down here to see me and he was asking all sorts of questions. He knows something's up, God damn it all. He was asking if Michael went home with anyone, for Christ's sake. Shit, he could really screw things up if he finds out. I can't believe this. I'll be here for another couple of hours. I'll call when I get home, and you sure as hell better answer. Got it, girlfriend?"

16

Some thirty minutes later Todd was driving along Lake of the Isles Parkway when he let his Grand Cherokee drift to a halt on the side of the road. Staring across the long, narrow part of Lake of the Isles, his thoughts drifted. How many miles had Michael and he jogged around this lake? Hundreds? It wasn't quite three miles around, and over the past two years they had run this course at least three times a week. Sometimes they made several loops, while in the summer they'd often do Isles, Calhoun, and Harriet. All three lakes. Well, they had only run that much once or twice a summer. That was plenty, certainly enough to keep them both trim and fit, which were the silent expectations of the gay community and the spoken expectations of the television industry.

Michael was everywhere down here. He knew every inch of the lakes, all these houses, and so many of the people. Michael had tons of friends in town, and he'd see most of them down here, for to walk or jog around one of the lakes was the quintessential Minneapolis experience. Being a native Minnesotan, Michael had played hockey as a kid, and so

in the winter he was often down here at night on the huge
rink, reveling in the frigid air. Michael loved this place, this
city. Oz on the Tundra, that's what he called it. He knew it
all. The parks, the theaters, the downtown buildings. Oh, and
the restaurants. And he hated the megamall, would rant and
rave about that bloodsucking giant tick of a suburban shopping center that existed, no, preyed off Minneapolis yet con-
tributed no tax dollars to the city itself.

So Michael knew a lot about the Twin Cities as well as life
in general, but did he know that night he was murdered how
much he meant to Todd? Staring across the dark waters and
off into the night, that was all Todd wanted. Just to know that
Michael knew. Jeff's sharp criticisms echoed in Todd's mind.
Sure, Jeff was right on some accounts. Todd had been a shit,
much too self-absorbed. But Jeff was only looking at the
outer world. He wasn't seeing how Michael and he had connected on the inner, how together they were bumbling and
struggling to find something quite profound. How they were
almost there.

Todd wanted to be close to Michael, and without thinking
he started up his Cherokee, put it in gear, and started driving
along the narrow parkway. At the narrow end of the lake he
took a right on Franklin and swerved around and up a hill,
passing colossal house after colossal house. Like a homing
pigeon, he turned right at the first stop sign, heading south on
Irving and passing the Mondales'. He braked at 22nd Street,
saw Lake of the Isles again appear off to the right, and continued up to 23rd, where he took a left. He was on automatic
pilot, driving the same route he'd taken almost every day
after work for these past few years.

But, like that part of Todd's life, Michael's house was now
dark.

Todd slowly cruised by the large white duplex, saw the
blackened windows. He hadn't been in there since the night
of the fight. Was the place still sealed?

He drove on for another block, pulled over, and took his

cellular phone from its holster. What were their names? Right. He remembered, and he called information and got the number of the couple who lived upstairs from Michael. Todd dialed, the phone rang, but there was no answer. No answering machine or voice mail either, which was unusual for two fledgling lawyers. So maybe they had moved out, as Janice had yesterday suggested was a strong possibility. In any case there didn't seem to be anyone home, so maybe he could get in without the police being called.

He took a small flashlight from his glove compartment and left his Cherokee right there, climbing out and proceeding down the sidewalk. Thinking better of it, he cut around to the alley, certain that there was less chance of being seen back there. Slipping through the darkness, he moved along quickly and soon reached Michael's place, where he ascertained that the whole building was completely dark.

Feeling more as if he were breaking and entering than coming home, Todd let himself in the rear door, which he shut and locked behind him. He stood completely still, listened for any movement, but could detect nothing. He reached for a light switch, thought better of it. Certainly the next-door neighbors were jumpy and certainly they'd been told to call the police if they noticed anything strange. With that in mind, Todd flicked on his flashlight and proceeded up the three steps to Michael's back door. It was hopeless though, for a new hasp had been screwed into the door and a police padlock slapped in place.

He stood there, thinking. Surely the front door would be similarly sealed. He turned the corner, aimed the flashlight up the back stairs to the second-floor apartment, then turned around and followed the stairs down and past the outer door. Continuing down the next flight, Todd descended into the basement, a cavernous space cut up by old coal bins, storage lockers, and a vast cedar closet. Running the flashlight from left to right, he saw the paint Michael had used last year when he redid the bathroom, Michael's skis, Michael's bicycle, Michael's Christmas-tree stand, and Michael's old table, the oak one that he bought and intended to refinish but never did. This would not be fun, thought Todd. At some point Maggie and he were going to have to go through all this.

He continued around the gas boiler and came to yet another staircase. One of the former owners had planned to build an extra bedroom or something down here, but aside from gutting a closet upstairs and dropping down a set of stairs, no progress had been made. Michael and Todd had, in fact, talked about building an office down here if and when Todd moved in. But like so many other plans, that wasn't going to happen, and now he aimed his light up the dusty stairs. Just as he'd hoped, this entry into the apartment had been overlooked and there was no padlock.

Pulling the apartment key from his pocket, Todd proceeded up the stairs and unlocked the door, which swung open with ease. In an instant he was inside Michael's apartment, perusing the dark space with the small beam of light. And facing the stain of death.

It was the first thing that his flashlight fell upon, a big splash of darkened blood on the wall, a huge pool on the oak floor. The shock overwhelmed Todd and he couldn't move. Of course it was all dry, every little splatter and drip mark that streaked the wall, as well as the vast puddle where Michael had fallen, either dead or dying.

Oh, shit, he thought, and hurried through the kitchen, bumping into a chair as he rushed to the sink. His stomach swirled in a huge wave, threatened to rise out of his body. He gagged, caught his breath, then turned on the cold water. After a moment he splashed his face, next took a sip of water. He'd seen death before. A number of times actually. He'd seen it on maybe sixty percent of the stories he'd done for the CrimeEye, from gang assassinations to butchered lovers. But that blood had always been so distant, so remote.

Avoiding the back hall, he caught his breath and exited the kitchen via the other door. Everything was so quiet, so deathly still, and he stood on the edge of the dining room, slowly running the flashlight over the dark wood dinner table, the chairs. And the broken sideboard. The large piece of furniture was still tipped over, the wood cracked and splintered. A wave of shame rushed through Todd. He moved forward, scanning the floor. Where were the shards of china? Someone had obviously cleaned up. No, that wasn't what had happened. The crime lab had gone over all this. Right. They'd probably gathered every little shard of Michael's grandmother's china, hoping to find a trace of blood, a bit of material. Turning, Todd saw fingerprint dust on various parts of the smashed sideboard. Shaking his head, he couldn't believe he'd done all this damage, broken it all in such a fit of rage and frustration.

The scene screamed out of his memory. Todd flicked off the small flashlight and stood there in the dark, transfixed by memories of his shouting, his fury, his threatening gestures, the violent act. And, God, so much noise. When he'd dumped that piece of furniture the whole house had shook. It was no wonder that he'd scared the hell out of Michael and no surprise that Michael had gone down to see Jeff, seeking council and advice.

Moving into the living room, Todd peered through the dark and saw the black couch where Michael had sat when he'd stated his ultimatum. Studying the wall next to the fireplace, he saw the champagne stain on the white bricks, heard the explosion of glass and liquid all over again. Jeff had undoubtedly advised Michael to leave Todd because, of course, Jeff had always seen how much Todd withheld from Michael. The problem, Todd now clearly understood, was that during the day, in the light, he felt, acted, was perceived—and perceived himself—as straight. Wasn't that what people had expected of him, wasn't he fulfilling their expectations? Good God, what a fool he'd been. And to think he'd exploded over Michael's request to come to a fucking Christmas party. A wretchedly boring one, at that, with nothing but—

Something creaked.

Todd caught his breath, stood there in the dark living room. What was that? It sounded like a floorboard. Oh, shit, he thought, listening for something, anything. Maybe it was just the heat coming on. Maybe it was cold enough outside to activate the thermostat in here. Could be. Or it could just be a rodent.

No, that had been a footstep. Someone else was in Michael's apartment. His heart bolted. His eyes flashed from side to side. But he didn't move. Someone had come into this apartment before and killed Michael. Someone had come into Todd and Michael's life and ruined it. And that person, Todd sensed, was now hidden somewhere in this dark apartment. But why? To recover an incriminating item? Fear began to comingle with anger. He glanced at the set of fireplace tools and slowly reached over and took the iron poker. Michael's killer, the man who destroyed their world, was here.

Todd slowly began to cross the living room. Slipping his small flashlight into the jacket pocket, he gripped the poker with both hands and raised it head-high. His muscles tightened as he reached the hallway that led to the bedroom and office. He heard something else, the faint rustling of clothing. Someone was back here. But where? The bedroom, Michael's office, the bathroom?

Todd came around the corner, moving with constrained yet absolute purpose. He came to Michael's bedroom, paused in deep concentration. In the faint grayish light seeping through the windows, Todd saw the large bed he and Michael had shared and made love in covered with a smooth bedspread. The closet door in the corner was shut tight, the dresser undisturbed.

He inched down the hall, one grave, hushed step at a time. The night-light in the bathroom was on, illuminating the small room with a yellowish glow. The door was open all the way, pressed back against the wall, so clearly there was no one behind it. The tub? Todd took a half-step into the room.

No. No one lurking behind the shower curtain either. Which meant, he thought, easing back into the hallway, the intruder was in Michael's office. Could Todd possibly have him cornered?

He was focusing on the next room when he heard it. Darting steps behind him. Shit, whoever was here had gone back through the kitchen, the dining and living rooms, and was now coming at Todd from behind. He spun around, tried to swing the poker. But the hall was too narrow and the poker caught the wall just as the figure came thrusting into him, grabbing him by the chest, twisting him around. Todd tried to jab him with his weapon, but the stranger swung out, punched Todd's arm, and then grabbed Todd's fist and smashed it against a doorjamb. The iron poker dropped to the wooden floor.

The man was terribly strong and he grunted, shouted something, but Todd exploded with fury, hurling him back down the hall. The guy stumbled, and Todd was flying forward. The intruder pulled to the side, ducking into Michael's bedroom. Todd charged in, grappling to catch him by the shoulder. But the intruder spun around, yelled again, and rammed a fist into Todd's stomach. As the wind shot out of him, Todd stumbled. The guy caught Todd by one arm and threw him forward onto the floor. In one huge heave he pounced on Todd's back, grabbing Todd's right arm and twisting it around, pinning it behind Todd's back.

"Cool it!"

Todd thrashed to the side, felt the pain zing up his arm, down his back. He tried to jerk himself free, but the pain cut even more deeply and sharply.

"Stop it!" shouted the man, straddling Todd and holding him firmly down. "You're going to hurt yourself, you idiot!"

Like some animal who'd been chased wildly through the woods and who now knew it was hopeless, Todd lay there completely still, awaiting his fate.

"It's me, asshole!"

Todd turned his head slightly, glanced upward, saw a somewhat familiar shape looming above him in the dark. "Wh-what?"

"It's me, Rawlins."

"Oh, fuck . . ."

17

Todd lay there, heart thumping, his face mashed against the floor. He thrashed once, tried to free himself, but when he moved another streak of lightning-fast pain shot up his arm.

"Just calm down, Todd," Detective Rawlins said sternly. "It's just me. I'm not going to hurt you."

"What the hell are you doing here?"

"My job. What about you?"

Totally exhausted, Todd only muttered, "My arm."

"I'm going to let you go. I'm going to let your arm go now, okay? Just your arm. Don't get up."

"Don't worry."

Todd felt his arm release and he pulled it over, dropped it to his side. He tried to move, but couldn't. Rawlins was still straddling him, sitting on his back.

"Get off."

Rawlins gently rubbed the back of Todd's neck. "You all right, buddy? You all calmed down?"

"Get the hell off me!"

"Not until you calm down. I don't want you jumping up and getting all excited. I don't want any problems."

"Okay," Todd forced himself to say. "I'm okay."

Rawlins lifted himself off, and then Todd spun to the side, rolling onto his back. He lay there, staring at the dark figure of Rawlins, who now sat not two feet away on the edge of Michael's bed.

Todd demanded, "Didn't you see that fire poker I had? I could have killed you."

"Big deal, I got a gun. I could've killed you." Rawlins scratched his head, turned away, looked back. "You still haven't told me why you're here. You know, if I report this you could be in big trouble. This place is still a sealed crime scene."

"I was looking for something."

"Like what?"

"Something that belongs to me."

"You weren't going to remove evidence from a crime scene, were you?"

"My checkbook," blurted Todd. "I think I left it over here."

"Yeah, you did. And we have it now. Downtown. It's evidence. You should've just asked. I could have saved you a lot of hassle."

"Gee, thanks. Next time I'll be sure and remember how thoughtful you are." Todd pushed himself to his feet and stood there in the dark bedroom. "If you're here doing your job, why did I just see you somewhere else, like in a very big gay bar?"

"What kind of hotshot investigative reporter are you?"

"What's that mean?"

"Just put two and two together, you idiot. You saw me downtown and now you see me here. My, what a big coincidence."

"Oh, shit," moaned Todd. "You followed me?"

"What a brilliant conclusion. You really are sharp. No wonder you won those Emmys."

"Fuck you." Todd shook his head. "And get off Michael's bed."

"Yeah, yeah, yeah."

Todd didn't like being in here, not in this particular bedroom with Rawlins, and so he turned, started out. And then stopped. He took out his small flashlight, flicked it on, and aimed it at the reddish stain, which seemed to glow. Stumbling into a hole, Todd wondered if there'd been much of a struggle. Much pain. If Michael had died slowly or quickly.

"Come on," said Rawlins, placing a hand on Todd's shoulder. "You shouldn't be in here. Besides, we got a cop checking on this place every night, and I don't think it would be too good for him to find you in here. I'll only lie so much, you know."

Todd didn't move, even as Rawlins slipped the flashlight out of Todd's hand. Rawlins returned to the bedroom, smoothed the bedspread, then came out and returned the poker to the living room. Leaning against the wall, Todd felt like the truth of what happened was slipping further and further away. He heard Jeff's sharp words, saw the dried blood before him. Michael was buried, but now what?

"Come on," said Rawlins. "Out we go."

With Rawlins leading the way with the flashlight, Todd let himself be steered along and past the blood stain. Todd took one look back, then stepped through the door, down the stairs, and into the basement.

As Rawlins stood up at the top of the steps closing the door, Todd muttered, "This door wasn't padlocked."

"Yeah, don't worry about it, man."

"Here," said Todd, reaching into his pocket. "You're going to need my key to lock up."

"Nope, I'm all set. Detective Lewis and I each have a copy."

"Oh."

Moments later they were passing up the other stairs to the back door, and finally outside.

As they passed across the lawn Todd asked, "Where's Michael's car?"

"We're all done with it. I think you can pick it up anytime now."

"I'll call Maggie. She should have it."

Walking down the alley, Todd seemed to grow more tired with each step. Had Michael's service only been this afternoon? It already felt like days ago. And that realization frightened him. Was he losing Michael that quickly?

At the end of the alley Rawlins turned left, and Todd stopped, nodded in the other direction, and said, "I'm parked this way."

"Right. I'll walk you to your car."

Todd continued up the quiet street, and Rawlins followed, keeping silent pace. As they neared the Cherokee Todd cleared his throat.

"Listen, I'm sorry about that," he began, his breath steaming in the air. "I mean, I'm glad I didn't clobber you with the poker."

"Me too."

"Assaulting a police officer is all I need." Todd stared down the straight street, put his hands in his pockets. "I didn't even see you down there."

"What?"

"Down at the lake. You know, on the parkway," clarified Todd.

"Oh, right."

"I thought I was the only car parked down there."

Rawlins shrugged. "What can I say? That's my job." He stared at the ground, then looked up at the night sky. "Are you going to be all right?"

"Oh, sure. The man I love is dead, I probably lost my job, and the entire fucking world knows I'm queer. Other than that, hell, things are great."

"And your arm? I twisted it pretty good."

"It's okay." Todd shook his head. "Hell, I don't know. I

think it's just all catching up with me. It's been a hell of a long day, not to mention week.''

"Yeah, well, get some sleep. And don't worry about tonight. I won't mention it down at the station.''

As Todd started to take his keys from his pocket, Rawlins moved forward. Todd flinched. He stood quite stiff as he felt Rawlins's arms wrap around his back and embrace him tightly. And then the moment of hesitation evaporated. Todd returned the hug, even pulling Rawlins's thick, hard body against his and reveling in it. Someone to lean on. It just felt so good, so solid. Todd breathed in, faintly smelled cologne mixed with bar smoke, and his hand slipped upward, sensed the short hair on the back of Rawlins's neck.

A car whizzing around the corner, the headlights sweeping like spotlights and exposing their embrace. Todd and Rawlins quickly broke apart, each of them pushing back a couple of steps. Todd flinched, feared what might happen. And it did. The brake lights of the big old Ford flared up as it came to a quick halt. Both Todd and Rawlins kept their eyes on the vehicle, fearing the next few moments. Sure enough, one of the doors flung open. Were there now going to be a bunch of guys with baseball bats? No, only one guy emerged, and he shouted to the guys in the car, laughed, and then jogged up to a big stucco house.

Relief rushed through Todd, and he said, "I've got to go.''

"Sure.'' Rawlins looked up at the night sky again. "Look, I'm going to give you a call tomorrow. You know, just to check in, make sure you're okay. You won't mind, will you?''

"No. No, not at all.''

Perplexed, Todd climbed into his Cherokee. He started up the vehicle and glanced in the rearview mirror. He had his foot on the brake, and in the red glow he saw the muscular Rawlins heading down the street toward his car, a lone figure disappearing into the night. Just what, wondered Todd, had the detective really been after?

18

The sidewalk sale was going full force. There were guys everywhere, milling about on the sidewalk, eyeing the goods, groping the wares, trying to make up their minds.

The bars had just closed in downtown Minneapolis, and a flood of queers was pouring out of the Gay Times onto the sidewalk. Last call for drinks had been issued a half hour ago. This was the last chance. If you hadn't met the boy of your dreams during the evening inside, then the sidewalk sale out front was the final opportunity of the night. And the hundreds of men milling about on the brightly lit sidewalk were by no means masking their desirous, alcohol-fueled intentions. Take me. Love me. Be mine. At least for an hour.

Seated inside his dark car, the man watched the goings-on. While a few of them paired up, most of them went home alone, sauntering away from the Gay Times, heads hung, pace slow, even dejected. Sure, the bar scene was exciting and fun, all the men, all the hormones, all that music. It grew old, though. He knew that. All that cruising took a lot of energy. Some gay friends of his just hated the bar scene. Or so they claimed, even though they still came down here all the time.

Each day since he'd done Michael he'd been surprised. Grinning, he realized he'd literally gotten away with murder. At least so far, knock on wood. No one suspected him, because, of course, all the attention was still focused on Todd Mills. In just this morning's *Tribune* one letter to editor had expressed shock that Channel 7 hadn't fired Mills on the spot. Another letter, signed *Two Dykes on Bikes,* cursed Mills for fostering homophobia and violence against gays and lesbians. And a teenaged boy asked how was he supposed to develop a positive self-image when gays in positions of power like Todd Mills and all those famous Hollywood actors denied their true identities?

Amazing, he thought. In the course of one short week Todd Mills had gone from stud muffin to killer fag. Not long ago he'd considered the possibility of doing Todd as well. And he still might want to. But not just yet. The pretty boy was making such a good decoy. Besides, if he did Todd like he'd done Michael, then would they suspect? No, better not to stir things up just now. It was playing out all too perfectly.

The door of the Gay Times opened again and finally there he was: Jeff. The big man who wanted nothing more out of life than to wear heels and belt out Broadway tunes. He sashayed out of the bar, a huge grin on that broad face, his eyes casting about the crowd of eager men. Yoo-hoo, any of you boys want to take a nice queen home? All the makeup was gone, his face was scrubbed almost as red as a fresh beet, and what was left of his thinning hair was brushed carefully and neatly back. His plaid shirt was crisp and pressed, as were the jeans that circled his large waist. Sure, Jeff made a neat, presentable package, but nothing nearly so glamorous and dramatic as Tiffany Crystal. What a pity.

He was going to have to do Jeff. There was no question about it. Jeff knew too much about him. That was now abundantly clear. The only question was when.

He'd thought maybe tonight, which was why he was down here, parked across from the Gay Times, scoping the scene. Sure, he could play the troll and fish Jeff out of that crowd. Absolutely. And like some old troll he could take him down by the Mississippi and do him under a bridge. But that would be too easy and for that reason far too obvious. No, far better to wait. Far better to throw a curve.

Right, he thought, starting up his car and silently laughing to himself. A curve. Something not only to keep the spotlight burning on Todd Mills, but to throw the police way off. And this was going to work perfectly. He was sure of it, he told himself as he backed out of the parking space, pulled out of the lot, and turned right on Fourth Street. He had his big kitchen knife with him, wrapped in a T-shirt under the seat, and he knew only too well where he could dig up trouble. A whole bunch of it right along the banks of Lake Calhoun.

Turning right on Marquette and heading south, this should prove easy. He just prayed he'd still be able to get the story on Channel 7's morning news.

19

Unaware of the time, Todd drove onto Lake Street and passed along the edge of Lake Calhoun. While Michael had had an affinity for Lake of the Isles, Calhoun was Todd's lake of choice. It was about the same distance around each lake—three miles—but Todd preferred the bigger feel of Calhoun, which was totally open and unobstructed. Isles was much more twisty with all its bays and islands. Todd also preferred the diversity of Calhoun. The houses ringing the parkway weren't as big as those on Isles, the people not as trendy nor as wealthy, yet on Calhoun there was the sailboarding beach, the yuppie beach, the kiddie beach, the Generation X beach, the black parking lot, and, of course, the gay beach. Todd had never sat along the long, narrow stretch frequented by gays, never joined in a volleyball game. But he'd often walked or biked along the eastern shore of Lake Calhoun, seeing who was who and what was what, his sexuality never falling suspect because both the pedestrian and bike paths ran through this area. He could pass as a harmless het, just out enjoying the day.

But there would never be reason to hide again. Todd stared

across the dark lake toward the gay beach. Would he be hanging out there in the future, either by day or night? No, he might take up sailboarding, but he doubted he'd hang out at the beach or pursue encounters in the dark bushes. He hated sitting around in the sun, and anonymous sex frightened more than titillated him. He realized that while his life had changed fundamentally, in many ways he was still the same person as before.

Just past the Lakes' Beach Club he turned right, then left, pleased that the hecklers and demonstrators in front of his building were gone. As he pulled into the parking garage he continued up the ramp and to his space, where he got out and locked the Cherokee. Instead of boarding the elevator and going all the way up to the fifteenth floor, however, he entered the elevator lobby and descended to the main floor. After Michael's funeral today he'd forgotten about picking up his mail.

As he headed for the bank of mailboxes he looked toward the security desk and saw not the younger Bob but the night doorman, Larry, sitting behind the desk. A heavy, older man whose red uniform jacket didn't quite make it all the way around him, he was almost completely bald, and he now barely nodded. Todd offered a solemn wave in return and wondered just what Larry thought about the infamous homo-anchor-psycho-killer in his midst.

Stop it, he told himself as he unlocked the small silvery box. You can't do that anymore. So what if this Larry knows? Who gives a shit? Just get a grip, get real. He reached into his box and pulled out a handful of mail. Bills. *Newsweek.* The requisite junk mail. A letter with no return address.

Shaking his head, he crossed the lobby and reboarded the elevator. As he punched the button for his floor he glanced at the postmark on the letter and saw that it was mailed from St. Paul. He hesitated for a moment. Recently he'd done a story on a woman—an abortion rights activist—who'd gotten a brown box in the mail, no return address, no markings of any sort. Fortunately the woman had had her wits about her, was aware of what it might be, and had called both the CrimeEye team and the bomb squad. The result was a nice bit of publicity for the woman's cause, because somehow Todd had persuaded the police not to open the package until shortly after 6:00 P.M. and was thus able to broadcast the resulting explosion live on the evening news.

So what did he now hold in his hands?

Todd carefully felt the envelope, sensing no object, no lumpy item within. He held the envelope up to the recessed light in the elevator. As far as he could tell there was only a sheet of paper inside. Ripping open the envelope, he found a note scribbled in pencil.

> *Dear Mr. Faggot Mills:*
>
> *So you're just a disgusting homo, huh? I hope you get AIDS. I hope you get oozing sores all over your body. I hope you get diarrhea and shit and shit and shit until you weigh nothing. That's right, I hope you shrivel up and die, you pathetic queer.*
>
> *A former Fan*

Todd crumpled the letter into a ball and slumped against the wall of the elevator. Right. This was what he'd been afraid of. What people would say about him. How they would hate him if they knew the real Todd. And no matter how much he jogged, no matter how often he worked out at the gym, no matter how many Emmys he won, he just wasn't strong enough to face up to this kind of stuff. Never had been. And he doubted he ever would be. This was his kryptonite. What people thought about him had the same mysterious effect as that glowing green stuff had on Superman.

The elevator stopped on the fifteenth floor and Todd scurried toward his door. A horrible voice in his head was screaming. See, you fool, I told you so, there's always been a reason, people hate you now, you have no more friends, your life is over, get back in the fucking closet. This very thing, this stupid note, was the very reason he'd always been so secretive. He couldn't be openly gay because his life was just too public; Michael had never comprehended that.

Rushing into his apartment, he sensed his exhaustion transforming into paranoia, yet he couldn't stop it. He slammed the door, bolted it as if someone were right behind him, ready to barge in, to slice him to pieces. Nearly delirious, he threw the mail on the kitchen counter, turned on the small light over the stove, then dropped his coat on the floor and hit the power button on the CD player. The deep, melodic music of Seal filled the apartment, and Todd rushed to his bedroom, where he stripped at a manic pace, yanking off his sweater, tugging at the buttons of his shirt. He tore everything away—throwing pants, black socks, blue-striped underwear everywhere—as if it were burning his skin. Then he ran naked down the narrow hallway and back to the kitchen, where he grabbed a pack of matches from a drawer. Next he grabbed a candle from the dining room table. He turned up the stereo even louder and rotated one of the speakers so that the song "Prayer for the Dying" was blasting toward the bathroom.

Seconds later the hot water was beating down on him. He stood in the shower, the gentle light of the candle flickering through the glass shower door, the water steaming all around him. Just relax, he told himself. Let go of it. All of it. Go back to the basics. Go back to what really matters. Mom said it was okay. Thank God for *Oprah*. Mom still loves you. And she said Dad knew, somewhere in his heart. He knew and he only came down so hard on you because he wanted you to fly beyond him. Well, damn him, thought Todd, pounding the tile wall of the shower with his fist. Didn't that stupid bastard understand that you don't teach someone to fly by telling them what they're doing wrong?

The images came whisking out of the dark. There was Michael's coffin at the front of the chapel. All those people. The deep hole Michael was to be dropped into. The pumping music at the Gay Times. The queens with the big lips and big hair. Ethel Merman's voice crawling through his ears like a worm. And then, of course, the blood. Michael's blood in the apartment. Rawlins, too, grabbing him, pinning him down. And the letter. He'd gotten fan mail, lots of it, but never hate mail. Let go of it. Just let go of it.

The shower pounded down on him, massaging his neck, his shoulders. Soothing his head, his back. Nearly twenty minutes later he reached down, turned off the water, and toweled himself off. He felt jet-lagged. One moment exhausted, the next overwhelmed and confused and longing for some sleeping pills, something to slow his heart and mind. Something to knock him out, if only for a few hours.

There was a pause between songs, and in this break there was banging. Oh, Christ, he thought, standing there at the edge of the bathroom. Someone was beating on his door. For a moment he didn't move, fearing Michael's murderer, or the letter writer, Former Fan. Wrapping a blue towel around his waist, he slowly proceeded down the hall, then stopped by the doorway to the kitchen, where the only light in his apartment, the stove light, was still burning. Another song started but had the knocking ceased?

No, definitely not.

Above Seal's deep, smoky voice he heard a fist pounding on his door. Who was it? Cindy Wilson, Mark Buchanan, and the roving camera of Channel 7? Another search squad? Someone with malicious intent? Or perhaps merely a neighbor complaining about the music?

Taking the cordless phone from the kitchen counter, he readied himself to punch in 911. Todd switched off the stereo. And stood completely still.

"Who's there?"

A muffled voice from the hallway called, "Todd, it's me."

Both alarmed and concerned, Todd tightened the towel around his waist and edged toward the door. What was he doing here so late? Hesitantly leaning against the door, Todd peered out of the peephole. Steve Rawlins stood there, and as far as Todd could tell his visitor was alone, unless of course a team of cops was waiting just down the hall.

"How did you get in the building?" Todd asked.

"I showed the doorman my badge."

"What do you want?"

"I need to talk."

"Now?"

"Yeah. Let me in. Please?"

Todd knew what it was about, knew what he wanted, but Todd didn't want to get into it. Particularly not tonight.

"It's late," replied Todd, still not opening up.

"This is important."

Todd placed his hand on the bolt, was about to twist it open, and hesitated. "Are you alone?"

"What do you think? Of couse I am."

He shouldn't be doing this, he thought. It was a whole can of worms, insidious ones at that. A mess that was sure to grow only worse if he opened the door. Yet even though Todd wanted to tell him to go away, to leave him alone, he couldn't force those words out. He found his hand compulsively twisting the bolt, turning the knob, pulling back the door. In an instant the dark figure darted through the opening. Todd relocked the door, turned around, and stared at the back of his late-night guest. Nervously scratching his naked chest, Todd reached down, firmly held the knotted towel in place around his waist.

Looking away from Todd, Steve Rawlins was leaning against the entry to the kitchen. His head was hung.

Todd demanded, "Why are you here?"

"I . . . I . . ." he began, shaking his head. "Shit, I'm sorry. This is really stupid of me, coming over like this."

"It's not a good idea."

"Of course it isn't."

Still without turning around and seeing Todd, Rawlins moved forward toward the living room. He stopped, stared across the space and out the windows at Lake Calhoun.

"I need to talk to you," began Rawlins, sounding troubled, even pained.

"So talk."

"There's something I need to tell you."

Oh, God, thought Todd, I don't want to get into this. Not now. Not tonight. Michael hadn't even been in the ground twelve hours.

"You need to know something," continued Rawlins. "There's something I haven't told you."

Todd was suddenly wide awake. Suddenly trembling. And he couldn't steady himself, couldn't make his body quit jittering. Oh, shit. This was heading for trouble. You don't want to be doing this. No. Go back to the door. Open it up. Tell Rawlins to get out of here.

"It's kind of complicated, and I really don't know how much I should tell you," said Rawlins, his voice almost quivering as he turned and faced Todd for the first time. "But—"

Todd's half-naked body was grazed by Rawlins's burning stare, and a prick of adrenaline shot Todd's heart. Michael said the chemistry of homosexuality was simply floating in the air, pheromones just lingering out there waiting for queers to pick up on them. Todd sensed it otherwise. The eyes. If the eyes met and held for a fraction of a second too long, he could see the truth. And looking into Rawlins's, Todd saw not only his sexuality but the depth of his lust.

An instant later he felt the eyes on his chest, where both his muscles and hair were the thickest. Then Todd sensed the stare upon his biceps, which Todd had worked and worked until they were full and round and hard. And next Rawlins's eyes were following the thin trail of hair that zipped down Todd's stomach, over his navel, and on down beneath the towel. Todd trembled as if Rawlins were caressing him with much more than those X-ray eyes. Oh, God, thought Todd. This wasn't right. This was a big mistake. Michael was barely in the grave. Michael? Did he matter now? This wasn't like cheating. Michael was forever gone and . . . and he'd been seeing someone else, hadn't he? Well, hadn't he?

Todd knew it was a helpless situation. There was no stopping it, and both men moved forward silently, abandoning words, recognizing that these events were way beyond their control. Something quite a bit stronger was taking hold, gripping the two of them, pulling them magnetically together. Todd moved farther into the living room, Rawlins stepped closer, and the last rational thought Todd had, albeit brief, was, why hadn't this lust been there for women? And then a little voice within him blurted: Shut up, Todd, who the fuck cares?

They stopped when they were less than a foot apart. Todd felt the other man's deep, hot breath on his neck and then trickling downward. He inhaled the now-familiar odor of smoky, musky cologne. And as Todd stared into the eyes of Steve Rawlins, the intensity excited as much as frightened him. Todd couldn't be alone, not now, not tonight. He needed comfort. Yearned to be held. Warmed. Taken care of. And he liked this strength, this power now before him. Had to touch it. Had to have it. Hesitantly raising his fingers, he was more than eager to explore. He was desperate to. Yes, explosion and release. Now. His fingers sensed the heaviness of Rawlins's jacket. And then, almost simultaneously, Todd felt a hand on his waist, a sure hand that rubbed his skin, then reached for the knot of the towel and popped it loose.

20

He was surprised to see so many men out here so very late. As soon as one guy succeeded in his pursuit and scurried away, another appeared, eager for the touch that would bring the release. Yes, these deep bushes along this dark stretch of Lake Calhoun were a beehive of sexual business, all of it desperate, all of it gay, and ninety-nine percent of it unspoken. Just do it and get out of here.

It was a notorious spot, this area that ran behind the gay beach. The streetlights were way up along the road, and the large cottonwoods, elms, and thick bushes sucked up most of the light. While the young straights were busy screwing on the Spoon Bridge in the Sculpture Garden or beneath a shrouded table in one particular bar, this was one of the prime gay cruising areas of Minneapolis, the other being along the steep banks of the Mississippi. Or it was, anyway, for just a few more weeks. The next heavy winds would blow off the last of the leaves and there would be no more hiding. To be sure, this dark, chilly fall night was one of the last of the season.

He stood on the grassy edge of the park alongside a towering elm. It was so dark and so still that he could barely see anything. But there was a still figure standing beside another tree. Or was there? He studied the spot, suddenly couldn't see anything. Wait, no. The figure moved, slipping into the bushes that climbed up the small hill and to the road.

And, yes, the man liked what he saw, for that guy, the one who'd just disappeared into the bushes, appeared none too tall or hefty. It didn't make that much difference, but why take on a big guy, someone who might make a bit of a struggle or even holler out? No, somebody like this guy was better. Do him and be done. Simple.

More important yet, thought the man, slipping forward and touching the knife cradled inside his jacket, was the fact that no one else was over here. Right. Some guy had strolled by in a suit not long ago, but he'd kept on going. And two guys in jeans and jackets had disappeared into the bushes way down there, some fifty feet away. But unless someone else was lying prey in this particular spot, the area should be quiet. Less chance of being seen.

Heading toward the hillside, he glanced from side to side, saw no one else, and then proceeded across the bike path to the very edge of the bushes. Just in front of him, perhaps only some ten feet within the bushes, there was a rustling. Yes, thought the man. This shouldn't be too difficult. Just be matter of fact about it. Very direct.

He ducked beneath a branch, followed a well-trodden path. It was a narrow passage that led into an inner chamber of sorts, a room trampled within the innards of the bushes. Stopping in this space, he realized he was alone in here. Had his friend-to-be disappeared, slipped out another way? His eyes scanned the faint light of the area, spotted another dirt path leading up and around a tree. It was a real maze down here. Not more than twenty minutes ago he'd followed one guy into another set of bushes, tailed him as he weaved in and out of these little outdoor bedrooms until he finally cornered him. Or thought he had, because then someone else appeared out of nowhere, a tall, thin guy with glasses, and the two of them had paired off.

A voice out of nowhere whispered, "Hi."

He jumped, spooked by the unseen man. Glancing to his immediate right, his eyes drank in the short, lithe figure. Yes, it was the same one he'd seen enter the area. And now getting a closer look, the man thought how perfect this guy was going to be. Very doable.

"It's getting kind of quiet down here," said the man.

"Yeah, it is kind of late."

But then for a brief second he didn't think he could do it again. Eyeing the shadow of the guy, sensing the fearful pulsing of blood within himself, he wondered if he could actually go through with it again. But, shit. He had to. He'd thought of every way to stop it, but there was none. This was the only choice. Just be smart about it. And quick.

He volunteered, "I'm kind of . . . of nervous."

"Me too."

"Do you do this very often?"

"Hell, no," laughed the short guy. "Only my second time."

"My first."

"Really?"

Yes, that was the right thing to say. Put the guy at ease. Make him feel like you were the shy, inexperienced one, and he had nothing to fear. Like he was the teacher, the one in control.

"Well . . ." said the guy, stepping closer, "let's have some fun."

"I saw a good spot over here."

The man backed down the trail, leading the way into the clearing. This was the right place. Plenty of room to move. And fall. Nothing to get in the way. Very secluded.

The short guy followed him, then came right up and kissed him on the cheek, saying, "You're cute."

He couldn't help but flinch. Of course there was no way he

was going to be able to get excited. Think fast, he told him-self. Don't lose him. He's perfect. How exactly are you go-ing to do this?

"Like I said, I'm a little scared," said the man. "I'm kind of new at this."

"Hey, don't worry. This'll be just nice and sweet. Okay? A little fun in the woods."

"Okay, but . . . but I might need a little help getting started, if you know what I mean."

"No problem."

"Just at the beginning. Once I get hot, then . . . then . . . well . . ." The man's heart was trembling. "Would you mind opening, you know, my pants, and . . . and . . ."

"Trust me, I'd be delighted to just nuzzle right in there."

Oh, God, this was perfect. The short guy was kneeling down, reaching out, tugging at the man's belt, popping the top button of his pants. And here it was, he realized as he stared down at the other. His little window of opportunity. Perfect. Yes, go for the neck. One quick slice should do it. Just be sure and lean into it. Lots of pressure.

It was only as he reached into his jacket for the long kitchen knife that he saw it. The slim band of gold on the short guy's left ring finger. Oh, well. All this would really be one hell of a curveball. Particularly since the man was going to leave behind one ratty old baseball cap.

21

Something started ringing, and Cindy Wilson started twisting in her dreams. She had been floating in this huge, placid lake. All so still. So black. And then this shrill, hideous sound came at her like a shrieking bird, a creature that plucked her out of that lake and thus out of her sleep.

In an instant she was sitting on the edge of her bed. Dear Lord. She opened her eyes for a brief second and saw the digital alarm clock: 5:13 A.M. No, it wasn't the alarm clock ringing reveille. It was the phone, and the stupid thing kept crying out. She forced her eyes open a bit more, forced herself to reach out for the receiver, knowing most definitely who it had to be. She just wondered what it was about.

"Yeah?" she mumbled into the phone.

"Cindy, it's me, Bonnie," said the young woman on night duty at the Channel 7 news desk.

"I figured."

"We just got a call."

"Oh?"

"It came right here, to the news desk," said Bonnie.

This was sounding familiar, and Cindy asked, "What?"

"I mean, whoever called in didn't do so on the CrimeEye line."

Cindy was waking up as quickly as if she had jumped into a cold lake. Could this be her second lucky break?

Cindy asked, "Another murder?"

"Right. About—"

"And you answered the call?"

"Yeah."

"Male or female?"

"Male," replied Bonnie. "At least I think so. The voice was kind of deep and hoarse."

"Just like the first one. Where?"

"Lake Calhoun. In the bushes up between 32nd and 33rd Streets."

"Oh, my God. That's the gay beach. Did he say anything else? Did he—"

"Hang on," said Bonnie, a tad frustrated by Cindy's impatience. "It went like this: The phone rings, I pick it up, this hoarse voice says there's another one. I say, another one what? He says, another body. In the bushes. By Lake Calhoun between 32nd and 33rd. I start to ask something else, he hangs up. And then I call you. That's it."

"So you haven't called the police yet?"

"No, but I—"

"Give Mark a call, tell him to meet me at 33rd and Lake Calhoun Parkway in ten minutes," instructed an eager Cindy. "Then wait two minutes and call the police. Got it?"

"Of course."

"Oh, and don't forget to save a spot on Sunrise Seven for us," she added, referring to the 7:00 A.M. news program. "I can feel it, this is going to be good. Call Locker too. Tell him I think we can begin Plan B."

It was yet another beautiful morning in this fall of extraordinary weather, and the rising sun spread a golden cast over the glasslike surface of Lake Calhoun. The perfect backdrop for the beginning of the story, thought Cindy Wilson. She and Mark Buchanan had it all planned out. She was going to be standing with the lake behind her, then he'd swing around and zoom in on the hillside, and next they'd cut to the segment they'd been piecing together since before six this morning. Perfect. Yes, her stock at Channel 7 was rising quickly, and this story very well might clinch her promotion. The CrimeEye might be all hers.

She opened her compact, stared at the small mirror, and noted that her blond hair was all in place. The deep red lipstick was fresh and expertly applied too. Good. Putting away her compact, Cindy smoothed her black leather jacket, which fit her trim body perfectly. She'd been wearing the same jacket since she arrived hours ago, and although she'd considered switching to her burgundy wool coat—which was up in the Channel 7 van and looked so great against the tones of her skin—management downtown had told her to stick with the leather. Much better, they'd said. Made it look like she was actively involved in the investigation. Which in a very real way she was. After all, she'd found the body.

"Thirty seconds," called Mark, tightening his camera on the tripod.

Cindy assumed her position, adjusted her earpiece, flicked at one stray hair. Clear your head. Think this through. Start with the sunrise. The beauty. Move into the murder. Yes, this was going to be great. And be sure, she told herself, be absolutely sure to mention the bit about the suspect. Tell them to stay tuned to Channel 7 for this unfolding story of murder.

"And five, four, three, two, one," announced Mark. "You're live."

A microphone in her right hand, Cindy looked directly into the camera. "It's a beautiful dawn out here on Lake Calhoun, with the morning sun cutting through the trees, reflecting off the glassy surface of this popular lake. It's just after seven in the morning, and already scores of joggers and bicyclists are out enjoying the day. But is this lake, this park, as beautiful and safe as we would all like to believe? Evidently not, for early this morning another man was murdered, apparently knifed to death in an area where gay men reputedly seek anonymous sex. Once again the CrimeEye team has been on the story from the very start, alerting the police and aiding in the investigation. Here's what we learned. . . .''

The camera turned away from Cindy, showed the bushy hillside, and then faded away. Cindy turned toward a small monitor and watched the clip she and Mark had prepared.

''Shortly after five this morning Channel Seven received an anonymous tip, claiming that a man had been killed in this area,'' came Cindy's voice-over as the video showed a large clock in the station downtown. ''Our night manager of the news desk then alerted both me and the police of the mysterious call, and all of us immediately rushed to this area of Lake Calhoun, frequently known as the gay beach.'' The video showed the police and Cindy Wilson searching the area, flashlights in hand. ''And what we found was indeed a body.''

As graphically as could be portrayed on television, the camera showed the sequence of events as Cindy Wilson narrated. There was shouting and hollering. Then Cindy gasping, trying to maintain control, trying to look both professional and resolute. Yes, the body, Cindy shouted. The cops came running, and the camera zeroed in on one hand poking out of the brush. Then there was a huge bloodstain on the hillside. An ambulance. Flashing lights. The arrival of the crime lab. More shouting and chaos. And lots of Cindy Wilson looking official, concerned, and professional. Always professional.

Then back to Cindy live, standing on the banks of the picture-perfect lake. ''The victim of this grisly murder was a white male, thought to be in his early thirties. While the police are not releasing the victim's name pending notification of relatives, the CrimeEye team has learned that the cause of death initially appears to be multiple knife wounds. This is speculation, but it is quite possible that early this morning the victim was seeking anonymous sex in these bushes and was attacked and killed in the process of that.

"It's much too early to reach any conclusions, of course, but off the record several police officers have already commented on the similarity of this murder to the one just last week. That murder occurred only ten blocks away in Kenwood, and I'm sure many viewers will recall seeing Channel Seven's own Emmy Award–winning Todd Mills led away by the police. Although he was released, Mr. Mills was held overnight for questioning for the murder of Michael Carter, his homosexual lover, who died from multiple knife wounds. Whether the man found dead this morning was also gay remains to be known, but police are not discounting a link between the two. However, I did personally note a wedding band on the victim's left ring finger.

"Needless to say, the tranquility of this beautiful autumn morning has been shattered by this grisly murder. While murder is by no means new to Minneapolis or St. Paul, it is rarely seen in the heart of the wealthy Kenwood area or in the beautiful Lake District, which really is the pride of the entire city of Minneapolis. I have been assured by the head of police, Captain Lou Olson, that these two cases are top priority.

"I should add, there has already been one very interesting development in this case that might lead to a solution of this murder and perhaps also that of Michael Carter," continued Cindy Wilson. "A piece of evidence was found near the scene of the crime this morning. While I'm not at liberty at this moment to divulge anything further, an item was found in the bushes that police feel might lead to an arrest. The police are excited and pleased about this, and I would like to assure you that the CrimeEye team will keep you completely informed for any developments in this exciting and fast-breaking story of murder and gay sex.

"For the Channel Seven CrimeEye team, this is Cindy Wilson."

22

"You look like shit," said Donna Lewis, sitting behind the steering wheel of the Taurus.

"Yeah, well, I didn't get much sleep last night," replied Rawlins.

His mouth opened in a huge, unstifled yawn, and he glanced down the hill at the collection of cop cars on the grass and along the bicycle path. Lewis and he had been down there for hours and had only just retreated to their car up on the parkway.

"What, were you out at the bars trying to find the man of your dreams?" she prodded.

"Something like that," answered Rawlins, trying to ignore her by looking through the dense trees and out over the smooth surface of the lake.

"And?"

"None of your business, Mom."

"But you did see Mills?"

"Like I told you, he was at the Gay Times."

"That's pretty nervy of him, wouldn't you say?" She reached toward the dashboard for the silver Thermos of coffee. "I mean, going out cruising just after you bury your boyfriend doesn't sound so very puritan, does it? Then again, if he did kill Carter and perhaps this guy, then obviously he isn't terribly ethical, much less sentimental."

Rawlins looked away in disgust and said, "After some of the shit I've seen him pull on TV, I wouldn't call him warm and fuzzy, that's for sure."

Rawlins shrugged and slumped against the passenger door of the Taurus, then closed his eyes. He hadn't been asleep more than an hour or two when the phone started ringing and he was called down here to Lake Calhoun. Then for the last few hours it had been nothing but chaos as everyone from the crime lab to the coroner to—of course—Channel 7 rushed around, doing their business. Although Lewis and he had yet to talk about it specifically, Rawlins most certainly knew their next task of the day.

Crap, he wasn't going to get any time for a nap. All he wanted to do was sleep. Things were calming down now though. They'd just taken away the body, and the guys should soon be done combing the hillside for any additional items. Already they'd found a number of condoms. And, of course, the hat.

"More," muttered Rawlins, holding out his chipped coffee mug. "Like about a gallon."

"Yeah, yeah," she said as she poured some for him, then for herself.

Of course the guy they'd found knifed in the bushes had been seeking anonymous sex. In Rawlins's mind there was virtually no doubt about it. Lewis had suggested a simple mugging; Rawlins had told her to stop being ridiculous. And he wasn't that surprised to learn that the dead guy was married and from the wealthy suburb of Edina, facts that had been confirmed within the last half hour. Sure, most of the men who hunted for sex in these bushes were gay, either the compulsive types or the perennial lonely hearts. But a good deal weren't. After all, anonymous sex areas like this were anonymous for a very good reason: Many of the guys had much too much to lose. Like wives. Or girlfriends. Or jobs.

"So you think this is connected," asked Lewis, "to the murder of Michael Carter?"

Rawlins hesitated, wasn't sure how he should respond, then answered the most simple way, saying, "Probably."

"Both were knifings, obviously. Both appear to involve gay men." Lewis sipped at her coffee, then added, "But it'll be interesting to see the coroner's report."

"He should be able to tell us if the wounds could have been made by the same weapon."

"Or if any sexual act had taken place. After all, they never found proof that Carter was actually doing anything." Lewis shrugged. "This guy's pants were open, but that was about it. I mean, it didn't look like he was doing anything hot and heavy."

Rawlins shrugged. "Blow jobs?"

"Could be. We'll have to wait to hear from the coroner on that one too. See what they find in his mouth and stomach."

With his head, Rawlins motioned toward the Cubs baseball cap perched carefully on the backseat and said, "So at last we have the mysterious Cubs hat. What are we going to do about it?"

"Even if it is his, it doesn't prove anything, not conclusively. Obviously, though, we need to talk to him."

"When?"

"The sooner the better. Actually, we could just go over there right now. I would imagine this early he'd still be there."

The possibility that the cap belonged to Todd Mills had been brought up almost immediately after it had been found in the bushes. Upon seeing it, both Cindy Wilson and Mark Buchanan had stood there dumbfounded. It wasn't that Cubs hats were all that rare in the Twin Cities, merely that Cindy and Mark so clearly associated a hat like this—a real wool

Cubs cap like the players wore—with one person in particular.

"Wait a minute, that's Todd's hat, isn't it?" Cindy had said, freezing in her steps.

"Christ," Buchanan had muttered, knowing fully what it implied.

Of course, it might not be, and in an effort to identify its owner the crime lab had been quick to study the hat and gather a number of hair samples from it. With any luck there were still a few follicles attached to those samples, otherwise they'd get an identification with only eighty-five percent certitude. Which wouldn't be good enough in court. Nevertheless, the hat was clearly attached to the murder via a stain on the brim, which one of the technicians had taken note of. He'd done a chemical test on sight, and the dab had barked up orange, meaning that the spot was in fact blood. They'd be able to ascertain a blood type within a few days, but it would take at least a month to get a foolproof DNA identification.

Rawlins downed his coffee and said, "You know what, why don't you let me go over?"

"Alone?"

"Yeah, I just want to get him talking. See how much he'll say. I think we'll get more information out of him if we keep this as nonintimidating as possible."

"Not to mention noncustodial."

"Exactly." Rawlins wondered if Lewis suspected anything, and he added, "Let me just go over and shoot the breeze with him. I'll get him to make me some coffee and just sort of work into it."

"You mean, you think he might talk more to you just because you're gay?" she asked, eyeing him suspiciously.

"Maybe."

"You fags," said Lewis, rolling her eyes. "You're like a private club, you know?"

"Let's not get into that now."

"No, really. You want to be accepted, but you can't accept that some straight people just might—"

Rawlins shook his head. "Listen, we'll have a group therapy session on sexuality some other time. Just not now. I'm too tired."

"Okay, fine. You go over alone and talk about boy things or whatever. I don't care. I'll get a ride downtown with the crime lab." She nabbed the Thermos off the dashboard. "Just don't forget to take a real good look around his apartment. Maybe he'll even let you do a search without a warrant."

"Yeah, he just might." Rawlins smiled. "He's starting to get real comfortable with me."

23

Todd just lay there in bed, his eyes open, his body not moving beneath the down comforter. For a moment he considered trying to catch the morning news on his small bedroom TV, but the morning light in his bedroom warned that it was already too late. After staring at the ceiling for five or ten more minutes, he rolled his head to the side, saw the clock. It was just after nine. Well, he'd missed the news by more than two hours. Oh, well, he thought. He should get up. He had to. But his arms felt weighed down and he just couldn't move. He hadn't slept this late in years.

He had reason to be exhausted, of course, and he was sure that he hadn't slept this soundly in weeks, most definitely not since the night before Michael and he had fought. His mind drifted over all that had occurred since that night. No wonder he was worn out, he mused, getting tired just thinking about it all.

So had he slept so soundly because he'd passed through the end of the beginning or because he'd had sex with Rawlins? Todd rolled onto his side, stared at the empty space. Christ, what had he done? How stupid. How . . . how . . .

Rawlins had really been here, and it had really happened. They'd started out there in the living room and ten, maybe fifteen minutes later proceeded back to this bed. And it had been great. Todd recalled the other man's body, the surprising bulk of his chest, the strength of his shoulders, the trim waist. How wonderful it had been to hold someone in his arms. And to be held. Absolutely. Through all of this short, intense week Todd had yet to realize how lonely he was already. And he recalled Rawlins's sure, firm exploration of Todd's own body, how naturally and easily things had progressed. It was almost as easy as being with Michael, he thought with yet another tinge of guilt. Perhaps even a little bit more exciting. Or had that been because of the novelty? Sure, it had been exciting to touch and feel and kiss someone altogether new. There had been something odd about it though, for while it had been passionate, it had also been so frenzied, so desperate.

But what did it mean?

Todd didn't know the answer to that one. Rawlins hadn't stayed long enough. The act itself had been protracted—three or four times they'd neared orgasm, only to hang back and stretch things out—and then once they were done, Rawlins had left, rather hurriedly so. When was it? Almost 3:30. He'd barely lingered afterward. Barely said anything as he slipped out of bed and trudged naked back to the dark living room, where he gathered his clothes. Todd had followed a few minutes later, stood at the end of the hall and watched as Rawlins dressed, looking . . . looking what? Angry? Todd had been so tired he couldn't really tell. Or rather, he'd noticed, but he'd been too exhausted to give it any thought. Instead, he'd given Rawlins a final hug, seen him to the door, then collapsed into bed and blacked out in a deep, lost sleep.

Despite how deeply he'd slept, Todd now felt nearly as exhausted as when he went to bed. He stared at the curtain-covered window and at the light that was seeping around the edges and thought: Michael is dead and I screwed Rawlins.

Sure, but Michael had been killed almost a week ago. He was never coming back. It was just that, well, Todd wasn't ready to move on, to let go of Michael. Yes, that was right, thought Todd, realizing he was as depressed as he was exhausted. He wasn't ready to start picking up the pieces, didn't want to be ready. Yet Rawlins had just dropped right in there, forcing a wedge right between Todd and the memory of Michael.

So what had been on Rawlins's mind? Why had he come over here in the first place? Rawlins had claimed there was something he wanted to talk about, something he wanted to tell Todd. Was that merely a ploy, a way to gain entry into Todd's apartment and his emotions? And why had Rawlins seemed so stern as he departed? Surely that had to do with his work. Perhaps Rawlins was afraid it would get back to the police force, where word of last night's liaison might not fly too well. Then again, Todd wasn't still a suspect in Michael's case, was he? Surely the statements from that gas station attendant and the waitress at the chili restaurant had taken care of that. And surely there were no ethical questions involved. This wasn't like a shrink sleeping with a client. Or was it? Then Todd wondered if the complicating factor wasn't much more basic. Did Rawlins have a partner, a lover, a longtime companion, or whatever you called the person of the same sex you couldn't live without? No, he'd claimed earlier that he was unattached.

Todd moaned and rolled out of bed. From the bathroom he took his robe, the big white, terry-cloth one, and proceeded to the living room, where he put on some music. As he turned toward the kitchen he saw it, the blue towel, right where Rawlins had dropped it after pulling it from Todd's waist. Todd had a vision of himself standing naked before Rawlins in the dimly lit living room. Okay, it might be complicated today, but last night it was hot. Definitely so. And he wondered when he might see Rawlins again, what might transpire at that time versus what he wanted to transpire. No, he thought, he couldn't handle anyone new in his life. Not yet.

In the kitchen Todd glanced at his new answering machine. Even as he looked at the small white box, he saw the digital number climb from five to six. Six messages? How was that possible? He studied the phone. Oh, right. He'd turned off the ringer last night, and his machine had been silently answering the phone all morning.

He shook his head and turned away from the phone, toward the coffee maker. He'd deal with the calls later; for now he'd tend to his number-one priority, namely, brewing some extrastrong coffee. As usual, he'd take his first cup of coffee into the shower, where he'd stand and let the water blast him into the morning. And then what?

He supposed it was time to think about picking up the pieces. He should call Janice, see if there was any news, ask her if it was okay to contact Channel 7. Oh, and he had to call Stella. She'd called three times last week, but Todd had yet to phone her back. There was the delicate matter of his career, of course, and what in the hell would happen now. Could it be possible that everything would die down, that no one would give a shit about his sexuality, that he could go back to work? Was the world that wonderful, that generous? Perhaps. Perhaps, too, all this publicity might fuel interest in his career and propel him into another stratosphere à la Harding and Kerrigan. On the other hand, his career might be over at Channel 7 and he might soon be interviewing in the boonies. No, that wasn't right. He couldn't go to a small town because that would certainly mean going back into the closet. And he couldn't, wouldn't. Well, then, maybe New York. Or San Francisco. Maybe he could get hired on one of the new gay cable programs.

As he was pouring that first cup of coffee there was a solid knock on the door. He guessed who it was, and was surprised to find himself smiling. Perfect timing. He'd just gotten up and the coffee was fresh. And maybe his visitor had picked up some bagels or muffins. It might be nice. They could talk. He took a deep breath, exhaled. Michael wouldn't mind this, would he? No, absolutely not. Move on with your life, his ghost would say. Enjoy. I'll be with you in spirit, buddy. Just don't forget about the flesh. You gotta take care of the real part of your life.

There was more knocking, and a voice called, "Todd?"

Of course it was him, thought Todd as he put down the coffeepot and called, "Just a minute."

"It's me."

Yeah, that was him. Sure it was. The forceful knock was familiar, and who else just arrived up here on the fifteenth floor? With the recent exception of Cindy Wilson and Mark Buchanan, hardly anyone. His neighbors usually called before dropping by. And the guards downstairs—Larry and Bob—always cleared any visitors coming in. The security was good here, yet they obviously had let Rawlins in unannounced because he was a cop. Carefully holding his coffee with one hand, he unlocked the bolt with the other.

An uneasy sense of paranoia came over him, and before he twisted open the door handle he peered out the peephole, saw the very familiar figure, and asked, "You're alone, aren't you?"

"No, my mother's with me."

Todd couldn't suppress a grin as he opened the door. "Hi. Want some coffee?"

"Sure."

As Rawlins brushed past him, Todd saw that he was carrying a brown paper bag. Muffins? Bagels? Just how serious, he wondered as he followed Rawlins into the kitchen, was this going to be from the start? He knew he couldn't handle a torrid affair. Not yet anyway. Friendship, yes. Companionship, definitely.

"You don't look like you slept too much," said Todd, an amused look on his face.

He watched as Rawlins deposited the brown bag on the

kitchen counter and turned, his eyes intense and deep. Todd felt a shot of arousal clutch his waist. Or was it fear? He didn't know, couldn't tell, and he backed up slightly.

"I didn't," replied Steve Rawlins, his voice deep and scratchy. "And it doesn't look like you did either."

Dressed only in his white terry-cloth bathrobe, his hair uncombed and still tousled with sleep, his teeth unbrushed, Todd felt oddly exposed. Or terribly vulnerable. He felt Rawlins's eyes running down his neck and burning through his robe. Was this to be a replay of last night's union?

"I . . . I was just about to take a shower," Todd muttered and then took a sip of coffee.

"A little groggy?"

"Yeah."

"Where have you been?"

"Nowhere. I just got up."

Rawlins stared at him, said, "But you weren't here. I tried calling."

"I switched my phone off last night."

Oh, shit, thought Todd. His heart pounding, his throat tightening. Rawlins was moving toward him, his steps slow but sure. Yet Todd wasn't sure he liked this. Something was different, not so easy, and he stepped back, felt the refrigerator at his back, realized he was cornered.

"I don't think I moved a muscle since you left." With a nervous laugh and his voice surprisingly faint, Todd added, "As if I weren't exhausted enough, you wore me out."

"It was great, wasn't it?"

"Yeah, but—"

"Sh."

"But, Steve—"

"Rawlins," he said in a hushed voice as he closed in. "Everyone calls me Rawlins."

"I'm . . . I'm not sure I'm ready for this."

"Just put your coffee down."

"But . . ."

Todd set his mug on the counter and couldn't help but close his eyes as he saw the hand reaching out slowly. An instant later he felt the sure, strong fingers of the other man wrap around the back of his neck. Todd gasped, then leaned over, pressing his cheek against Rawlins's thick, hairy wrist. He opened his mouth, softly bit at the skin. Then Todd sensed Rawlins's right hand on the other side of his neck, and as Rawlins began to knead and massage him, Todd's breath began to come in short, deep gasps.

"Oh, my God," moaned Todd. "That feels incredible."

He reached up with his right hand, wanting to touch Rawlins, satisfy, please him in some way as well. But just as his hand descended on Rawlins's shoulder, Rawlins removed it, gently pressing it down and back against the cool refrigerator door.

"Just relax," instructed Rawlins. "Just take from me."

Todd tumbled into a nervous kind of bliss as the other man's fingers massaged his neck, the back of his head. With a deep, gentle, and circular motion, Rawlins's strong, steady fingers worked their way over Todd's ears, up his scalp. Todd dreamily opened his eyes, saw how intently Rawlins was inspecting him.

"Close your eyes," ordered Rawlins. "Just receive."

Trapped in the corner of his kitchen, held captive by a deep surge of desire, Todd did as he was told, feeling the hands next on his forehead, next softly descending to his temples. A finger brushed over Todd's lips, and he lunged out at it, bit and sucked on it. But Rawlins wouldn't be entrapped, and slowly, steadily, his hand moved down. A moment later Todd felt the hands on his chest, then sensed his robe tugged totally open. Oh, Christ, he thought. Here he was, all of him, including the extent of his arousal, totally exposed, as easy to read as a thermometer.

He couldn't help but reach out. Couldn't help but open his eyes as Rawlins's right hand skimmed over his stomach. But what was this? This was definitely different from last night, when the charge of energy had been coming from both of them. This felt lopsided, as if Todd was being used, nothing more.

No, realized Todd, grabbing at his robe, pulling it shut. They had to talk. They had to work things out. Perhaps—hopefully—there'd be time for this later. For now it was all wrong. He didn't know why. He just knew it was.

"Rawlins," began Todd, pushing away, "this is a little too soon for—"

"Please."

"Don't," said Todd, pulling free of his grasp.

Surprised at himself, amazed that he was breaking away, Todd grabbed his mug. He quickly crossed to the coffee maker where, with a trembling hand, he poured himself a refill.

"I've got to take a shower."

His body surging with desire, his head churning with confusion, he rushed down the narrow hall, coffee splashing out of his mug and onto the beige carpet. He charged into the bathroom, shut the door, and locked it. Michael, Michael, Michael. He took a sip of coffee, stared at the door, then purposefully unlocked it. Not knowing at all what he wanted, he took another swallow of coffee, slipped out of his robe, then climbed into the shower, coffee in hand. He set the mug on a back shelf, then disappeared beneath a pounding stream of steaming water. Breathing as hard as if he'd just climbed several flights of stairs, he wondered if the door would be pushed open and a naked Steve Rawlins would join him, wondered, too, if that was what he wanted after all.

Nothing happened however.

He was not disturbed as he bathed, and eventually the shower cooled his desire and warmed his flesh. He washed and shampooed, then stood there, the water beating against his back. Drinking more coffee, he was relieved to feel in control once again. Control? Fuck that, he thought. For so long he'd been so tight, so worried. He had to let go. Nothing mattered, not anymore. But did that mean giving in to Rawlins? Maybe. Maybe eventually. He just didn't know, and finally he climbed out of the shower, calmed but no less confused. As he toweled himself off he heard a noise from somewhere in his apartment. What had that been, a door closing?

He cracked the door and called out, "You're still here, aren't you?"

"Indeed I am."

"I'll be right there."

"Take your time," replied Rawlins. "Hey, where do you keep your knives?"

"The silverware's in the drawer beneath the coffee maker."

"No, the sharp ones."

"Oh. They're in the drawer left of the stove."

So what was Rawlins doing, cooking breakfast? Things could be worse, thought Todd as he turned to the sink, lathered up his face, and began to shave. Actually, a good solid breakfast, some company, and a calm morning were just what he wanted and needed. It would be only too great if Rawlins and he could back up a bit and start the day from a different angle.

Minutes later Todd had tugged on his favorite blue jeans, the faded ones that gripped his body smoothly and snugly, and pulled on a dark blue T-shirt that hugged his chest. He ran his hands through his hair, ruffled things a bit, and started back to the kitchen. Wondering what Rawlins might be cooking, Todd took a deep whiff. He smelled only the rich aroma of coffee. Not even the warm scent of toast. Cereal? Was that to be the morning's fare?

But then Todd entered the kitchen and found it empty.

"Rawlins?" he called rather desperately. "Where are you?"

Shit, he thought, when his question was answered by silence. Rawlins had left after all. Within the last few minutes he'd slipped out. That wasn't what Todd had wanted. No, he realized, the disappointment stinging him. He shook his head, dumped his now-cold coffee down the drain. He hadn't realized it when he'd first gotten up, but this promised to be an extremely lonely morning. The phone, he thought, remembering his lifeline of human contact. As he crossed to it and flicked on the ringer, he checked the answering machine and saw that there were now eight messages. What was all this about? It seemed odd that there'd be so many calls, particularly so early in the morning.

His eye was caught by an object: the brown bag, which still sat on the counter. Well, whatever Rawlins had brought, at least he'd been decent enough to leave it. Stepping over to the bag, hungry for any kind of baked good, Todd peered in and found a hat. A crumpled Cubs hat. He reached in, pulled it out. What was this all about?

"That yours?"

Todd jumped, turned around, saw Rawlins standing in the kitchen doorway, and said, "Shit, you scared me."

"Sorry."

"I thought you'd left."

"Nope, just out on the balcony." Rawlins nodded toward the hat. "Is that your hat?"

Todd turned the cap in his hand and recognized the creases and folds, the faded tones and the soft wool. All of it seemed familiar except for one thing.

"I'd say sure, but mine doesn't have an orange spot like this." He glanced suspiciously at Rawlins. "Why?"

"Someone found it down by Lake Calhoun."

"Then it's not mine," Todd replied quickly. "I haven't seen it in a while, but mine's probably in the closet."

"Which?"

"The front hall one right there. Why? What difference does it make?"

Rawlins didn't answer him, instead turning around, stepping toward the closet, and opening it. It was only then that

Todd saw the large knife that Rawlins was clutching in his right hand.

"What are you doing with that knife?" Todd demanded.

Rawlins ignored the question, peered into the closet, pushed aside a few coats, and said, "There's no hat in here."

"It's on the shelf if it's there."

"Nope. Nothing." Rawlins turned around, pointed with the knife at the hat in Todd's hands. "That's gotta be yours, doesn't it?"

"What the hell are you getting at?"

"And this is your knife, isn't it?"

"Of course it is. You just took it out of the drawer." Todd didn't like any of this and he stepped toward Rawlins, his hand extended. "Give it back. I don't know what you're getting at, but I don't like it."

"Someone was killed last night."

"What?"

"Or rather, early this morning. Right out there by Lake Calhoun. Right by blow-job beach. You can even see the spot from your balcony."

"What the hell are you talking about?" demanded Todd.

Rawlins nodded at the cap. "And they found that by the body. That orange spot is the guy's blood. The crime lab ran a test."

His eyes wide with shock, Todd stared at the hat he held. The next instant he threw it on the counter.

"It's not my hat," Todd said quickly.

"They took some hair samples, so they'll be able to tell for sure."

"It can't be mine."

"What if it is?"

"Well . . . well, then someone took it from me. Someone came in here and stole my hat." Todd remembered throwing it on the floor at Michael's. "Actually, I haven't seen it since that night Michael and I fought."

Rawlins asked bluntly, "Todd, where were you last night?"

"What are you talking about?" demanded Todd. "I was at the Gay Times, then at Michael's, and then here. Here, fucking you. Remember?"

"What about after?"

"Are you kidding? I . . . I was asleep. I didn't even move until ten minutes before you showed up."

"Are you sure you didn't make a—"

"Don't. Don't even dare suggest it."

A horrible realization whooshed through him. This entire morning was coming all too quickly into focus.

"Holy shit," said Todd, "that's why you're here, isn't it? You didn't come here to coo in my ear. You came to check me out, see if you could find anything. Well, I don't have any scratches, do I? No bruises either. Nothing except maybe some of your little paw marks."

"Todd, you need to—"

"Get out."

"You can either tell me everything or we can haul you back downtown."

"Great, you take me in for questioning and I'll tell them, among other things, that you're a size queen," threatened Todd, referring to Rawlins's penchant for well-endowed men. "I bet the guys downtown would get a bang out of that, so to speak."

"Todd, if we bring you in, the press will be all over you. They'll eat up whatever's left of your career. You'll be completely ruined."

"I'll tell you this much," snapped Todd in disgust, "I don't know anything about anyone getting killed last night. I wasn't down at Lake Calhoun. Now, give me my knife and get out of my home."

Rawlins raised the gleaming blade, saying, "Someone was murdered with a long knife, perhaps one just like this."

"Get out! Get the fuck out of here!" Todd charged forward. "I can't take this and I don't have to. Now leave!"

"Not until you tell me how your hat got down there."

"Well, why don't you tell me where you went after you left here last night? Actually, that's a pretty good idea. How the hell do I know you didn't head down to the lake and do a little trolling? Well?"

Rawlins flushed red with anger. Standing only inches in front of him, Todd saw the other man's hand tighten on the handle of the knife.

Todd's hand shot through the air, grabbing the knife by the blade as he shouted, "Give me that!"

He wrenched the knife from Rawlins, stormed past him, and yanked open the door, saying, "Get the fuck out!"

Rawlins stared at him, but instead of leaving he ducked into the kitchen, where he snatched the Cubs hat and stuffed it back into the paper bag.

"What the hell are you doing?" demanded Todd, letting go of the open door and hurrying back to the kitchen.

"This is a piece of evidence."

"But—"

"But what? It's yours? I thought you said it wasn't." He glanced in the bag and shrugged. "Sorry, I've got it now. You want to try and stop me? You've got a knife. Go ahead. I dare you."

"Just get the hell out of here and leave me alone!"

Without further words, Rawlins heaved past Todd and out the door. Charging after him, Todd twisted the bolt shut and stood there, flushed with anger. A moment later he sensed a hot, wet sensation in his right hand, looked down, and saw a steady stream of blood curling from his hand down the shiny blade of the knife.

"Shit," he muttered.

He started for the kitchen, but just then the phone began ringing. Todd threw the knife on the counter, grabbed a kitchen towel, wrapped it around his hand, and picked up the phone on the third ring.

"What?" he snapped.

"Jesus Christ, Todd, where the hell have you been?" demanded a voice.

"Who is this?"

"It's me, Janice, you idiot. I've been calling you all morning. Didn't you get my messages, all five of them?"

"I turned my phone off. And—"

"Listen, you've got to get down here. We have a problem. Or, I should say, you do. You've heard the news, haven't you?"

Todd tightened the towel around his hand. "Rawlins was just here."

"Oh, God. Officially or unofficially?"

"That's a good question."

"Well, get your butt down here right away. We've got to figure out what's going on."

Todd replied, "Janice, if I didn't know better, I'd say someone was trying to frame me."

24

"Cindy, Cindy, Cindy," said Locker, beaming. "What can I say? You're doing an excellent job. An incredible one."

"Thank you."

Still wearing her black leather jacket, having not changed at all since this morning's shoot, Cindy Wilson sat in her boss's office, a proud smile on her face. She knew it too. She was doing fabulously. Upon arriving here at the station she'd watched the entire clip that had run on Sunrise Seven. Not only had her delivery been calm and professional, not only did she look wonderful on screen, but Mark's camera work had been great. It truly looked as if she'd been critical in assisting the police in their search for the body. In other words, her horror at discovering the body hadn't come across. No one had been able to discern her fright, her disgust at spotting the maimed corpse and all that blood. Just thinking about it now—the blatant knife wounds, the pants open, the ghostly white legs—made her tense all over again. No, just push it away, she told herself. You've seen plenty of bodies.

"And I think you're absolutely right," continued Locker.

"Plan B?"

With a broad grin Locker said, "Hang him."

They'd talked about it the other day at the staff meeting, a horrendously long meeting that had focused on how to handle this explosive situation. Just how were they going to treat Todd Mills, both officially and unofficially? How long did they want him associated with Channel 7?

"Dear Lord, I can't believe how he's screwed every last one of us," Locker now moaned.

Cindy said, "Well, we just can't go down with him, can we? I mean, I like Todd, but—"

"We all liked Todd," interrupted Locker, completely aware that he was referring to his once star reporter in the past tense. "I mean, he did good work here. He won those Emmys. But you're right, Cindy, that's not the point. The point is that we can't let Channel Seven go down the tubes just because his life is all screwed up. The station has its ratings to bear in mind, we've all got careers, and it's just not right to let one guy come in and ruin the whole thing. Right?"

"Absolutely."

"So what choice do we have? The death of Michael Carter was one thing—maybe Todd really didn't do it. But this one is entirely different. No one knows what really happened down at Lake Calhoun early this morning, but rightly or wrongly our viewers are going to see Todd Mills as a gay serial killer. We have no choice but to distance ourselves from him. And who knows, maybe he actually killed his boyfriend and now this other one too. Like I say, who knows. I was grooming Todd. He was doing wonderful things for the station. Hell, we were going to offer him an anchor position." He shook his head, ran a hand over his bald scalp. "But, good God, maybe he's this pent-up faggot who's gone on a killing rampage."

"If that's the case, we've got to find out if he hurt anyone before," volunteered Cindy. "What if he has a history of violence?"

"Exactly. And that's the story," barked Locker from behind his desk. "Did we have a murderer in our midst and not even know it? Had evil crept into this building, into these rooms? We were accepting and loving of Todd. We treated him with care and dignity and respect. He was a member of our family, and, hell, we made him a star. But now? Now?"

Cindy sat there watching her boss, who was round-faced and bald and hyper, and she knew what Plan B meant, for they'd discussed it at length. Guilty until proven innocent. Or Save-Your-Ass TV. Of course they had to distance themselves from Todd Mills. This station—any station—cultivated and garnered viewers as though nothing else mattered. Ratings were everything, and Channel 7 was undoubtedly the most respected station of the Upper Midwest. The one people had turned to for generations. They couldn't toss it all aside for some reporter who very well might be the poisoned apple in the barrel.

"So we've got to give him the O.J. treatment," continued Locker. "And you're the perfect person to do it."

Cindy's gut knotted. Perfect because she was a woman or perfect because she'd worked by Todd's side and she was a good reporter?

"We've got to look like innocents, Cindy. That's the angle I want you to come from. We can't go down with Todd. We've got to rise to the surface and then float like angels up to heaven. And we need to get a call-in number, a special number viewers can call for recorded updates."

"Or maybe a couple of numbers. One for updates, another for biographical information on Todd. Maybe a third for a gay crisis line or something."

"Oh, God, our viewers are going to eat this up."

"And I'll focus on how we were betrayed," said Cindy.

"Exactly."

"And how we were deceived."

"Perfect."

"It's actually a pretty good story," mused Cindy, her mind clicking along, formulating the steps she'd take.

"Of course it is."

"Here's this guy, this hunk, who's approaching the pinnacle of his career. He's won these Emmys, everything looks perfect from the outside. But then his life is shattered when the world finds out who the real Todd is."

"That's it. We're all tempted by evil. Or tainted by it."

"And our golden boy, it turns out, is no different."

"Right," said Locker with a laugh. "Let's get someone working on a couple of side pieces. You know, the pressures of being homosexual, not being out at work. Being married and gay. That kind of thing."

"So I have to find out what happened to Todd. When he crossed over the line into darkness."

"Oh, I like this."

"I have to focus on the bad side of him. And these days and in this liberal state it's got to be more than his sexuality. Specifically, I have to keep murder always in the forefront."

"Absolutely. A killer always fascinates viewers." Locker leaned forward, a sly grin on his face, and said, "But don't forget to keep sex and sexuality right up there too. Everyone finds that interesting. Particularly famous queers who've buried themselves deep in the closet. You know, like Rock Hudson, Malcolm Forbes, and Calvin Klein."

"Patricia Ireland of N.O.W. too."

"Right. People are gossipy by nature, and there's no better way to hook 'em than talk of who's doing what to whom. But you're right. In the South you could get more mileage out of homosexuality, but not necessarily up here. On the other hand . . . on the other hand AIDS has everyone afraid of homos, and a murdering fag is an entirely different beast."

Cindy nodded and looked down at her long red nails. "I'm

going to have to do some research, see what I can dig up. Can I get some help? Obviously there's a part of Todd that he kept hidden."

"Cindy, my dear, you can have anything you want. Channel Seven is at your disposal."

She liked this, for it was already perfectly clear what Todd Mills and his predicament were doing for her career. When she'd first been hired at Channel 7 they'd treated her like this nice little girl. She was pretty. She had nice white teeth and bright blond hair. She looked good on TV. But Todd and Channel 7 had kept her in the wings at best until suddenly, almost overnight, things had changed. Now there was respect. Seated across from Locker, she could see how he no longer viewed her as someone to be merely tolerated, nor even as a magnet to draw female viewership. Hell, no. Now Locker understood she was a key player who could deliver something he needed. She liked this. She was vital. He needed her.

"He was married before, wasn't he?" asked Cindy.

"Sure."

"Maybe we can find his ex-wife."

"I hear she's beautiful. And way up there. Someone important. A lawyer maybe. Or a doctor. I don't know," said Locker with a wave of his hand. "But that's a great idea. You should find her and see if she knows her ex was a homo. Maybe that's what caused the divorce. Hell, maybe she caught him in bed with some guy. And maybe she knows if Todd has a history of violence. When you do talk with her, see what you can learn about their sex life. Find out if they had one at all. And if he was violent with her."

"Or better yet, I should find her divorce lawyer."

"Brilliant."

"I should check that other station too, the one in central Illinois. Todd was there for five years, wasn't he?"

"Something like that. Just check everywhere. Dig up as

much dirt as you can. Who knows, maybe something like this happened before.''

"Right," replied Cindy, nodding.

"His father was an alcoholic, wasn't he?''

"I don't know.''

"I'm pretty sure that was the case. And I know for a fact that Todd saw a shrink up here.'' Locker paused for a moment and grinned. "God, I wonder how we can find out if Todd's been on medication. And don't forget to check the gay bars. Do a lot of snooping at the Gay Times in particular. Maybe Todd was down there all the time.'' Locker paused, surprised by his own chain of thought. "Good God, maybe Todd was a regular at those anonymous sex places. Isn't there another over by the Mississippi? Shit, maybe Todd even has AIDS. Has he been sick—a cold or anything—lately? Christ, I wonder if we all shouldn't get blood tests. Maybe you better. I mean, you've been working side by side.''

"I'll get someone to pull his medical files.''

There was a whole laundry list of things to check, thought Cindy. And it would take a team of researchers to pull together a story like this. But the challenge was irresistible. A version of the story started to appear in her mind's eye: Todd as a strapping kid who pulled himself from an abusive, dysfunctional family—maybe he'd been beaten by his drunk father, perhaps even sexually abused—and then struggled to fame and wealth, only to be toppled by sex and murder. Everyone would want to watch that, for it was the stuff that miniseries were made of. Only this one was real, which made it all the more compelling. In fact, there was so much information and this was such a captivating and shocking story— who hadn't trusted Todd, either at the station or on the screen?—that Cindy could easily imagine a number of segments. Which meant a lot of exposure for her. She'd have to keep it personal too. That would be the best. She'd emphasize how she and Todd had worked so closely. How he'd been her mentor and how they'd become such good friends.

And Cindy sensed that she should even bring in some personal elements of her own life, like how she'd been mugged and nearly raped in college, and especially the story of her cousin Sandi, who was both a lesbian and a police officer in Chicago. That would soften Cindy's coverage, keep it from seeming overtly homophobic. The last thing she wanted was something like a backlash from the gay community.

"There's a whole lot of stuff spinning in this head of mine," said Cindy, unable to hide her excitement. "There's so much material. So much potential. This is going to be a great story."

"I know. And it's all yours. I'm sure we can get the nationals to pick this up too. I'm sure they'll want a few spots. You do realize, don't you, that this is the kind of stuff that Emmys are made of?"

Despite mention of such a golden carrot, Cindy maintained her trademark composure, saying, "Well, I'll get someone started on Todd's personal history and all. But . . . I've got to stick with the story of the day, namely the murder down at Lake Calhoun. Can I do an update on the evening news?"

"Absolutely. In fact, I'll make you our lead." Locker ran his hand over his smooth, bald head. "You're the perfect person for this, Cindy. There's no one better. You worked right by Todd's side. You know him better than almost anyone. So you've got to show the world how you were deceived. How all of us were deceived. This is your baby, Cindy. Go get him."

Good God, she thought. For a brief moment she couldn't move. This was unbelievable. Locker was talking to her as if he were a football coach and she were his star player. It was too good to be true. Finally, her big story.

She rose and extended her hand, saying, "Thank you, Mr. Locker. I won't let you down."

"Of course you won't."

She couldn't quite comprehend it. Who could have imagined she'd be given Todd Mills to crucify? Certainly not she. So what if he was innocent? This was power. Big power. And she was going to use it to blast her all the way to the top.

25

Todd was speechless when Janice told him. They sat in her twelfth-floor office downtown, and he stared out the window at the grassy plaza on the south end of Government Center. It seemed to Todd that his stomach had fallen away. He could barely breathe, let alone move. The day, like his life, was careening out of control.

"Todd, you do understand how serious this is, don't you?"

Slowly turning toward her, Todd tried to say something, couldn't, and when he finally managed a few words his voice was small, almost childlike. "Janice, that's impossible."

"Not according to the lab tests."

"But . . ."

"Todd, listen to me," she implored. "Just a few minutes ago, just before you walked in, I called Detective Rawlins at the police department. They've gotten the initial results back from the lab. The hairs match."

Deep inside he was shaking. This couldn't be happening. They'd analyzed the hairs from the Cubs cap and found them to match the samples plucked from his own scalp. How was it possible? Suddenly this spacious modern office felt like a prison. No, a trap. He'd come down here and now he was caught.

"Janice, that can't be my hat," he said desperately. "I'm sure the last time I saw it was at Michael's. Like I told the cops, I threw it on the floor. You've got to believe me. I haven't been over on that side of Lake Calhoun in weeks. And I certainly wasn't down there last night."

Janice rose from her large wooden desk, and as she started to pace she said, "Oh, my God, why did I ever quit smoking?" She shook her head, shrugged, and muttered, "Todd, this is bad, real bad."

"Are they going to charge me with killing that guy?"

"I get two cigarettes a week," she said, pulling open a drawer. "And just watch, I'm going to smoke them both right now."

"Janice, are they going to charge me with anything?"

"I don't know. Nothing's been really proved. I mean, you can't kill a guy with a baseball cap. Still, this looks bad. It really does. This could be enough to put you on trial."

"But . . . but . . ."

"Todd, you can say whatever you like, but they found your goddamn Cubs hat by that body. Of course, if they charge you with murder, I'll insist they do a DNA test on the hairs. That could take a month or so, but maybe that'll clear you. Maybe, somehow, they'll find that the hairs don't match after all. But if they can somehow prove that's your cap and that's his blood on the visor—"

"But I wasn't down there! I wasn't down at the lake last night!" Todd looked up at her and begged, "Janice, you've got to believe me. I didn't kill this guy, whoever he was!"

"His name was Brian Fisher."

"I've never even heard of a Brian Fisher!"

"Oh, God, Todd . . ." Janice stopped, struck a match, and lit her cigarette. "I shouldn't be representing you. This is too hard."

"Janice, no. Don't talk like that."

"But—"

"You can't leave me."

"I know you too well, Todd. Maybe one of my partners should be handling this."

"I don't want another lawyer."

"I think it's a conflict of interest, Todd. I don't think I'm the right person for you." The cigarette shaking in her lips, Janice took a puff, then shook her head and started pacing again. "I'm just not sure you wouldn't be better off with someone else."

"Jesus Christ, Janice," Todd shouted, coming to his feet and moving toward her. "You're talking like I did it, like I killed this guy!"

"Todd, I just—"

"Janice, please don't say this."

"I'm just not so sure you don't need someone with a little more distance, someone with a better perspective. You're one of my closest friends, Todd. We've known each other for over twenty years. I mean, we even dated in college. And I loved Michael. He was my friend too." She shook her head hopelessly and said, "I'm afraid I'm too involved to be impartial."

"I have to have somebody gay."

"Well, we're one in ten, so there are a whole lot of queer lawyers. I can rattle off a dozen names of gay and lesbian lawyers who'd jump at the chance to represent you. This is a hot one. Unfortunately, I'm just too close to the fire."

"Don't do this to me."

He went to the door of her small office and leaned against it, his forehead touching the cool wood. Could he actually be charged with murder? Only a month ago he was being lauded with praise, wined and dined, and awarded with Emmys. How quickly things had changed. And if they were going to charge him with killing a man he'd never even laid eyes on, did that mean they'd charge him for the murder of Michael as well? Good God. His career and a good part of his life were now ruined, and if Janice left him there was no way he'd ever get through this. Hell no, he couldn't imagine working with another lawyer. The mere idea of trying to get a new attorney to understand the complexities of his life was just too daunting.

"How many times did we go out?" he asked, turning away from her, pacing a few steps to the other side of the small chamber.

"What?"

"How long did we date in college?"

"I don't know. Two months. What in the hell are you getting at?"

"More like three, I think. Anyway, I fell in love with you."

"Oh, Jesus, Todd. Don't." She snuffed out her cigarette and dropped herself into a chair. "We can't get into all that now. You're in much too much trouble."

"Okay, you're right. I didn't fall in love with you," said Todd, going over to the window and staring out again. "But ever since then I've loved you."

"Stop it, Todd!"

"I mean it."

"You're going to make me cry," warned Janice. "And I'm telling you, I might look like a nice lipstick lezzie in this business suit, but if I start bawling I'm going to lose it. This is way too hard. I'm going to start crying, my makeup's going to run, and I'm going to walk out of here looking like some wimpy suburban housewife."

"Funny, and here all these years I thought you just didn't want to look like a diesel dyke." Todd steered the conversation back down his intended path, asking, "You've loved me too, haven't you? I mean, ever since then?"

"Of course."

"There was so much that was right about us," he continued. "Everything . . . everything except, of course, the sexual part. It all makes such sense when I look back. It was always awkward when we kissed and fooled around.''

With a short laugh Janice said, ''Somehow we both knew that we were queer, didn't we?''

''Probably. But you accepted it a lot sooner than me. Like decades sooner. When did you come out, that next fall?''

''Right. I went to Europe that spring and summer, which is when I had my first big affair with another woman.''

''It scared me, you know,'' volunteered Todd, looking at her over his shoulder. ''Your honesty, I mean. When you came out I was afraid what it might mean about me. I knew, of course, that I had same-sex feelings, but I was doing my damnedest not to admit it.'' For a moment Todd was carried away by their shared history. ''And that's one of the things I've loved most about you—your honesty, your integrity.''

''Todd, have you flipped or what? Why the hell are you talking about this now?''

''Because I've been trying to learn from you.'' He turned from the window and said, ''Just look at me, Janice.''

Seated at her desk, she looked up, staring at him with reddened eyes. He crossed to her, pushed aside a few papers, and sat down on the edge of the desk. Reaching out, he took both her hands in his.

Clearing his throat, Todd said, ''We've been through a lot together. All these years, all these problems. You've always told me the truth, even when it hurt. And I've been trying to do the same. Hell, you were the first person I told about Michael and me.''

''Oh, sweetheart, you've always been so hard on yourself.''

''So ask.''

''Ask what?''

''Go on, ask me what you're worried about. Ask me what I did or didn't do. You've got to know.''

''But . . .''

"No buts. Be a big old bull-dyke lawyer and walk all over me. Be as direct as possible."

Janice blotted her right eye, asked meekly, "Did you kill Michael?"

"Absolutely not." Todd waited, then added, "Go on."

"Did you kill Brian Fisher?"

"No, I don't even know who he was."

"Were you cruising down at Lake Calhoun last night?"

"No. I've never even done that, gone down there and had sex. It scares me too much."

Todd watched as she closed her eyes and bit her bottom lip. Then she let out a huge sigh, sat back in her office chair. The next moment, she was leaning forward, wrapping her arms around him. He bent over, hugged her back, clutched her, and held on.

"I'm sorry," said Janice. "I was just so worried. I was just—"

"Sh. It's okay."

"God, this is a mess." She pushed back, wiped her eyes.

"No shit. This has turned into a pig roast, I'm the pig, and the media is swarming in for the feast."

"Channel Seven was down at the murder site this morning. It was on the early news."

"Oh, great. What did they say? Was my name brought up?"

He listened as she related the entire story. When Janice mentioned that Channel 7 claimed to have received the initial call, Todd took special note.

He shook his head and said, "Janice, I have to tell you all about last night."

"Of course you do."

He got up, went around, and sat down in front of her desk. "I went down to the Gay Times."

"Oh, that was smart. I'm sure a jury would find that very interesting. I mean, it doesn't sound very good, you going out to the bars right after Michael's funeral. You weren't trying to pick up someone, were you?''

''No.''

''Thank God for miracles.''

''I just wanted to talk to Jeff.'' Todd studied Janice as he said, ''I . . . I don't know, I just wanted to know if Michael was seeing someone else.''

''What? Michael? You two didn't have an open relationship, did you?''

''No. It was just a thought, a worry.'' A worry with no resolution, he realized, looking away. ''Jeff wasn't particularly happy to see me though.''

''I bet not.'' She lit her second cigarette, then reached into a drawer and took out a fresh yellow legal pad. ''What else? Did you just leave then? Did you have a drink or anything?''

''Yeah, one. Two maybe, I can't remember. I watched part of the drag show.'' He added the most important aspect of the night, saying, ''And I ran into Rawlins.''

''What? Detective Rawlins?''

''Yeah, he's gay.''

''Of course he is.''

''You knew?''

''Absolutely. And you didn't?''

''I was, well, surprised.''

''Todd, sometimes you are so dense.'' She eyed him suspiciously. ''What was Rawlins doing down there, following you?''

''I . . . I don't know. And that's what scares me.''

''Okay, pal, out with it.''

''What?''

''What's going on with you two? I'm no dummy. I can tell by the way your voice is all tight.''

Todd knew, of course, that he had to tell her. ''Janice, I—''

''Did you talk to him last night?''

''Yes, but—''

"Well, what did he say?"

"He . . . he . . ."

"Come on, out with it, Mr. Honesty and Integrity."

"Give me a break, I'm trying." Todd looked away and blurted, "He came over to my apartment. We had sex."

"Oh, shit, Todd."

"It just happened. I don't know. I was depressed, I was tired."

"You screwed Rawlins?" She dropped her pen and smacked her forehead with her palm. "God, but you're getting good at complicating your life. I think maybe I was wrong all these years. You should have stayed in the closet after all. At least then you weren't a danger to yourself."

He started at the beginning, telling her everything. How Rawlins had offered him a drink and seemed to hit on him down at the bar. How Todd had gone over and slipped into Michael's house.

"You did what?" she asked.

"I went in through the basement."

"Not good, Todd. His place is still a sealed crime scene," moaned Janice. "That's sure to come up if this goes to trial. Or, I should say, when."

Todd went on, explaining how he'd gone home, peacefully, quietly. He'd been totally exhausted, and then there was a knock on his door. Rawlins had come in, and . . . and . . .

Janice cut to the chase, asking, "Did he stay the whole night?"

"No."

"Slam, bam . . . and there goes your perfect alibi."

"I think it was about three-thirty when he left. Maybe four," added Todd, recalling how quickly Rawlins had departed.

"We'll have to wait until the coroner's report, but they think this Fisher guy was killed even later than that."

Todd slumped back in the leather chair. He understood the

evening, how one thing had led to the next and the next, from bumping into Rawlins to Jeff to going to Michael's. There'd been an odd rhythm to the evening, a natural progression of events, and in its own weird way it made sense that Rawlins had come over to Todd's and that they'd ended up in bed.

"The only thing I don't get about any of this," said Todd, "is my hat. I mean, this morning Rawlins brought over the one they found. But if it's really mine, how the hell did it wind up at Lake Calhoun?"

"That's what we're going to be up against." Janice jotted something down on her pad, circled it twice. "I mean, strictly between us, what do you think? Was or wasn't that your hat?"

"Actually, I'd . . . I'd say it probably was."

"Okay, so there's not much sense in disputing that."

"But I thought I left it at Michael's. I don't know. I can't remember." He paused. "Did the police find anything? Did they report any evidence like that?"

"Not that I'm aware of. But if you left it at Michael's, then whoever killed Michael could easily have taken it."

Todd sat back in the chair and disappeared into thought, then said, "This really has all been premeditated, hasn't it?"

"It's beginning to look that way." Janice shook her head. "Either someone's trying to cover their tracks by making you look guilty as hell, or . . ."

"Or someone's trying to frame me for some other reason." He stared at her, suddenly afraid. "But who? And why?"

"You got any enemies? Anyone in that wonderful world of television who might want to sink your career?"

"I . . . I . . . don't know. I sure as hell didn't think so."

"Well, you better think twice, toots," advised Janice. "You're about to be charged with first-degree murder."

26

It was almost noon when Todd neared his towering condominium building, a monolithic structure that shot through the trees and over the neighborhood, and he began to slow, wondering what or who might be awaiting him. As he drove around the northern edge of Lake Calhoun, he stared up at the beige structure, tried to pinpoint the exact location of his apartment. Rawlins and Lewis could have received a second search warrant and might be tearing apart his place yet another time. Or, he realized, they might simply be waiting downstairs, ready to arrest him and take him into custody. On the other hand, in a very real way the media could be worse. Would the likes of Channel 7 and other stations be swarming around his building again, hoping to catch a glimpse of the marauding Todd Mills and paint him as the next homo killer à la Jeffrey Dahmer?

Turning right onto Dean Parkway, Todd expected to see television crews and newspaper reporters lingering outside his building, not to mention that religious fanatic and the Radical Faeries. As he approached he scanned the boulevard, knowing that if he'd been working this he'd be camped out front. But as far as he could tell there wasn't anyone. Not even one of the Channel 7 vans with the antenna perched on top. He turned left into the drive, and with a bit of surprise and a lot of relief he drove slowly past the entrance and up the ramp to the second-floor garage. Perhaps there were no reporters here, not yet anyway. Or maybe they'd been here and missed him. Maybe they'd all rushed downtown, assuming they'd catch a glimpse of Todd under arrest. Whatever, but there'd be a mess of them later, and Todd knew what he should do: pack a suitcase and leave. But where would he go? He couldn't leave town, obviously. Not only would that rile the police to no end, it would make him look guilty as hell. He could go to a downtown hotel for a week or so, but he'd probably be recognized by the staff. Word would eventually get out. What about Janice's place?

Todd opened his window, leaned out to a keypad, and pressed in the code. The doors automatically eased open, and he proceeded into the dimly lit garage and to his space, which was at the far end of this level. Shutting off the engine and climbing out, he considered how perfect hiding at Janice's would be. The police could be apprised of his whereabouts, and Janice could shield him at least until things began to die down. But how long would that be? And then, as he locked his car door, it came at him yet again, that wave of fear that slapped him: They weren't really going to arrest him, were they? They wouldn't, couldn't, could they?

He shuffled across the garage, a broad, concrete space that was only half full. It was amazing to Todd that his life could be so quickly and totally ruined, that everything he had worked for could fall apart so quickly. He took a deep breath, choked, wanted to cry. He just wanted to hear Michael's laugh again, that burst of life that said no matter what, everything would be okay. If only Todd had given it all up and the two of them had taken off, disappeared into the Greek islands, as they had often fantasized. Michael had wanted to escape the daily grind and have Todd completely to himself, while Todd had merely wanted to find a place where he could disappoint no one, where his sexuality was of no consequence. Yet it had only been big dreaming, big talk. The escape, of course, had never taken place. And Todd had never been able to bring the two—his public life and his sexual one—into harmony. Now this disaster was the apparent punishment. Actually, wasn't it something just like this that he'd feared all along?

A sound somewhere behind quickly drew him out of his self-pity. Midway through the garage, Todd hesitated and turned around. He glanced toward the garage doors, saw them still closed tightly. He then scanned the vast chamber. There was no car coming or going, and there was no one walking about, at least not that he could see. A second later he heard it again, a long, slow noise, like the sound of a shoe moving slowly over cement. He tensed inside. Someone was in here. And just as soon as he realized that, he understood that someone was watching him.

As he quickly made his way to the steel door that led into the elevator lobby, Todd pulled out his key. When he went to slip it into the lock, however, it would only go in about halfway. He pulled the key out, rammed it in again. Shit. He checked, saw that it was definitely the right one.

He bent over and in a flash realized that someone had jammed the lock with a broken match or toothpick. There was a short, quick sound off to the left, and Todd glanced over, saw nothing but a row of cars. He hurried to the right, passed around the rear of a small van, and broke into a run. When he finally reached a second door, he rammed the key into the lock, pushed down on the handle, and bolted into a stairway. He shoved the door shut behind him, then turned and realized there was no elevator here. He checked the cool, concrete-block room and saw only a steel staircase that led down.

Todd quickly started for the steps, then paused. He could now clearly hear steps in the garage, for whoever was trailing

him was no longer making an effort at concealment. Someone was running toward the door, hoping to catch him. And
as he stood on the first step, Todd stared at the door handle
and watched as someone pushed it down. The door was
locked though, and the lever caught. All appeared fine—until
there was the jingling of keys.

His heart quivering, Todd spun, ready to bolt down the
steps. Just as quickly he stopped himself. All his life he'd
been running; all his life he'd been hiding. He just couldn't
do it anymore. That meant standing up to the truth, including
this one.

Todd spotted a light switch on the wall, rushed toward it,
and flicked off the lights. In an instant the stairwell was so
deeply black that it took Todd's breath away. He groped for
the wall and positioned himself behind the door. Seconds
later he heard a key turning and then sensed the door slowly
opening.

"Shit, it's pitch black," said a deep male voice.

"Well, go on, we can't let him get away. He's in there
somewhere."

Recognizing the voices, Todd became so angry that he
couldn't stop himself. He yanked the door back and lunged
forward. Just as he suspected, he saw the black device cradled in the guy's arm. Not wasting a second, Todd grabbed
for it. Someone screamed, a struggle ensued, and as soon as
Todd had what he wanted he rushed back across the small
space and flicked on the lights.

Holding up a videocassette, Todd said, "Gee, Mark, I
hope you got my good side."

"Shit, Todd," replied Mark Buchanan, huffing and clutching his camera. "I'm just doing my job."

Cindy Wilson flicked back her blond hair as she moved
into the space and demanded, "Give it back, Todd."

"Fat chance."

"You do know you're a suspect for this new murder, don't
you?"

"Cut the crap, Cindy."

"They found your hat by the body. I was there. I was the one who found the body, and—"

"Shit, Cindy, we worked side by side. You know me. There's no way in hell I killed anyone."

"We all thought we knew you, Todd, but none of us even guessed you were gay." She let the words hang, then asked, "So what have you told the officials?"

"Stop it. I know the routine. I taught it to you."

"Todd, give me the tape or—"

"Or what?"

"I'll do a piece on tonight's news on how you attacked us and stole a videotape. I really had no idea you were so violent."

Todd's entire body tightened and he stared at her. At first he wanted to tell her to fuck off, but then he looked into her eyes and saw a reflection. His own.

"Cindy, they've made you as desperate as I was."

"What?"

"I'm out of the loop and I can see it now. But you can't, can you? You're in it so deep you don't even realize it."

"Todd, just answer a few—"

"You want to succeed every bit as much as I did, don't you?" He hesitated, but then couldn't stop himself from saying, "What the hell are you trying to prove?"

Clearly perturbed, she hesitated before asking, "Come on, Todd, what about a five-minute interview? You can tell us your side, the pain of being closeted, how much you cared for Michael Carter. And you can keep that tape. Mark, you've got another one, don't you?"

"Right here," he said, patting a shoulder pack.

"Forget it," replied Todd, shaking his head. "How did you two get in here anyway?"

It flashed through Todd's mind that someone in the building had given them keys. Maybe Bob, the security guard, had sold them a set. But then he looked at the steel door, saw the keys still dangling from the lock.

"Oh, shit," muttered Todd, recognizing the round key ring and yanking it from the door.

"Sorry, buddy," said Mark Buchanan. "I meant to return 'em to you last week."

It was a complete set of Todd's own keys, which he'd given Mark Buchanan several weeks ago so he could pick up a videotape. So how many other times had they gotten in?

Todd said, "Were you two just up in my apartment?"

Cindy said, "What about—"

"Fuck, you were, weren't you?"

Mark urged, "Todd, come on, let's not—"

"Shut up, Mark. And get out of here, both of you, before I call the police."

"My, a party," sneered Cindy. "Wouldn't that make for some great TV?"

"You bet it would," snapped Todd, "because I'm sure the cops would be interested to find your fingerprints all over my place, Cindy. Who knows, maybe you even snuck into my place the other day. Maybe you took my Cubs hat and just sort of dropped it in the bushes so you could work that into your coverage. Now that I think about it, I bet the police would be really curious to find out just how far you'd go to further your career."

"Don't be ridiculous."

Mark added, "Cut it out, Todd."

"And, Mark, I bet they'd want to hear just why you had an AIDS test a few weeks ago."

"Shit, Todd, I told you that in confidence."

"Exactly what did you do in San Francisco that was causing you concern? Some dope and some swinging, wasn't it? Mixed crowd, right? Of course, unless you were anal receptive you probably don't have too much to worry about. But I'm sure the police would want to know all about your sexuality, not to mention the fact that you've had an extra set of all my keys. After all," he said, lifting one in particular, "this one's the key to Michael's." Todd glared at the two of them. "So I don't want to see anything on the news tonight about my apartment or about this little incident. Got it? Now get out of here."

27

_____

If by night it was heaven, all sequins and heels, makeup and lush song, then by day it was hell: starched shirts and neckties. Jeff wedged his finger into his tight collar, tugged at it, tried to get a little breathing room. Oh, God, how he hated this . . . this corporate bondage. Though he had no desire whatsoever to get his you-know-what chopped off, he much preferred his life as Tiffany Crystal, *chanteuse extraordinaire,* to Jeff Barnes, the bank teller. Oh, confusion. Oh, dilemma. That was the story of his life. Of course he was a guy and of course he was gay, but could he help it if he just loved the glamour of beautiful, sparkly clothes? Did it really matter if he didn't happen to look so absolutely fab in a gown and wig?

An elderly woman appeared at his teller window, and Jeff looked up, smiled. "Sorry, ma'am, I just closed. See, my light's off."

"Oh, yes. Sorry."

"Barb right down there can help you."

"Oh, yes. I see."

The customer moved down two windows, while Jeff continued counting his drawer of funds and making sure everything added up just right. He prided himself on never being off, which was one reason he'd become the bank's star teller. He never broke any rules, but he couldn't help it just now, and he looked around, reached up, and strictly against bank policy undid his top button. Either the damn shirt had shrunk or he'd gained still more weight. So what if he was going to look a tad casual? If one of the managers questioned him about that upper button, Jeff would just say it was his lunch hour. Which it was. Never mind that today unlike any other, Jeff was taking part of his break right here at his window. While the head teller, Sue Bayer, was gone for her lunch, there was something Jeff had to find. No stroll for Jeff along downtown's Nicollet Mall today. No sitting outside and leisurely eating his sandwich. He just needed to find and take care of one little document tied to Michael's death.

Carefully sorting the cash drawer, Jeff ascertained that he'd made no errors. Next he locked up the drawer, but he didn't sign off on his computer, for this was the perfect time for him to do his snooping. The lunch hour had brought in a good crowd of office workers, and Barb and the two other tellers now on duty at First Midwestern were swamped. Which meant they'd more than likely be too busy to notice what Jeff was doing over here. He glanced at the rear offices and saw that they were empty, just as he'd figured. The bulk of the staff was gone for this hour. There was one manager, Mr. Uptight What'shisname, at one of the front desks, and Shirley the receptionist was at her desk as well. Aside from the guard by the front door, that was it. This indeed was the time to do the research, which he most definitely knew had to be completed today.

Not long before his death Michael had come to Jeff and asked a few questions that scared the hell out of Jeff. Ever the ethical accountant, Michael had stumbled upon something, a trail of dollars, and he'd followed it all the way to First Midwestern. Which was why poor Michael had been killed. Good Lord. Hacked up like a fish just because of what he'd discovered. It made Jeff sick, but looking back on it there was nothing he could have done to prevent it.

Jeff studied his computer screen and scrolled through some commands, knowing full well that he'd be fired on the spot for doing this. Or dropped in jail, which would be a real drag because he knew a queen like him would have a rough time in prison. But it was all coming to a head and he had to act quickly. His hands flying across the keyboard, he punched in the name and the account appeared immediately on the monitor. Okay, he thought as he read, everything still looked legit. Good. No one had monkeyed with anything. As far as he could tell, no one had suspected, no one had even looked at the account since Michael's death. He scrolled down, bringing up the entire transaction history, and there it was. Slightly over seven hundred thousand dollars, and every penny of it still there. Bravo. Someone was pretty fucking rich, and he couldn't hide a smug smile, because he knew who that was. Oh, he thought, he was just so brilliant. He'd have to swing by Saks and buy a new gown. Sure, he'd celebrate in real style.

He glanced around. No big deal. With a couple of quick keystrokes he entered the command. A few seconds later he could hear the printer in the back begin to hum away. This was the only part he was nervous about, and he scurried away from his computer. There'd be questions if a manager saw him printing out someone's account record, particularly this one. And there'd be trouble if Jeff was spotted stuffing that printout into his pocket.

All the information filled up three pages. Jeff stood by the laser printer, collecting each page as it came spitting out. Then, as if it were perfectly normal business, he took the pages back to his teller window. There he feigned interest in the papers—oh, just checking on a possible discrepancy, he'd say, if anyone asked—circling some numbers, running a finger down one column. And when no one was watching, he folded the sheets in half.

Okay. Out of here, he thought. He signed off on the computer, nabbed the documents, and waltzed off.

"See you, Barb," he called to one of the tellers. "I'll be back in thirty."

She glanced over as she counted out something, saying, "Bye now."

Less than five minutes later, his brown-paper lunch sack in hand, Jeff was making his way quickly through the Skyway. There was a bit of a chill in the air, nothing like what was coming in a month or two, for sure, but the system of interior second-floor corridors that linked most of the buildings was pretty full. Jeff strolled along, passing from his bank building across the glassed-in pedestrian bridge and toward City Center. He paused once, zeroing in on a flashy display of women's shoes. God, he thought, the shiny gold ones with the clear plastic heels were magnificent. They'd go perfectly with one of Tiffany's dresses. But were those clear, spiky heels strong enough to hold someone of Tiffany's voluptuous proportions?

Later, doll, he told himself. The big party would come later, but for now there were more important things.

The Skyway splintered off, and instead of heading across Sixth Street toward City Center he followed a narrow corridor into a more anonymous building. Passing through a double door, he took a left at a copy shop and then, just before the sub shop, turned down a little corridor, a deadend passage that led to some storerooms or something. He liked this pay phone down here. Except for Jeff, no one ever used it. And no one was ever lingering about and listening in, which was quite different than at the bank, where you couldn't say a peep back in the employee lounge without being overheard. That was why Jeff always used this phone for his private transactions.

He dropped a quarter into the phone, looked up and down the little hall, and dialed the number.

Just after the third ring a deep voice said, "Hello?"

"Hi, gorgeous, it's *moi,*" said Jeff, feigning Tiffany. "Is that really you? I'm speechless. Truly I am. Tell me it isn't so. Tell me I haven't reached your answering machine."

"Did you check?"

"Oh, I did indeed."

"And it's all there?"

"All of it. All that luscious money," replied Jeff with a soft, heated laugh. "More than I could ever spend in a month."

"Great, then I'll pick you up tonight."

"The show's over at midnight."

"I'll be waiting just off Fourth."

"Kiss, kiss," said Jeff into the phone. "See you then, Sweet Prince."

28

Todd wasted no time in packing a bag. He threw some jeans, a couple of shirts, a sweater, underwear, and socks into a small duffel bag, grabbed a sports coat, and then called Janice at her office. When her secretary informed him she was in a meeting, he told her to interrupt whatever Janice was doing, it was an emergency, he had to talk to her. After a couple of desperate minutes Janice finally clicked onto the line.

"Todd, are you all right?" she demanded. "What's wrong? What happened?"

"I'm okay, I guess," he told her over his cordless phone as he paced back and forth in his living room.

"Where are you?"

"At home, but there's no way I can stay here."

"Calm down, Todd. Everything's okay for now. I just talked to the police. I don't think they're taking any immediate action."

"Well, I just had a run-in with Channel Seven down in the garage." He couldn't stand this. "I've got to leave. I've got to get out of here. Reporters are going to be swarming around this place like flies on shit.''

"You can't leave town. You know that, don't you?''

Yeah, but, he pleaded, couldn't he stay at her place? He just had to get out of here. He couldn't stay at his condo. He was afraid. Did she understand? Afraid. There was a moment of hesitation, she mumbled something about legal propriety, and then she replied, sure, what the hell.

"But I won't be home until almost six.''

"Fine, there's something I've got to do.''

"Like what?'' And then she quickly added, "No, I don't want to know. Just don't do anything stupid, and stay out of trouble, you hear me? And call me in a couple of hours.''

"Yeah, yeah.''

Todd hung up, slipped on a loose cotton jacket, grabbed his bag and briefcase, and started for the door. He put on a pair of sunglasses and rode the elevator down to the garage. When the lift stopped on the seventh floor and a young couple boarded, Todd stood in a corner, his head slumped. Much to his relief, they were much too involved with each other to notice him.

Car key in hand, Todd bolted out of the elevator and into the garage, his eyes shifting from side to side. He made straight for his Cherokee, nervously opened the door, threw in his things. Slamming down on the automatic locks, he brought the vehicle to a roar of a start and simultaneously slammed the gears into reverse. His temptation was to come screeching and barreling out of the garage, but instead he kept his speed down. When he saw the Channel 7 van now parked out on Dean Parkway, he bit his bottom lip. Nice and steady, he told himself as he passed the vehicle, which appeared to be empty. Were Cindy and Mark still lurking down in the lobby? Within seconds he was turning down Lake Street and heading toward Highway 100, and Todd realized he'd gotten away undetected.

As he eased onto the highway he took a deep breath, tried

to get his thoughts in order. He placed a quick call on his car phone, making sure it was all right to come by, and about twenty minutes later he was once again driving along the edges of Lake Minnetonka. When he turned down the twisty, leaf-sprinkled drive leading to Michael's sister's house, the golden retriever greeted him as always, barking as Todd pulled the Cherokee to a stop.

"Hey, there, Pronto," said Todd as he got out and patted the dog.

When he looked up, the dark gray door of the Cape Cod house was opening, and she stood there, hair dark and curly, those brown eyes big and inquisitive. It took him by surprise. He had never really paid much attention, but her resemblance to Michael was just so strong, now more than ever.

"Hi, Maggie," he called as he made his way up the low stone steps.

She embraced him long and hard, wrapping her arms around him, saying only, "Todd."

Hugging her back, he said, "I think you could say I'm not having a good week."

"Come on in. You want some coffee?"

"Sure."

"Did you have lunch? You want a sandwich?"

"Sure." Todd grinned and said, "You're reminding me why Michael liked to come out here so much. It's like coming home to Mom."

"Oh, stop."

"It just feels safe out here."

"Thanks. You make me sound like a dour old matron when I'm just a depressed suburban housewife." As she led the way in she said, "Rick should be back in a few minutes. He'll be glad to see you."

"Back? What's that mean?"

She shrugged and ventured a hesitant-yet-hopeful phrase, saying, "We're kind of giving it another whirl."

"And?"

"It's only been a few days, but so far so good. He's been staying here most nights since . . . since Michael died. He's pretty busy during the day, but he's been helping with the kids as much as possible. I hate to say it, but a crisis like this brings out the best in Rick, and he's been a big comfort to me. Who knows? He took this afternoon off—he just went to the store to get some hamburger—and we're going to have a little family barbecue tonight. Doesn't that sound encouraging?"

"I hope it works out."

"Thanks. So do I." She hesitated, then added softly, "It's just been so hard losing Michael."

"I know."

Todd followed her across the oak flooring of the front hall, and then he stood above the sunken living room. The last time he was here it had been filled with Maggie's friends who'd gathered to offer their sympathies and condolences. Now, with the room cleared, it was filled with memories of Michael. Todd saw him everywhere, in every corner, on every piece of furniture. Michael building a fire in the large fireplace. Michael setting up his nephew's train set after Christmas. Michael napping on the couch after Thanksgiving dinner while a football game blared.

"Take off your jacket and have a seat, I'll be right there," called Maggie as she slipped into the kitchen.

He descended into the living room, looked around, saw the ghost of Michael traipsing about quite normally. Todd went over to the sliding glass doors and stared out over the lawn and Lake Minnetonka. Michael . . . Michael . . . Michael . . . There he was, teaching his nephews how to water ski. With no children of his own, a fact he'd always regretted, Michael had been the consummate uncle.

"Todd?"

He turned around. Maggie was just setting a tray on the coffee table. How long had he been looking out the window, lost in memory?

"Sit," she said as she took a place on the couch. "You look a little pale."

"Things are kind of going from bad to worse." As he sat on the couch he let out a deep, exasperated breath of air. "Did you hear the news? This other murder?"

Taking her mug of coffee from the table, she nodded and then muttered, "Unbelievable."

"I'll say. The police—"

"Let's not," she said, wincing. "Not now anyway. I just can't." She shook her head. "Do you mind?"

"No," he said, for he'd come out here for altogether different reasons.

Getting up rather quickly and going to a bookcase, Maggie switched eagerly to a different subject, saying, "Rick and I got out some pictures last night. I don't think you've seen them. They were Mother's photo albums from when we were kids. There are some adorable ones of Michael. I want you to have some of them."

She carried over three huge albums, all bound in red leather, and plunked them on the couch between Todd and her. For the next twenty minutes they thumbed through the pages, disappearing into the past, reminiscing about Michael. Todd drank his coffee, ate the sandwich, and listened as Maggie went on and on about her big brother.

"He was such a little pistol," she said, tears twinkling in her eyes. "You know, a big brother can be a real pain in the ass. Not Michael. He was the best. The greatest. He always let me hang out with him and his friends."

"What did he do in exchange," joked Todd, "make you play waitress and serve them Kool-Aid?"

"Well, actually, that's about right. That's probably when my waitressing career bagan."

There were black-and-white pictures of them at Christmas, sitting on Santa's knee down at Dayton's department store. And there was Michael in a little bow tie, all dressed up for Easter. There they were, brother and sister, visiting the

grandparents. And the childhood dog, Rusty, the golden retriever that had inspired the gift of Pronto to Michael's nephews. Michael at day camp. Michael at summer camp. The
two of them at the Aquatennial Parade on a hot, hot July day.

"Look at him in his shorts and his little cowboy boots. It
was broiling and he just had to wear those boots. He got
horrible blisters too. I'll never forget it. He could barely walk
for days after that, but he never cried," said Maggie.
"Wasn't he cute?"

"Yeah."

As she delved further and further into her memory, bathing in the images of Michael as if it were some sort of sacred
ritual, Todd began to lose his nerve. He just wasn't sure he
could ask. He'd come out here determined to see if Maggie
knew, for Michael had been closest to her of all people. If
Michael had had anything to confess, more than likely it
would have been to her. Sensing how fragile Maggie still
was, however, Todd just wasn't sure he could broach the subject.

Maggie turned yet another page, and a group of young
boys stared up at Todd. Probably about age ten in the photo,
all three boys wore raggedy shorts and stood knee-deep in
some water.

"That's down at Lake Harriet," volunteered Maggie.

"There's Michael." Pointing to a chubby kid in the middle, Todd guessed, "And that's got to be Jeff."

Maggie nodded and grinned. "He's always been a little
overweight. But this is them, the famous Banditos. They
were best buddies from grade school all the way through
high school."

She turned the page, exposing a large black-and-white
class photo. There were four rows of kids, the front row
seated on the floor, the back row standing on a short riser. A
sign in the corner read, MRS. FITZ'S SIXTH-GRADE CLASS, LAKE
HARRIET ELEMENTARY.

"See," said Maggie, pointing to the same three boys

standing at one end of the back row. "Here they are in the little graduating class, the three of them. I think they terrorized half of Linden Hills, actually. Everyone knew the Banditos—they went everywhere on their Schwinns and were inseparable."

"Michael had a lot of stories, from capturing raccoons to toilet-papering houses." Todd looked more closely. "Who was the third kid?"

"Um . . . um . . ." Maggie leaned back. "Shoot, he was over at our house all the time, almost every day. What was his name? I must be losing my mind."

Todd leaned over, suddenly captured by the picture of the three boys. Michael. Jeff. And who? He stared at the third boy, who stood there, squinting his left eye in the sun. Just what was so familiar about him? Though still a child, you could see he was going to be a stocky, perhaps muscular man. Perhaps a little tough. Odd, thought Todd. While faces of some kids changed dramatically as they aged—Todd had gone from having a skinny face to a rugged, square one—others retained an element of their initial bone structure as they moved into adulthood. A few years ago in a Chicago bar Todd had recognized a grade-school classmate simply by the deep cleft in his chin.

"He really looks familiar," said Todd.

"He was kind of quiet, I remember that. Kind of had a temper too." She shrugged. "Beats me, I can't remember . . . wait, it was Corky. That's right. That's what everyone called him. Corky." She laughed. "He was the troublemaker, if I recall correctly."

"I don't recognize the name. Maybe I've just seen this picture before."

Corky was obviously a nickname and did not help to explain the child's real identity or why Todd had an odd sensation of knowing him. Maybe Todd actually did. More than likely Todd had met this third kid via Michael, perhaps at a party or maybe just out on the street. Michael and Todd could have bumped into him while strolling around Lake of the Isles, for Michael was always running into someone he knew.

Okay, get to the point, thought Todd. You've come here to ask her something specific. You have to know. So ask, he told himself. You've got to, no matter how much it upsets her.

"Maggie, I've been wondering something."

He sat back, looked out the window and at the lake. Maybe, he thought, I'm nuts. Maybe I'm just a jealous asshole. But one way or the other he had to put the pieces together.

"Michael talked to you, Maggie, more than anyone else. I mean, he told you everything, didn't he?"

"Just about."

"Was . . . well, do you know, was he happy with me? I mean, I didn't make things easy for our relationship, and—"

Maggie gently took Todd's right hand in both of hers, looked him straight in the eyes, and said, "Todd, he loved you. Michael was crazy about you."

"But . . ." He took a deep breath, for here was the real question. "But was he seeing anyone else?"

She flinched, her hands abruptly squeezing his. And in that instant she seemed to separate somehow. To drift away. Maggie sat motionless there on the couch, but every bit of her seemed to rush away. She turned away from Todd, stared at a blue and green pillow on a chair across the room.

"I'm sorry, Maggie," began Todd. "I didn't want to ask you. And . . . and I don't mean to imply that Michael was sleeping around. I—"

"It's all right," she said, raising a hand to silence him. "The police stopped out here. Those two detectives—"

"Rawlins and Lewis?"

"Right. They were out here the day before the funeral, and they asked all sorts of questions, including that one." She hesitated, said, "I don't know why, but I always worried about losing Michael. I worried about him and AIDS so much, which was why I was so glad when you two got together. You were both healthy and . . . and . . . who could ever have thought he'd be murdered? A car accident maybe. But not this.''

"That's why I'm asking. It doesn't make any sense." Todd bent forward, rubbed his eyes. "The police think that it wasn't random, that Michael knew whoever killed him. There was no sign of forced entry into his apartment, after all.''

"Right." Her voice very faint, Maggie said, "The police told me everything.''

"The whole idea hurts, I can't say it doesn't, but maybe Michael was seeing someone else." He hesitated. "And maybe that someone else killed him. I mean, I wouldn't blame Michael if he was looking around. I certainly didn't make it easy for him. Our relationship, I mean. I was an asshole, just so worried what people were thinking. I'm sure I was slowly and methodically driving him away. And . . . and . . .''

"Todd, don't. Please don't." Pronto started barking out front, and Maggie said, "That's Rick."

She closed the photo albums, placed them on the coffee table. Silently she rose and headed for the front door. Halfway through the living room she stopped and turned back to Todd.

"Sure, Michael and I talked a lot, and I know . . ." Her eyes became misty yet again. "I know that your career was very hard on him and your relationship. Frankly, he complained a lot about it, how the stress of being so hidden was wearing him down. He just didn't know what to do. But he was crazy about you, Todd. He really was. So to answer your question, I'll tell you the same thing I told the police: No, he never said anything to me about dating anyone else. Then again, Michael also knew how much Rick and I care for you, so maybe he wouldn't have told me." She ran her hand along the back of a chair. "Actually, I've been thinking a lot about this since the detectives were here. Michael and I talked a lot about where our heads were at, what kind of problems we were having. Particularly relationships. But if Michael was sleeping around, I sure didn't know. Then again, I think Rick and I wore him out talking about our troubles. On the other hand, Michael and I never talked about sex. I mean, after all, he's my brother." After a long pause she corrected herself, saying, "I mean, was."

Todd watched as Maggie climbed the three or four steps up to the front hall, and then heard her go out the front. At a loss, he sat on the couch. What now? What had he been hoping he might find out here? Something the police might have missed? Of course Rawlins and Lewis would have quizzed Maggie and Rick about every detail of Michael's life, from Todd right on down to the possibility of another lover and every other man Michael had ever encountered. And quite obviously they hadn't learned anything new either.

Todd glanced toward the front door, saw no sign of Maggie and Rick returning yet. Rather compulsively he reached for one of the photo albums, taking it in his lap and flipping quickly through the pages. He stopped at the picture of the three boys standing knee-deep in Lake Harriet, stared briefly at the mysterious third boy, then turned the page to the class photo. Without thinking whether he should or shouldn't, he reached forward and ripped the large photo out of the album. Hearing Maggie and Rick coming in now, Todd quickly put on his jacket and tucked the picture against his shirt. He then slammed the album shut and shoved it back on the coffee table.

"Todd, what a surprise!" called Rick, a bag of groceries in his arm. "How good to see you. I'll be right there, just let me get rid of this stuff."

"Hey, Rick," said Todd, rising to his feet.

There was the sound of scratching nails scrambling through the front hall, and a moment later Pronto came bounding down the steps and into the living room. In a second the dog was jumping up at Todd.

"Pronto!" shouted Maggie, charging behind. "Your feet are all muddy. Out! Get outside!"

She rushed through the living room and over to one of the sliding glass doors, which she yanked back. Shaking her head, she snapped her fingers and ordered Pronto into the backyard.

"Some things change," she said with a sigh, "and some don't." She took one look at Todd with his coat on and said quickly, "Oh, don't go. Sit back down and take your coat off."

With thinning red hair, Rick emerged from the kitchen and stepped down into the sunken living room. As he smiled, he extended his hand and shook Todd's warmly.

"Stay for dinner, won't you? Please? I've got to pick up my mail and do another errand, but we'll be having an early dinner," he said. "The kids would love it if you stayed. We've got plenty of food—the best burgers in Minnesota. And I was going to make grilled french fries too."

"Actually, I have to be going," replied Todd, checking his watch.

"The boys will be home in another twenty minutes," said Maggie. "Can you stay at least until then?"

"I'd love to, but . . . but I have to see Janice," he replied, lying slightly. "Sorry. Things are a little intense right now."

"I hate to imagine," said Rick, shaking his head.

Wanting to be gone as quickly as possible, Todd kept his left arm pressed against his coat. He hugged Maggie and said good-bye, promising he'd be back soon, promising to keep in touch. And Rick made him swear he'd call if he needed any help.

"Oh, and Michael's apartment," added Rick. "We're going to have to deal with it sometime. The three of us, I mean. It's not going to be any fun, but it's got to be done."

"Of course," said Todd, "but I don't think we'll be able to get in until next week."

"Probably not," interjected Maggie.

Rick escorted him out of the house and to his car, walking by Todd's side, saying how much he hoped Todd would stay in contact. His boys had only one uncle, he explained, and they adored him. Now that Michael was gone, Rick's entire family needed Todd.

"Thanks, you don't know how much I appreciate that," said Todd, pulling out his car keys.

As they neared the Cherokee, Rick slowed to a stop. He glanced back at the house, making sure Maggie couldn't overhear.

"There's one more thing," he said, keeping his voice low. "Maggie told me what you were talking about. I mean, when I came home just now she told me what you asked. You know, about Michael and whether he was seeing anyone else."

"I hope I didn't upset her."

"She'll be fine. The police already asked the same question, after all."

Todd looked at him, saw him start to talk. Then stop. So there was something else.

"What is it, Rick?"

"Well, I didn't really think about it when we were talking to the police. It didn't occur to me, actually. There was just so much other stuff going on. But . . . but . . . Michael and I had lunch a couple of weeks ago. We usually got together once a month or so, and this last time I was talking about my marriage. You know, the problems Maggie and I were having. I went on and on. Michael was always the good listener, but . . ."

"But what?" pressed Todd.

"You really want to hear this?"

Todd looked up at the trees, saw how most of the leaves had already dropped. Then he heard barking, saw Pronto bounding through the woods after a squirrel. No, he really didn't want to hear anything more, wasn't sure he could.

He replied, "Sure."

"Well, I don't know if I cut him off. I was just so absorbed in my life, what was happening with Maggie and me." He kicked at the gravel. "But he did talk about recently bumping into one of his old boyfriends. I don't know who or from where, but Michael said an old love had just reappeared and . . . and he implied how it was too bad things between the two of them hadn't worked out. He said it had just been such an easy relationship."

Part of Todd was crumbling inside. "More open probably."

"I don't know. But he did mention that he was going to be getting together with this guy for a drink."

"Oh."

Oh, fuck, thought Todd. Oh, shit. This was news to him. Sure, he knew Michael had dated lots of guys over the years. There'd been a couple of serious ones before Todd too. But Michael hadn't mentioned the recent reappearance of any particular one, certainly hadn't admitted that he'd gone off and had any little social time with an old beau. And that fact alone didn't bode well.

"Unfortunately I sort of dominated the conversation, and Michael didn't say much else," added Rick. "Sorry. I . . . I . . ."

"No, it's okay. I'll tell the police. I'm sure they'll follow up on it."

"Have them give me a call."

"Yeah."

Todd didn't say much more. He couldn't. Feeling like he'd just been hit by a truck, he climbed into his Cherokee, started it up. He waved good-bye to Rick, slowly turned his Jeep around, and headed down the drive. It was more than he could handle, more than his brain could imagine. Michael and some other guy. He'd been such a fool, thought Todd, cursing himself. He'd had it all . . . and lost it.

As he turned onto the main road he reached up, took out the photo, and glanced briefly at it. Well, at least he knew where he had to go next.

29

Rawlins told Detective Lewis down at the station that he was just going over to the bank. Maybe he was being paranoid, he didn't know.

"I'm going to deposit a check," Rawlins had said.

She had stared at him suspiciously, quizzed, "So what's up?"

"Huh?"

"You getting rich on the side or something? Didn't you just go to the bank yesterday?"

"That was to get cash. This is to make a deposit," he lied. "A friend just paid back a couple of hundred bucks he owed me. I'll be back in twenty minutes."

But of course there was no check, just as he'd gotten no cash yesterday. Instead he was headed for the main post office, and as he now turned into the small parking area just to the north of the long structure, he supposed he was being silly. He just didn't want to tell his partner that he was going to the post office and then have her say, You got a letter to mail? Here, give it to me, I got lots of stamps. I'm going downstairs now. I'll drop it in the box for you. Or, What are you doing? Paying your bills or sending off love letters?

As he parked, Steve Rawlins supposed he hadn't told Lewis about where he was going because he didn't want to give her even the slightest reason to suspect. He didn't want her looking at him, saying, main post office? What in the hell are you going all the way over there for? He didn't want to explain that he was going to the sprawling central post office, a long art deco building that ran for several blocks along the banks of the Mississippi River, because it was so anonymous. When he checked the box no one would take note.

Walking to the main entry of the post office, Rawlins pushed his way through the brass revolving doors. It was an elegant structure, cool and graceful, and this vast central hall stretched on and on. A polished black stone floor. Native Kasota stone walls that were sleek and beige. Brass signs. Brass chandeliers. Brass writing podiums for jotting that last message.

And few people.

It always surprised Rawlins how empty this place was, how hushed and still. There was an older man silently pushing a big, long broom along. Five people lined up at the service window. A couple of people checking boxes. Someone heading into the passport office. But no one else. He knew that the mail for the city and region was being sorted back in the depths of this building, so somewhere within these walls were constant activity and constant work. But out here you'd never know it. So quiet. Like a library.

Rawlins walked nearly a half-block through the hall, came to a long bank of mailboxes. He pulled the piece of paper from his pocket and glanced at the number he'd scribbled. Then he slowed. His eyes ran up and down the small brass boxes. There. Right in the middle. But he didn't stop. Not yet. He kept moving. There was another entry down at the other end, and he just wanted to make sure. Right. Rawlins glanced way down there, saw a woman come in. No one else.

And then he turned around, looping back. He glanced again at the service window, this time having to squint because it was so far away. One. Two. Three. Four. And the fifth person? There she was, just heading toward the far door. So no one had followed him in here.

Excellent, he thought, as he turned toward the mailboxes. He checked the slip of paper again. Yes. That box. Right there. Reaching into his pocket, he pulled out the key he'd been given and slipped it into the lock, which opened effortlessly. As he pulled open the small door Rawlins glanced to his left, to his right, then leaned forward and peered into the box. And yes, there it was, the nice small envelope. Perfect.

30

Five miles from downtown Minneapolis, the Linden Hills area was a quintessential Middle-American neighborhood and the city's most stable area in which to live. The only common gripe was the noise of jets approaching the nearby airport.

Circling the western edge of Lake Calhoun, Todd caught a glimpse of the recently built towers of downtown, then turned down Xerxes Avenue and into Linden Hills proper. As he passed beneath the last of the yellow and red and brown leaves, he thought of Michael, who referred to this, his childhood neighborhood, as Familyland. And he was right. As Todd drove beneath the last of the massive elms, turning off Xerxes and onto 43rd, he took note of the solid wood houses, replete with friendly front porches, that lined block after block. With bikes and kids everywhere, this was one of the last corners of Norman Rockwell's vanishing America.

"But it's so white and so incredibly straight!" Michael had always complained even as he waxed nostalgic about growing up here.

While not a large building, the area library was nevertheless a neighborhood landmark. A dark red brick structure with a thick slate roof and a bright, newly refinished oak front door, it resembled a Carnegie library, which it might have been. Todd just hoped that somewhere inside would lie the answer to his question. Taking one last look at the class photo he'd taken from Maggie's, he headed up the front walk, passed inside and climbed the split stairs on the right. As he approached the main counter he admired the tall arched ceilings, the leaded-glass windows, the fireplace, and took note of the unfortunate beige linoleum flooring.

"Excuse me," he asked the librarian. "I'm looking for some class albums. Do you know where I might find them?"

"Albums?" A short, bland woman with blondish-gray hair and pale glasses studied him judgmentally. "You mean, school yearbooks?"

"Right."

"Sorry, we don't have anything like that here." She tugged at a yellow sweater draped over her shoulders. "As you can see, this is a small library—just these rooms up here and the children's library downstairs. You might try the downtown library, but I'd call first. Most libraries don't have room for that sort of thing anymore; a lot of them cleaned house in the sixties and seventies and sent things like yearbooks to the historical society."

"So I could try there for Lake Harriet Elementary yearbooks?"

"Actually, no." She stared at him, then cleared her throat and continued. "They wouldn't have that either. Not for that particular school."

"I'm sorry, I'm a little confused."

"Well, if I'm not mistaken, none of the grade schools in Minneapolis had yearbooks."

"I see," Todd muttered, unable to hide his disappointment.

"Only the high schools," continued the librarian, proud of her acquired knowledge. "So the closest you could come is the yearbook for Southwest High. That's where all the kids from Lake Harriet Elementary went.''

"Of course.''

Todd stood there, baffled and at a loss. He just wanted one name. That was all. Jeff would know, of course, but Todd didn't want to approach him with this question, which he might in turn avoid.

"It's too bad Lake Harriet Elementary was torn down,'' mused Todd, rubbing his forehead, wondering what to do next.

"Oh, yes, indeed. A real pity. That was, what, maybe fifteen years ago? Something like that.''

"I just wanted to see a picture of one of the graduating classes, and I'm sure they would have had that at the old school.''

Her eyebrows raised, she pushed her glasses up her nose, and said, "Say now, maybe I'll be able to help you after all. When they tore the school down, the school offered us all sorts of stuff, but we just couldn't take it. Not enough room, like I said, so they passed most of their historical photos and data on to the historical society. I imagine it's all in boxes in some warehouse somewhere over in St. Paul. But . . . but it seems to me we might have something of interest in the pamphlet files.''

Her hand to her chin, she muttered something, then pulled again at the shoulders of her draped sweater. She mumbled a few more words to herself, reached into a drawer, and nabbed a key attached to a large paper clip.

"Yes, maybe we do,'' she said, tapping on her front teeth with the nail of her right index finger. "Follow me.''

Leaving the main counter, she turned immediately to the right and unlocked a narrow door. She flipped a light switch, then led Todd up some stairs to a small room with a balcony overlooking the rooms below. Perhaps, thought Todd, this had once been a charming reading alcove, a place to hide away with a book. Now, however, it was crammed full of stuff, from clunky old computers draped with a sheet of translucent plastic to stacks of books, broken chairs, and a wall of old oak file cabinets.

"People live in this neighborhood for years and years," explained the librarian. "Even if they do move away, they come back, either to retire or just to visit. People are very loyal to Linden Hills. And that's why it seems to me that we kept a few things from Lake Harriet Elementary."

Todd felt his heart pick up speed. "Like photos?"

"Maybe." Running her finger down the wooden file cabinets, the librarian stopped at one drawer and pulled it open, saying, "Here, you can try looking in here."

As Todd approached the open file she backed away silently, circling around a pile of books. He bent down, began studying the hanging green folders. If he had any luck—which lately had seemed to desert him—there'd be something in here. His fingers started thumbing quickly through the plastic tabs.

Todd heard rustling, glanced over, saw the librarian standing there at the top of the stairs. Fidgeting with her sweater, she smiled oddly, hesitantly, at him. Had she only just recognized him?

He said, "This should only take a few minutes."

"Yes," she replied nervously. "I'll just wait."

He came to a file on streetcars, which had linked this cloistered neighborhood with the rest of the city. Then several green folders on the Lake Harriet bandshell and its various inceptions. Another on the history of the music at the lake's bandshell. The Rose Garden. A file containing photos of the fountain moved to the area from Gateway Park downtown. The historical highlights of Linden Hills were all captured here. Including, at last, Lake Harriet Elementary.

Eagerly, Todd lifted the green folder marked with the school's name from the drawer. And there it was, an early black-and-white photo of the large and once proud educational building. Some early group pictures. Next a more recent photo of the triangular piece of land, now cleared of the building and all rubble, once the wrecking ball had done its job.

"Shit," muttered Todd under his breath.

He dropped the hanging file back in and ran his fingers to the next plastic tab, which was marked *Lake Harriet Elementary, Graduating Classes.* Todd smiled, lifted the file, opened it. So this library had declined the vast majority of historical data from the school, but they'd kept the tip of the iceberg. Quite rightly too, thought Todd, as he flipped through the first photos, those of the graduating classes from the early part of the century. He lifted one marked *1927,* turned it over, and saw a typed listing of names carefully taped to the back. If someone had grown up in Linden Hills, moved away, then returned and sought out old memories, the library would want to have at least a few things on hand.

His fingers flew through the stack of black-and-white photos, soon reaching the fifties and eventually the sixties. So when would Michael have graduated from the sixth grade? He would have been ten or probably eleven. Sure, eleven. So, toward the late sixties. Todd skipped through the first part of that tumultuous decade, and then the familiar picture flipped right in front of him. Todd's heart jumped. It was the same photograph from Maggie's album, and he lifted it out. There was Michael. Jeff. And the mysterious third boy. Turning it over, Todd was relieved to find the names once again carefully typed and attached to the back. His eyes ran over the list, reaching the back row. Michael Carter. Jeff Barnes. And . . .

Todd caught his breath, read the name two and three times. He turned back to the photo, stared at the third boy. No wonder he seemed familiar. The third of the famous group, the Banditos. Michael Carter. Jeff Barnes. And Steve Rawlins, Junior. All of them childhood chums. All of them as queer as a three-dollar bill from the get-go.

31

Standing at the sliding glass door of his apartment, he stared at the late-afternoon sky. And thought about the man he'd killed last night.

Just last night? How odd. It already seemed days ago. Weeks. He took a deep, cleansing breath, then sat down in his leather chair. Closed his eyes. Smiled. He'd thought it would be so hard taking someone's life like that. It had seemed incomprehensible. Yet, he'd killed two men, and it had proved so . . . so easy. And challenging. That was what surprised him the most. The thrill of the hunt. It was like the biggest dare you could ever imagine, one that he'd actually succeeded in committing, which in turn left him with this great big buzz.

That was fun, he thought. Stalking like that. The sport of it. First, of course, he'd had to scout the area, decide where. And he was pleased he'd chosen the bushes along Lake Calhoun, for it was right in a residential district. Right on the edge of Uptown. He'd figured it would send big shock waves through the city, and it most definitely had. Big ones. Better yet, the link with Michael Carter was drawn almost immediately. Both killed by knife wounds. Both gay. Both found dead in south Minneapolis.

And both killed by Todd Mills?

He smiled, rubbed his forehead. That was the buzz in town. Everyone was talking about it, speculating, pointing fingers. He'd been out and about today and heard people gossiping, whispering. Todd Mills, good Lord, could he really have done such a hideous thing? And gay too? How creepy! He was on television, he was in our homes! Our family watched him, hung on his every word. And those Emmys, for God's sake!

Seated in his comfortable chair, he wondered what defined a serial killer. Was it simply more than one murder? As few as two? Or perhaps three? If so, would this next one do it, qualify him for that very special club? Or was it more, say, a half-dozen? No, that seemed awfully high, he thought. Or could it be linked by style and method, perhaps the length of time between each killing?

He really couldn't linger here at the apartment. Too much to do. And if he sat there much longer he was going to fall asleep. It had been a long night and only the adrenaline rush of the kill had kept him cruising all day. Soon he was going to crash big time. But he couldn't. Not just yet. Not now. Just one more big decision. It wasn't so much a question of how and where. He'd do the next one with a knife, of course. For better or worse, he was sort of stuck with that one already. And where? Not so important either. In a back alley. In another pickup area. In the guy's bedroom. It didn't really matter just so long as it looked gay. Very gay. Maybe a little kinky. Perhaps a trifle perverse.

Well, he'd work out the simpler details later. The only thing he needed to figure out right now was when he should do the next one. He'd been thinking about right away. Tonight? Or should he wait a few days, a week even? No, that wouldn't work. Too risky. His next target might talk. He might suspect that he was next in line and go running to the police. So actually, now that he thought it through, the answer was perfectly clear. No sense in letting the newspapers and newscasts cool down a bit only to stoke them again by the end of the week. No, he had to throw gas right on the flames, make everything explode. Then stand back, arms calmly crossed, and watch the spectacle while everyone else scurried about.

He rose from his chair, crossed to the small kitchen, and poured himself a nice glass of chilled water. The cool, refreshing liquid soothed his parched throat, refreshed his weary mind. He'd strike again tonight. Two days in a row. Sure. Boom. It would make the front page. Perhaps even the headline.

Oh, Todd Mills, thought the man as he grabbed his lightweight jacket and headed out. Oh, Todd, where are you? If you think things are bad now, you ain't seen nothing yet.

32

It could mean nothing. It could mean everything. As Todd drove through the bustling Uptown district, up Hennepin Avenue, past the Guthrie Theater and the Walker Art Center and the sprawling Sculpture Garden, his insides twisted into a knot of confusion. Michael, Jeff, and Rawlins—a.k.a. Corky—had been childhood chums, and they'd all turned out to be gay. Which in a very subtle way didn't surprise Todd at all.

He'd had a best friend. Eric, also the son of Polish immigrants. They'd gone all through grade school and the first couple of years of high school together until Eric's dad was transferred and the family had moved. Where was it? Detroit. Up to that time Eric and Todd had been inseparable, exploring the back alleys of Chicago's north side, busting bottles beneath the El, hanging around Wrigley Field, searching the sidewalks for a dropped ticket, and in fact once finding one, then fighting about which one of them was going to get in. They'd never talked about anything personal, as boys seldom did. And virtually the only talk of sex was when they'd stolen one of Eric's father's *Playboy* magazines and stared at the huge breasts of a smiling, blond woman. Wow! Fuck! Look at those boobs! HUGE! They'd seemed like typical, average boys. Which they were. Yet with no coaching or even acknowledgment from each other, they'd both turned out ''different'' in one fundamental way. Four or five years ago Todd had heard from another old classmate that Eric had died of AIDS in San Francisco. Todd realized that part of their childhood friendship, perhaps the glue that had mysteriously bound them in companionship, had been their unrecognized and unrealized homosexuality.

In view of the recent murders though, Michael's trio of childhood chums was too much of a coincidence. This was all connected. But what did it mean? Instinctively Todd understood there was something of great significance here. The very fact that neither Jeff nor Rawlins had mentioned Rawlins's connection meant something. And why in the hell hadn't Michael ever spoken of Steve Rawlins, one of his closest childhood buddies, a guy who was not only on the police force, but gay? What had happened between the two of them, what kind of rift had occurred? After all, Jeff and Michael had stayed good friends. Michael talked to him frequently and saw him regularly down at the Gay Times. So had Michael and Rawlins merely grown apart? No. If that had been the case Michael probably would have mentioned Rawlins sometime, even just in passing. And after Michael's death Rawlins would surely have mentioned the connection. Obviously something had happened to cause a bitter end of friendship, to make both Michael and Rawlins never want to utter the other's name.

Todd wanted an immediate answer. He continued up Hennepin, past the formidable stone basilica, and finally reached 7th Street, where he turned left. He parked in a lot and strode quickly back across Hennepin, through the mall of City Center, across Nicollet, and around the corner. Breaking into a jog, Todd checked his watch. There was just enough time this afternoon.

A block later he pushed through some heavy old doors and entered a two-story, wood-paneled hall. Todd glanced to his right, saw a handful of people at their desks, looked to the left, saw a row of tellers. Jeff was at the third window, helping an older man with a transaction. Rushing into line behind two people, Todd stood there trying to seem as calm as possible, his mind on fire with questions and anger. It was only a matter of moments. There was just one person left before Todd, a woman, and Todd abruptly cut in front of her when Jeff became available.

"Excuse me," he said, barging ahead of her. "That teller down there screwed up my account. I've got to talk with him. This is going to cost me a hundred bucks."

"But—"

"Trust me, lady, you don't want that guy touching your money—unless of course you want to risk losing it."

"Oh, heavens no."

Todd moved across the deep red carpet, blotting a few drops of perspiration from his brow. Jeff, who was sorting some documents, didn't even look up.

"Hello, Jeff," said Todd, his voice hushed, as he leaned on the counter with both hands.

Jeff, who assumed his customer had merely read his name tag, raised his head and with a bright smile replied, "Hi, and how . . ." When he saw Todd, his voice trailed quickly off. "Oh, it's you. Hi, Todd. What the hell are you doing here?" He looked at him nervously. "Let me guess, you want to start doing drag and you've come to *moi* for some beauty tips."

"No."

"You want me to teach you how to pick up guys?"

"No."

"Then, heavens, you must have an account here. I had no idea. How nice."

"No, I don't."

"Oh. Well . . . well, then would you like one? You can

step right over there to open an account. You see those nice people at the desks? Unlike me, one of the personal bankers would be more than glad to help you."

"I have to talk to you, Jeff."

He looked nervously from side to side. "Can't you see that this isn't a coffeehouse, darling? Some of us have to work, you know. The bank's still open. Isn't that kind of obvious?"

"When are you done?"

"I . . . I have lots of catching up to do once the bank closes."

"I'll wait."

"No . . . no, please don't bother. I'll be here for hours," said Jeff, glancing around. "Today really isn't good. I have to work late and . . . and then I have a show tonight. I have to rehearse. After all, I don't want to look like a fool. Dressing poorly is one thing, screwing up the lip-synch is another matter altogether. One on which I pride myself deeply. I'm working on a new Barbra Streisand number."

Todd leaned forward and blurted, "There were three boys. They all grew up in Linden Hills."

Jeff ran his hand around his heavy throat. "Todd, doll, are you okay? I know you've been under a lot of stress."

"Their names were Michael, Jeff, and Corky."

"You don't look too good, Todd. Maybe . . . maybe you should sit down. I heard the news on my break. Another murder. It's horrible, isn't it? So creepy. I'm sure the police have been asking you all sorts of nasty questions."

"Listen to me, you old cha-cha queen, quit fucking with me. You know all about Corky. I want the details."

"Really, you big old brute, I don't have the faintest idea what you're talking about," he said nervously. "Now please, Todd, enough of this chitchat. I have to get back to work. Look, look over there. See? See, there are people in line, waiting to do their banking. Some want to make deposits, some want to cash checks, and some—"

"Corky was the nickname for Steve, Junior."

"Todd, do I need to call the guard over here?"

"As in Steve Rawlins, Junior. As in the very same Detective Steve Rawlins assigned to Michael's murder."

"You know, all I have to do is raise my hands and scream in my sissiest voice, 'Help me, help me, robber, robber!' and you're dead meat, pal." Jeff glared at him, lowered his voice as deep as it would go. "Get out of here, you bitch, before I make that big old butch guard over there shoot you full of holes."

"Go ahead. Then you'll be responsible for two murders—mine and Michael's."

"Ah . . . ah, what are you implying?" Jeff flushed red and started sorting through some papers. "No, I'm not going to talk to you. Not another word. Get out of here, you fucker. Now. Leave. Leave or I'll really call security. I have a buzzer under my desk here. All I have to do is tap it with my knee and security will be all over you. You'll get thrown in a cop car and hauled away by the police. Or maybe you'd like that. I bet you like body searches. Oh, and a night in prison with the guys—wouldn't that be a real treat for a closet queen like you?"

"Just tell me one thing, you fat piece of shit," demanded Todd. "Were Michael and Rawlins lovers?"

"Oh, heavens," he muttered, shaking his head with disgust. "Who knows why God made you gay, because you certainly sound like the straightest, narrowest suburban jerk I've seen in a long time."

"Were they?"

"Girl, you are such a bitch." Jeff leaned forward again. "All right, I'll tell you this much—sure, they did it, Michael and Corky. They had sex. They sucked. They fucked. I don't know. They got naked together, that's all I know." He grinned. "There, is that what you want to know? Is that what you came here for, to satisfy your curious, jealous little mind? Now go on, get out of here. I don't have time for closet cases like you.''

''When?''

''What do you mean, when?''

''When did they have sex?'' Todd felt the blood rushing to his face. ''Answer me, damn it.''

''You are too fucking ridiculous, Toad.''

''I'm not leaving until you tell me.''

''What do you want, times of day? How long it took before they came? Who was top and who was bottom? And maybe what phase the moon was in? You're nuts, you know it? Do I look like a fucking social secretary or something?''

''I mean was it last week, last month, last year?''

''Oh, honey,'' he laughed. ''Is that all you're concerned about? Well, let me tell you, it was long before you.''

Of all the answers this was the only one that took him by surprise, and Todd replied, ''What?''

''They were both pencils. Or pistols. I don't know what you call 'em these days, but back then they were horny little dudes. I mean, Todd darling, they were nineteen. Twenty at most. It was the first time either of them had sex of any kind . . . wink, wink.''

''What are—''

''So you see, it's all history. You don't have anything to worry your jealous old head about.'' Jeff cocked his head, stared at him out of the corner of his eyes, and taunted, ''Of course, they say you fall hardest the first time, which is also to say, Corky never, ever got over Michael. For that matter, I don't think Michael ever really got over Corky.''

''But . . .''

''Oh, Lordy. Enough. I've got work to do. Now get out of here, you pathetic old troll. Michael, bless his soul, is dead, and there's nothing any of us can do to bring him back, so get out of here before I have you arrested for bothering the shit out of this old gal.''

33

―――――――

"I want you to talk to him," said Todd.

"Eat your meat loaf."

He stared out the front window of Janice's dining room into the night, down toward the narrow, twisting Minnehaha Creek. Her house, a sprawling Spanish-style place on a wooded hill above the creek, was beyond serene. Todd was so agitated, however, that he could barely sit still, and he turned, looked out of the dining room's arched doorway, across the red tile floor of the hall, and toward the spacious living room. He glanced briefly at a large fireplace, next a large aquarium, then just sat there shaking his head. Ever since his conversation with Jeff late this afternoon, his thoughts had been multiplying and dividing, ricocheting off every possibility.

"You're a lawyer."

"I know," replied Janice, taking a hunk of bread. "How else do you think I can afford a place like this?"

"He knows more."

"You're probably right there."

"But he hates my guts." Todd poked at his plate with his fork. "I don't think I'll get anything more out of him."

"Todd, I'm serious. You've got to put something in your stomach. You're pale. Have you eaten at all today?" she asked. "Besides, I thawed this meat loaf especially for you."

"But maybe you could. I'm sure Jeff is easily intimidated. Maybe you could say we're going to sue or something like that."

"All right, all right. I'll talk to him."

"You have to ask all about Rawlins." Todd made a faint attempt at spearing a piece of meat. "I don't get it. Isn't it unethical to have Rawlins, a friend of Michael's, assigned to the case? Or is it just unwise?"

"Probably just stupid. I don't know. I'm not sure there's anything on the books against it. I'll have to check on that tomorrow." She looked at her watch. "What time does Jeff finish?"

"Late. Let's have some coffee."

"Only after you eat your meat loaf."

They parked in the small lot next to the downtown library, crossed Hennepin, and as soon as Todd opened the door the noise of the Gay Times rolled over them. He and Janice entered the main room, saw a couple of male dancers—gorgeous hunks with Mr. Universe bodies—performing on the far end of the bar, dollars hanging out of their skimpy G-strings.

"Wow, look at those guys," said Janice, stopping still and staring at the dancers. "My latent heterosexuality is stirring."

"Come on, the drag show's upstairs."

"After this is all over I'm going to send you down here with a bunch of one-dollar bills. You can play horny old man and ogle those guys."

"Thanks. You're the second person today to call me a troll."

"Won't someone tell me why there aren't any good dyke bars like this in town?" she asked, eyeing all the activity and glancing toward the main disco room. "Or in the country, for that matter."

"It's called testosterone, Janice. Now come on."

He led her up the staircase, past the free condom stand, and into the Show Room, where this evening's performance was already under way. A loud song rolled over Todd and Janice as they entered the darkened room. Up on the short stage a tall, thin black queen, her nails big and polished, her hair big and orange, her legs long and oh-so beautiful, belted out a Tina Turner tune. Moving about gracefully in a teeny metallic silver dress that barely came down to her crotch—a crotch that had been bound and flattened to make it appear as smooth and beguiling as a woman's—she sang about life as a private dance. The audience was captivated, caught by the music, enchanted by the queen's perfect lip-synching and rhythmic dancing.

Just to Todd's left, a deep, seductive voice said, "Oh, hello, gorgeous. I just knew you'd come back. I've been counting the days. Let's see, it's been Monday, Tuesday, Wednesday, and then after Wednesday comes . . ."

In the dim light Todd spotted a huge head of dark hair, a sagging, wrinkled face caked with makeup, a beaming smile, and a very full body squeezed into a tight dress. Once again she wore large, silvery earrings and a glimmering black dress, a real vision of cocktail-dress glamour.

"Hi, Limoge," said Todd.

"Oh, kiss, kiss, you remember." She came over and gave him a very light but noisy smooch on his right cheek. "Say, your name's mud these days, isn't it, handsome? I saw a piece about you on TV, and I read all about you in the paper too. Just what have you been up to? That's okay though. I just love a man with a soiled past—once I dated an ex-con who was ever so much fun. Then again, I love just about any man that's breathing. Can a girl buy you a drink?" She looked Janice up and down and said, "Oh, hi, dear. That maroon sweater really looks awful on you. Makes you look all pasty. I think you're a winter. You know, all those frigid blues. You really ought to have your colors done, you know. Just look what it's done for me." Reaching for Todd's hand, she added, "Oh, and it's all right, I'll take him from here. You can go now. He's all mine."

Janice was staring at Limoge's shiny black heels. "Why the hell can you walk in spikes like those and I can't?"

"It just takes a little . . . *je ne sais quoi* . . . practice, I suppose. Now be a good tart and say ta-ta before I scratch your eyes out. You're not his type—wink, wink—if you catch my drift."

"No shit, Sherlock," she retorted. "I wouldn't want him anyway. Just in case you can't get those cheap eyelashes up high enough to see past your nose, I'm a member of the tribe too."

Taken aback, Limoge couldn't hide her surprise. "Oh, girl fight, girl fight, tell me it's not so. A bull dagger, are you?" She took a long judgmental look at Janice. "Sorry, sister, I guess we do come in all flavors, but heaven help me, how's a nice-dressed girl like me to know just what you are? You're not wearing any plaid flannel, no leather either. But wait . . . wait, let me see there," she said, bending over and peering at Janice's shoes. "Oh, dear *Gawd*, no wonder you can't do heels. Those are pretty nasty little loafers you got there. Where'd you get them, from a catalog or at a discount mall? So you're really a lezzie, are you? I know, I bet you rode your—wait, what do they call those muddy things with those big butch tires?—oh, yes. I bet you rode your mountain bike down here, didn't you?"

"No, my big fucking Harley." Janice couldn't hide a grin as she said, "Todd, I'm sure you never thought you'd be caught between a drag queen and a dyke, did you?"

But Todd was too busy to pay either of them any attention. Instead, his eyes were searching the room. He saw a big pile of auburn hair off to the right, yet the figure was much too thin. Just up ahead, leaning against a pillar, was a shapely figure with huge shoulders and a huge mound of platinum hair swirling and curling over a silvery dress. But that wasn't Jeff either. He scanned all the crowded tables, each with a small candle flickering on it, and peered through the crowd. Jeff was nowhere to be seen.

"Limoge, have you seen, uh . . ." His mind went blank for a moment. "Have you seen Tiffany?"

"Lordy, are you hung up on that big queen or what? Is that what this is all about?" she said with a big scowl. "And here I thought you'd come especially to see *moi.*"

"I don't have time for any bullshit, Limoge," he said. "I'm in deep trouble, and I need to find him—now. Janice here is my lawyer, and we need to get some information from him."

Limoge cleared her voice, and it became deep and serious. "I see, of course. Let me think. Tiffany finished up about fifteen minutes ago—she did a brilliant piece, a Streisand song—and I saw her head to the dressing room. She wasn't changing into another gown. No, I think she was leaving, so you might still be able to catch her."

"Thanks."

Todd took Janice by the hand, and they weaved in and out of the tables and chairs of the crowded room. They came to a side door, pushed through, and entered a bright corridor. A straight couple was standing there, drinks in hand, talking and laughing, smooching. Todd and Janice cut through another small group of people to the right and down another corridor. When they reached Jeff's dressing room Todd pushed open the door and found it empty, a pair of red heels tossed on the floor and a white billowy dress thrown on a chair.

"Jeff?" shouted Todd. "Jeff, where are you?"

A soft voice from down the hall called, "Now what are

you kiddies doing down here? Don't you know you shouldn't be back here?''

Todd turned, saw a queen poking out of the next dressing room, her makeup not fully applied, the jet-black wig not quite right, and demanded, ''Where the hell's Jeff?''

''Who the hell wants to know?'' She squinted, studied them, and scowled. ''Oh, it's you again, what'shisface. My, but it's hard to teach old dogs new tricks, isn't it? I really don't think Tiffany wants to see you. And you're really not supposed to be back here.''

''Where the hell is he?'' yelled Todd, moving briskly toward him. ''Tell me before I beat the shit out of you!''

''Oh!'' Screaming like a little girl, she slammed her door and locked it. ''Go away! Go away! You're too late! Now leave before I call the guys in the Leather Bar and have them beat the shit out of *you.''*

His fist hard and solid, Todd pounded once on the door. ''Where the fuck did he go?''

''I don't know! Honest! He just left. He went out the back just a couple of minutes ago! Now go away, you horrible thing. Leave me alone before I scream bloody fucking murder!''

Janice came up behind Todd, grabbed him by the arm, and pointed to an exit sign down the hall. ''Come on.''

They bolted through the narrow corridor and came to a staircase, which doubled back and down. Reaching the ground floor, they rushed out a side door and into the cool night, stopping awkwardly on the sidewalk. At first Todd didn't understand where they were, then he saw Hennepin Avenue to his right. And there was the library and the parking lot where he'd left his car. He scanned the street, saw only a few guys walking along. A young boy and girl necking against the side of a building. A daring young gay couple holding hands. A handful of cars moving down the broad street.

"He couldn't just vanish that quickly," quipped Janice, looking all around. "Where the hell is he?"

Todd saw a familiar car. A low, medium-sized sedan. Four doors. A Taurus. He saw it coming up the street, noted the flashing turn signal.

"Shit," said Todd, grabbing Janice by the arm and pulling her into a shadowy corner of the building. "That's Rawlins."

The car slowed, then turned into an alley. All at once Todd understood. This was either very good or very bad, he thought. With Todd leading the way, they hurried up the sidewalk, then crouched behind a car. And there, down the alley and in the dark light, stood the lone figure of Jeff, waiting for his ride.

"Keep an eye on them!" said Todd, and then turned and darted off, for he knew they had only seconds before losing them.

He ran as fast as he could, cutting across Fourth Street, tearing toward the library. Not waiting for traffic to clear on the busy Hennepin Avenue, he rushed through the moving cars as if he were fording a stream. One driver honked madly at him. Todd pressed on, jammed his hand into his pocket, yanked out his keys, and seconds later reached his Cherokee. With a huge roar, Todd brought the vehicle to life, but instead of pulling out of the parking lot and turning left on the one-way street, he turned right onto Fourth, proceeding the wrong way and directly into traffic. Gunning the engine, he drove quickly across Hennepin and slammed to a halt a half-block later. Janice rushed around the front of the vehicle and climbed in.

"Jeff got in and they drove off!" she related. "Rawlins turned left about midway down that alley."

Todd quickly formed a mental map. "So he must be cutting back to First Avenue."

On that chance, Todd drove along the edge of the street,

still against traffic. Several angry motorists honked. And then, a few moments later, Todd's prediction proved correct.

"There!" shouted Janice, pointing to the busy cross street.

Deep in traffic, Rawlins crossed Fourth and continued up First, and at the very moment when the light turned, Todd raced around the corner. Rawlins's car, clearly visible beneath the streetlights, was less than a block ahead. Todd pressed hard on the gas, then eased up.

"I don't think they saw us," said Todd, his heart beating hard.

"No, I don't either. But now what?"

"We see what they're up to, I guess."

Following Rawlins past the Target Arena and out of downtown, Todd was careful not to approach too closely. He wanted to see where they were going, just what they might be involved in. At the same time an underlying sense of fear kept pushing within him. He'd had two horrible thoughts nagging at him all day, and they now began to surface. Could the man Michael have let in that fateful night have been his first lover? And after leaving Todd's last night could Rawlins have snuck down to Lake Calhoun? Both were distinct possibilities, placing Jeff in certain danger. Or might the two be involved in some sort of sick relationship? Still again, they could easily be involved in a scam of some sort, this one definitely not a childhood prank but perhaps involving Jeff's connections at the bank and Rawlins's police work. If that were the case, Michael could have discovered it and been killed to ensure his silence.

Todd's head began to ache as he tailed Rawlins and Jeff into south Minneapolis. The Taurus veered to the left and headed directly down LaSalle, a straight street where the traffic picked up speed. A mile or so later Rawlins turned left on 28th Street. Soon after crossing 35W the Taurus slowed and turned right, entering a neighborhood lost between the highway and larger businesses. Hadn't he, Todd wondered, once done a story on a crack house somewhere in the vicinity?

"Where the hell are they going?" asked Janice. "This is kind of a rough area, isn't it?"

"Yeah," replied Todd, "but I remember Michael saying Jeff lived over here. I think somewhere near a lumberyard."

For fear of being spotted, Todd didn't risk turning down the same street after them. Instead, he continued to the next, where he made a right. Immediately they passed two abandoned cars, one missing its rear wheels, the other with all its windows smashed in. Todd glanced to the side and saw three boarded-up houses, one of them blackened with smoke stains. Only two houses on the entire block had lights on.

Todd turned right at the next corner, thereby cutting back to the street that Rawlins had taken. Here an entire row of houses had been leveled, their sad plight bulldozed into the ground.

"Down there," said Janice, leaning forward.

She pointed to the left, where the taillights of the Taurus were veering off the road and into a driveway. Todd waited a couple of moments, then turned left after them. Nearing the drive, Todd slowed and pulled over, then turned off the engine and lights. Past some overgrown lilac bushes he could make out the last house on the street, a tall Victorian that stood isolated and dark in this neglected neighborhood. A couple of lights in the house came on, and then Todd looked past some train tracks and saw a lumber barn.

"This is Jeff's place, I'm sure of it," said Todd.

"God, this is about as marginal as you can get," commented Janice. "What the hell is Jeff doing living over here?"

"I think he inherited it. Something like that. Like maybe his great-grandfather or great-great-grandfather owned that lumberyard or something and built that house. I can't quite remember."

"Well, now what do we do? Wait?"

"I've never been very good at that."

"Do tell," remarked Janice.

"Besides, who knows what's going on in there?"

"Okay, so let's just go up and confront them. We knock, go in, and see how much the two of them will tell us."

"That won't work."

Staring at the large, dark structure, Todd didn't want just part of the truth. He wanted all of it. And if Janice and he asked them directly, pushed them even, he doubted they'd get everything they needed to know.

"No," he said, reaching for the door handle. "I'm going to just check something out. You wait here."

"What?"

He took a pen from the dashboard, found a scrap of paper, scribbled something, and said, "If I'm not back in fifteen minutes, call this number. My car phone's right here."

"That's ridiculous."

"Just wait here, you'll be fine."

"Of course I'll be fine, but, Todd, you can't do this."

"What do you mean?"

"God, when it comes down to it, you're just a boy after all, aren't you?" began Janice, raising her hands in frustration. "You can tell a bimbo to wait in a car like a dog, but you can't tell a dyke. Particularly, *especially,* a lawyer dyke. Got it? It's just too stereotypical."

"But—"

"Todd, I'm not going to wait here like Barbie while you go off and play G.I. Joe."

"Okay, you want to go see what's going on?"

Janice rolled her eyes, but said nothing.

"You go and I'll wait here. See, there's a phone in the car," said Todd, picking up the receiver, "and in case anything weird happens, one of us should stay here to call."

"Oh, good Lord."

Janice peered out the side windows. She turned and looked out the back. Then leaned forward and looked toward Jeff's.

"All right, all right. This is a shit neighborhood and I don't want to go traipsing around. Not up to that house any-

way,'' she admitted. ''But you're going to pay for this—
literally. My meter's running, got it? I'm billing you for every minute. My firm's regular rate.''

''Just call this number if I'm not back in fifteen minutes.''

''Right. And I'm going to smoke inside your car too!''

''Fine.''

Todd climbed out and shut the door. As he rounded the
front of the car the passenger window opened quickly and
Janice poked her head out.

''Todd, just don't be real butch and do something stupid,
okay?''

''What do you want me to be, a fairy?''

''Yeah, just this once, would you?'' She added gently, ''I
mean it, be careful. We've already lost Michael.''

34

"Oh, God, Corky, I just couldn't believe it," said Jeff, turning from side to side and checking his figure in the front hall mirror. "I looked up and there he was. Jesus H. Christ, I never thought he'd just come marching right into the bank like that. God, he's ballsy. I thought I was going to have to call the guards and have them drag him away."

"What did he say?"

"I don't know, he's such a prick. He wanted to know all about you, actually. All about when you and Michael did it. You know, fucked. My Lord, some people just get so hung up on sex." Jeff waited a moment, then flopped his right hand at the wrist and added feyly, "Of course, I didn't tell him everything. Only a few tidbits. You know, the real juicy ones."

Rawlins shook his head, took off his leather coat, threw it on a chair, and said, "I'll have to deal with that later."

"I'll say. You know, Todd would be absolutely crazy with jealousy if he ever found out you went over to Michael's after he was at the Gay Times."

"Hey, like I told you, I bumped into Michael down at the

bar just after he'd seen you. He was all upset, so later on I just went over to give him a little comfort.''

"Yeah, right, you testosterone tiger, I know the comfort you give. All I'm saying is Todd would go ballistic, so watch it.''

"And I'd be reprimanded if my department ever found out, so keep that flaming trap of yours shut. Shit, you haven't told anyone already, have you?''

"Good heavens, no, Corky dear," he said. "But be careful. Todd's hot to find out what really happened. He really is the suspicious sort. Persistent too.''

Jeff leaned forward, dabbed at the blue shadow that still remained on his lids. It was too blue, he thought. It really hadn't gone with the dress he'd worn tonight, the silver one. It made him look too cheap. Then again, maybe it was just these lights. Maybe onstage it was okay. He looked again, closed his left eye, then made a face.

"Oh, ish," he moaned. "This color I wore tonight is just so tacky. I mean, how could I have been so stupid? I wonder if anyone was laughing at me.''

"Come on, gorgeous," said Rawlins. "Let's get to work.''

"Yeah, yeah, yeah. Work, work, work. That's all I do. By day I count money, by night I belt out tunes.''

"And now you count money again.''

"Oy, what a life.''

Jeff hit another light switch and led the way through the front parlor, which was filled with overstuffed furniture and covered with woodwork—oak and mahogany—used in Victorian extravagance. One of Jeff's forebears had built this place, an entrepreneur from Boston who'd come out here, wiped out the northern woods, and made a small fortune.

"This place always amazes me," commented Rawlins.

"Yeah, my great-granddaddy, the lumber queen. He was as much a show-off as me. Look at this millwork—it's everywhere and as thick as frosting on a wedding cake.''

Jeff led the way into the dining room, where the floor was

inlaid with strips of mahogany, the doorways framed with wooden lattice, and the walls decorated with mahogany wainscoting and an intricate built-in buffet. In recognition and respect for the money—albeit dwindling—they'd inherited, his heirs had never painted any of the wood, leaving it as a memorial to their one semigreat relative. Yet one hundred years later Jeff, the family outcast, was the only one in his extended family who dared live in this dilapidated neighborhood, all the others having picked up their skirts and fled to the suburbs.

"Personally, I think the old man got a little carried away. I mean, I've always said, woodwork is like makeup: Too much can ruin the whole effect." Jeff went over to one of the old gas fixtures on the wall, struck a match, then opened the valve and brought a flame to life. "That's not to say I'm not all for a little flair and drama. Aren't these old fixtures marvelous?"

"Looks a tad dangerous to me."

"Think romance, Corky. Hot romance."

"Yeah, right. You have all the papers, don't you?" asked Rawlins.

"I told you I did. Don't worry." Leaving the fixture burning, Jeff nodded and patted a small leather briefcase. "I did it at lunch when most everyone was gone. It wasn't that hard, really, once I knew what to look for. Here, let's spread it all out on the dinner table and see what we've got. How about you, you didn't have any problems, did you, sweetheart?"

From his pocket Rawlins lifted the small envelope. "It was right there in the mailbox, just like I'd hoped. One little bill that had all the account numbers on it, that's all."

"God, I work in a bank and I just had no idea that embezzling was so easy." Jeff laughed slightly and then yawned. "Why didn't I think of this? With this kind of money I could be dressed in diamonds from head to foot. Can't you see me in some sparkly tiara?"

"As if that wouldn't be a dead giveaway that something was amuck."

"Oh, good Lord, you're as much a stick in the mud as TV Todd. Just think, I wouldn't have to work at the bank and . . . and wouldn't I look great with some real jewels? After all, diamonds are a girl's best friend. A red wig and maybe I could pass for Fergie."

"I think the Queen Mum is more like it."

"Oh, stuff it, Corky, would you? You gotta live, you know. You gotta take a bite of something and enjoy it while you're here. That police job really has made you all uptight, you know it?" He stifled another yawn. "I'm bushed, and this is going to take a while to go through. You want some coffee? I make it with a lot of character."

"Sure. And black."

"Strong and black. Just like that boyfriend of yours. Remember that one, what was he, number thirty-five?" Jeff said coyly, starting toward the kitchen.

"Like you say, stuff it."

"Silly boy, after all these years don't you think I know absolutely everything about you and where you've put your heart?"

Rawlins shook his head and muttered, "Just give me the fucking papers, would you?"

"Right there in my briefcase. It's all in a file. All in order too. Three years' worth of data."

Jeff lingered in the doorway to the kitchen, staring at his longtime friend Steve Rawlins, Jr. He was good at hunches. Remarkable, actually. And there was something he'd been meaning to ask Corky. But, he wondered, should he? Might it not stir up things? Well, who cares? He had a right to know. This could affect him as well.

A fluffy gray cat slithered by, and Jeff said, "Hello, Pussy-wussy. How are you tonight? Bet you're ready to go out and gobble up some naughty little mice." Jeff picked up the cat and cuddled it. "Say, Corky, there's not something going on between you and TV Todd, is there?"

"What the hell are you talking about?"

"I don't know, just the way he looked when he mentioned your name. You know, he was more than upset. He was kind of in knots." Stroking Pussy, he added, "And you kind of get the same way whenever I mention his name. Here, I'll say it again and again: Todd . . . Todd . . . TV Todd . . . Todd . . ."

"Shut up, Jeff," snapped Rawlins, glaring at him. "You know, sometimes you're a real pain in the ass."

"Well, I can sense these things. After all, I'm quite tuned in to my feminine side."

"Everyone knows that, Jeff."

"Well, just don't forget a zillion years ago I was the first to figure out about you and Michael." He took a deep sigh. "Poor Michael, what a pity. If only he hadn't been such a goddamn good accountant."

Oh, dear Lord, Jeff thought sadly as he passed through the pantry and into the kitchen. What a world. Poor Michael, mutilated like that. Awful. The first of the Banditos to leave this pathetic place. Who would have imagined? And it wasn't AIDS that got him either.

"Didn't we have fun, the three of us?" called Jeff, crossing through the kitchen and to the back door. "I mean, it was the greatest, wasn't it, growing up in Linden Hills?"

"Yeah, it was fun."

"Fun? Fun? It was magic." Jeff opened the door, tossed out the cat, and said, "Eat 'em up, Pussy." Then he mused, "That lake and our bikes. Shit, we got into a lot of trouble, didn't we? Do you remember the time we toilet-papered that teacher's house? What was her name? The biology teacher. Miss . . . Miss Thatcher, wasn't it? *Gawd,* was that hysterical or what? All that toilet paper hanging from that old pine tree in her front yard. I've never thanked you, have I? You know, no one else would let me hang out with them. Do you know that? You and Michael were the only ones who were friendly to me.''

From out in the dining room Rawlins offered, ''You were funny.''

''Funny? Funny my ass, I was queer. And you two were too. We just didn't know it. No, correction. I always knew I was queer, I just didn't know what it meant. None of us did. No one knew diddly about sex, really. Not until puberty anyway. But all the other boys were afraid of me, I think, because I was different. You know, the sissy. Unlike you and Michael, I was the obvious one. But you and Michael, well, you didn't see how different I was from everyone else, but how similar I was to you two. Right? Don't you think? And then miracle of miracles, we became this cool little group.'' Jeff listened, waiting for an answer, then realized that his friend had put on some music. ''Corky, you faggot, can you hear me? Corky? Turn down the fucking music and answer me, you ding-a-ling!''

When no reply came over the voice of Al Jarreau, however, Jeff shook his head and started bustling around the kitchen, losing himself in memories. He didn't know what he would have done without Corky and Michael. Gone crazy, perhaps. They took Jeff everywhere with them. Fishing. Skating. To the movies. And sliding. Oh, God. They loved sliding. On cardboard. The faster the better, even when it was twenty fucking degrees below fucking zero. Once they'd put him on a toboggan and sent him down this icy hill over by the picnic pavilion. And then he'd smashed into a tree and broken his ankle. As Jeff now put a pot of water on the stove, struck a match, and lit the gas, he laughed, for he'd never looked more butch in his life than in that clunky foot cast. Oh, the girls at the Gay Times wouldn't believe it. Sometime he'd have to show them a photo.

He heard some floorboards creak in the old house and called over his shoulder, ''Is that you, girlfriend? Want anything to eat?''

When no reply came, he glanced back, saw no one. Oh, that Corky. He was probably deep into the papers already, trying to figure out how to find even more money. All work, that boy. Always had been.

Well, Jeff, for one, was hungry as hell. All that dancing, he thought. And singing. The stage lights too. They sucked energy out of you. Performing always made him famished, and he turned to the refrigerator. Screw the diet, he needed to eat. Today had been much too stressful. No, the whole week had been too stressful. Peering into the fridge, he found some cold pasta and picked out a bit. Divine, he thought, and knowing he had to have more, he pulled out the whole bowl and set it on the counter.

There it was again. That noise of someone moving quietly. He licked his fingers, peered past the blue flame of the stove and out the other doorway. What was Corky doing in the back hall? He obviously had passed from the dining room, through the pantry, and into the bathroom.

"I'm in here, darling," called Jeff. "What the hell are you doing back there? Are you in the john or the back hall? It's such a mess. Be careful, will you? There's mops and stuff. Dear Jesus, I don't want you taking a tumble."

But no reply came. Jeff shook his head and quickly picked at a bit more pasta, slurping the long noodles into his mouth. Gobbling them down, he walked toward the rear passage.

"Corky?" He saw a figure standing there in the dark. "Oh, there you are, you silly. Here, let me get you some light."

As Jeff reached for the switch, the figure suddenly leapt forward. Instinctively Jeff jumped back, but the other man was faster and caught Jeff by the wrist. Jeff was about to shout out, but he was clipped on the chin, and pain shot through his head and down his body. An instant later a powerful fist rammed his gut and knocked the wind completely out of him. Jeff grabbed at his stomach, doubled over, gasped for air. Bent over and trying to breathe, he glanced to his right, saw the basement stairs. No, please. Don't throw me—

Suddenly something hard and solid hit him on the back of his head, and Jeff's world went as dark as a blackened stage.

35

Todd hesitated at the stand of lilac bushes and looked through the branches at the tall Victorian with the burning front-porch light. He glanced back at the Cherokee, saw the black figure of Janice and the tiny glowing orange tip of her cigarette. Then he cut around the end of the lilacs and across an empty lot where a house had undoubtedly once stood. Bending forward slightly, he jogged across the lumpy, uneven ground and hurried for a tree, where he paused and took a semblance of shelter. The lights in the front of the house were lit, as were those in the room with the large bay window. That had to be the dining room, he thought, peering at the curving window that was covered with a light, lacy curtain. He saw a figure move—someone strolling through the room, pausing, then sitting down—but couldn't tell who it was.

So how was he going to handle this?

He had no idea, really, but his best reporter's instincts kept pulling him forward, urging him to slip through the shadows of the night. He knew that he shouldn't expose himself. Not yet anyway. His entire life, of course, had been about maintaining secrecy. From a life of hiding he had learned the techniques like a master spy. Everyone has a crack. Move forward; find it in the darkness. Expose that crack. Break the armor. Discover the truth.

As his feet thumped across the dirt he peered through the thin, frilly curtains and saw a figure at the dinner table. Broad-shouldered, steady. Todd moved closer still, crouched behind a bush. He heard the deep bass of music from within the house. And there was Rawlins. The bastard. Sitting at the large table, he was sorting through a stack of papers. Periodically his hand would reach up and touch something. A calculator, Todd realized. Sure, he was tabulating an account of some sort. Money, to be sure. Didn't it always boil down to either money or the passions of love and hate?

The now-vile memories of the previous night stirred Todd's gut. Rawlins's firm but gentle touch, his deep, earthy scent, his—

To hell with the bastard, thought Todd, still shocked that he had been so thoroughly duped. His first instinct was to hurl a rock at the window, charge forward, and yell at Rawlins or some such thing. But he had to ascertain where Jeff was in this sprawling house. It wouldn't do to confront Rawlins and then have Jeff spring out of nowhere. God only knew what the two of them were up to. And in any case, in this neighborhood Jeff was more than likely to have a gun, perhaps only a purse-sized one, but deadly enough, for sure.

Still bent over, Todd scurried across the drive past the dark garage. There was a light on in the back. Jeff had to be back there. The kitchen? A den? Todd crossed into the side yard, paused at a large old fuel tank—a rusty cylinder that smelled of heating oil—and leaned a hand against it. He surveyed the backyard and saw no other houses, only a weedy slope that led down to the railroad tracks. There was no other drive either, which was good. If by chance there was someone else involved, they wouldn't arrive unnoticed. Janice, at least, would take note.

His hand was oily and grimy from leaning against the tank, and he wiped it on his pants as he trotted toward the corner of the house. Reaching the corner of the clapboard structure, he hesitated one more time, listened. Throbbing music still emanated from the house. Todd could hear it seeping from the windows. But no voices. Could Jeff be upstairs? Sure. He could be bathing or changing, perhaps slipping into some gown or caftan. Todd stepped back a bit and spied the upper windows, which were all dark. Still, Jeff could be in another room up there, perhaps on the far side of the house. Or he might yet be in the kitchen.

He saw the rear stoop, some four steps that led up to a small enclosed porch and then the back door. As Todd neared that he peered through another window and spotted a round fluorescent light attached to the middle of a ceiling. Obviously the kitchen. So Jeff must be back here. And with any luck the back door would be open. If not he'd have to go around, try to slip in through the front door. And then? Locate them both, then corner and confront them? Something like that, and all before fifteen minutes expired and Janice made the call. All before Todd got himself killed as well.

Hesitating in the dark, Todd studied the kitchen window, saw no movement from within. Silently Todd moved closer to the stoop, froze, and spied into the kitchen, now clearly seeing a counter and the corner of a stove. A wisp of steam was rising from a kettle. But where was Jeff?

Todd climbed up the steps, pressed down on the old handle, pushed open the flimsy door, and entered the back porch. A pair of muddy shoes against one wall, some empty flowerpots next to the shoes. A broom in the corner. Todd took a step, froze when the floorboards creaked. With great care he moved toward the rear door of the house, a wooden door with a large, curtain-covered window, and reached for the brass handle. He twisted the knob, hoping against the improbability of it all. And it caught. Sure. Why shouldn't it be locked? Shit, cursed Todd. That meant he'd have to try the front door. Or perhaps the basement windows. Perhaps he'd be able to kick one in, crawl in that way.

Then, however, his attention was caught. The window in the door was mostly covered by a red-and-white-checkered curtain. But there was a crack. The two pieces of material didn't quite meet, and Todd leaned forward, peered in. Shit, was that a leg? Hell, yes. And an arm. Good God. He pressed against the glass. It was Jeff, lying unconscious in the back hall.

So, thought Todd, his heart racing with fury, this was all becoming clearer by the moment.

36

A big grin on his face, Rawlins rapidly went through the stack of papers, amazed at how much it was totaling. Much more than he had expected. He sorted through three more statements and calculated that on an average it totaled about $23,000 per month. Quite a substantial sum, no doubt about it. And all of it pure profit.

"Holy shit," he muttered with a smile on his face. "Someone's getting filthy rich."

And he knew who, of course.

Good God, who wouldn't kill for this kind of money? This operation was nearly perfect in its simplicity. A scam like this could go on just about forever. A true cash cow, one that kept on giving. Reaching for the calculator, Rawlins started crunching the numbers. At $23,000 per month times twelve months, that equaled $276,000 a year. Multiply that times 3.3—all this had been in place and working without flaw for over three years now—and you had over $900,000. Shit. Almost a million bucks as of now. If you added in interest, then maybe it was a million. No, you had to take out taxes too.

After all, even a crooked operation like this had to have a clean face.

He sat back, ran his hand through his short brown hair. Who would have ever thought that embezzling could be so easy? It was as surefire a way to get rich as any he'd ever seen, and he'd seen and studied a good number of ploys in his years on the force. Of course, there were any number of ways to make bigger money, and faster too. But in his opinion this was far superior. The tortoise way: start slow, finish first. Nothing so big that it would attract attention. You don't want the feds descending from the heavens. And you definitely don't want to go strutting around in a glitzy diamond-studded tiara as Queen Jeff had suggested. To act like that was as foolish as it was ignorant. A way to send up fireworks. Yo, cops, yo, IRS, over here, look at all the money I got. Diamonds and gowns too. Come and arrest me, *pleeaasse*.

No, to quote one particularly nasty little asshole, evil was patient. Most definitely so.

Okay, so you start a business, a little one, perhaps, just as they had. And it's all legit. You even get in some outside money. And then you set up another company, a phony one, say, the ABC Corporation. Next you get some nice fake bills printed at one of those instant places—the kind that do the work nice and cheap and don't ask questions—and then you get a mailbox, preferably at a big anonymous post office like the one downtown. Lastly, but most important, you start billing the legit company on a monthly basis. For consulting services rendered. Sure. That's it. Twenty-three grand. Okay, that's a lot, so you pull a few little punches. You vary the monthly bill every now and then—maybe only $18,000 in August, then nearly $30,000 in November when new product development is on the front burner. As long as the first company shows a profit, however, everything is fine. All is good. The investors would be delighted. After all, you can't go broke making a profit. Then you deposit the funds in the ABC Corporation's money-market account, declare taxes and so on, and live happily ever after. Oh, sure, there were a few expenses, like paying off the accountant at the legitimate company. But that was peanuts. The important thing was to keep quiet, be steady and consistent, and eliminate any obstacles along the way.

Right, thought Rawlins, you always have to get rid of the obstacles, the things that want to trip you up.

Rising from the table, Rawlins stretched, then stepped over to the stereo and turned it up even louder. Too bad about Michael. Murdered merely because he'd asked a few questions and followed up on a few things. So smart. Too smart. He was one of the obstacles that had to be gotten rid of, for he'd garnered too much information, thereby threatening the entire arrangement.

Who would have thought their trio—Michael, Jeff, and Rawlins—would have ended like this, in murder? As boys they'd been such innocents. Devious little shits, true. But innocents first. Three little boys, laughter rising from their throats as they bombed around Linden Hills on their Schwinns. But now . . . now nothing but tragedy. He never would have imagined such a sad ending.

Rawlins shook his head, forgot all about the money, and thought about Michael. The first and only person Rawlins had ever truly loved. Nothing had been as pure nor as intense as what he had felt for him, for handsome, wonderful, funny Michael. He'd been the first person that Rawlins had ever slept with. And while he'd known right from that instant— what were they, nineteen?—that Michael was the only person for him, he'd made one critical mistake. He'd pushed too hard. He'd come on too strong. And that had sent the young Michael, who had yet to accept his homosexuality, fleeing as fast and as far as he could. Which had devastated Rawlins. Like a broken wing, it proved a rejection that Rawlins had never been able to get over. From then on every potential suitor was judged against Michael—against his charm and warmth—and all of them came up short in one way or another. Well, nearly all. After his tumultuous break with Michael the two had avoided one another, seeking out separate friends, different parties, entirely distinct careers. In the three or four times that they had bumped into each other over the years, they had turned quickly and silently away, scowling, even fleeing the situation. Until, of course, the other evening at the Gay Times, in a conversation initiated by none other than Michael. Michael, who'd seen Rawlins across the bar and come over to him. Michael, who'd begged his counsel. Things are souring with my lover, Todd, Michael had sobbed. I can't take the pressure of being with someone so uptight, so closeted. Rawlins had listened, said little, stood there smirking, thinking, Now you know what it's like, asshole, let me see you cry, and . . . and silently wondering if Michael, the object of his obsession, even realized that Rawlins had never, not for a moment, fallen out of love with him. But of course Michael hadn't, as Rawlins had learned later when he'd stopped by Michael's.

Oh, forget it, thought Rawlins, moving toward the window. It was far too late. There was no fixing things. Nor would there ever be. That time had come and gone, an opportunity missed yet again, this time forever.

There was a brief pause between songs on the CD, and in that instant of silence Rawlins heard not only the screaming of the tea kettle from within the kitchen, but something else. He froze. What the hell was that? A sound of some sort from outside. Running, pounding steps. Someone was out there. He automatically moved away from the window and pressed himself against the wall. And there it was, a figure, that of a man scurrying through the dark. Oh, shit. This was no ordinary burglar, Rawlins sensed at once.

He rushed over to his leather jacket, which was thrown over a chair in the living room, and lifted his department-issued gun from its holster. Then he slipped back over to a side window, pushed aside the curtain, stared into the dark night. There was nothing, only his car, the deserted lot next door, and the thick bushes beyond.

Wait, no, up there. By the front bush. Yes, whoever was out there was now crouched by the corner of the front porch. Rawlins studied the figure, but couldn't ascertain who it was. He had an inkling, for sure, and most definitely feared who it might be. And when the man outside moved from behind the bush and around the front of the porch, Rawlins immediately rushed through the living room and into the front hall. For an instant he thought about charging outside, but then he thought far better of it. Right. Just let the unsuspecting bastard in. Make sure he was the vulnerable one.

With that in mind Rawlins bent over and scurried to the front door, which he silently unlocked. Then he slipped deep into the back hall. And waited. Just let him come to me, he thought, lifting his gun.

37

"Oh, crap," muttered Janice as she sat in the dark vehicle. "Crap, crap, crap."

She opened the door and climbed out. Standing on the tips of her toes, she tried to see over the bushes. Just what in the hell was going on down there in the big house? While there were a few lights on, she couldn't make out any movement or even the faintest sound of life. Where in God's name had Todd gone and what kind of trouble was he in now? Fifteen minutes was nearly up. So what was she supposed to do, go ahead and call the number, or go right on up to the house and find out what was going on?

"Come on, Todd," she said to herself. "Give me a signal. Let me know you're okay."

Todd had nothing, no weapon of any kind. Still, he knew that he had to gain entry to the house. Perhaps Jeff was merely knocked out. On the other hand, perhaps he lay dying.

He couldn't stop himself. Inside the house was the nugget of truth, the reason why Michael had been killed and Todd's own life thrown into such disarray. If only he could get a closer glimpse at the papers Rawlins had been sorting through in the dining room. It might reveal the true nature of what Rawlins and Jeff were involved in. As the tension rushed through his body however, Todd knew he wanted much more than to simply find out what this was all about.

Edging up to the front door, he hesitated, then stared at the large window to the right. He moved closer, but the curtain was thick and he couldn't see through, so he turned back, making it to the front door. Reaching for the old brass handle, he turned it, found that it gave easily, and pushed. It was the first of two doors however, and he entered a tiny chamber that was meant as a stopgap to the cold Minnesota winds. Todd gently closed the door behind him, stood still on the tiled floor. Then he moved up to the next door, which was made of thick oak and had a large curtained window set into it. Looking through the thin window covering, he could make out the lights of both the living room and dining room. But there was no sign of Rawlins. Was he still in the living room? Had he slipped back into the kitchen?

He turned the doorknob and to his surprise and relief felt it click open easily. Pushing it open a crack, Todd slipped quickly inside. He closed the door and was standing in the front hall, his heart thumping along, every one of his senses keenly piqued. To his left, the Victorian fireplace, a gas affair surrounded with a heavy mantel and extensive woodwork. Next to it, a dark wooden staircase with an ornate balustrade that rose up to the second floor. A dark hall right in front of him that might lead to the rear stairs or a back door. And the living room on his right.

For maybe thirty seconds Todd stood completely motionless, listening for any sound of Rawlins. He moved several feet forward and glanced into the living room and then into the very edge of the dining room. An assortment of papers was still spread across the table, a calculator. The papers on the table were bank statements—active ones, by the long lists of numbers. Todd slipped forward, moving out of the dark entry and through a corner of the living room. He paused at a large round column that marked the passage into the dining room. If only Rawlins were seated right there, his back to him.

He heard something, movement of some sort, perhaps from the kitchen. Quickly he pulled back, slipping out of the dining room, back into the dark entry hall. He pressed himself up against a wall, heard nothing else. It would be foolish to try to make it through the dining room, which was so open and well-lit, and he turned. Yes. This other hall, the dark one, had to lead to the rear of the house. Surely it connected to the kitchen. Perhaps he could sneak up on Rawlins from this side.

As Todd entered the passage a board moaned under his right foot. He froze. Fortunately the music was loud enough to have drowned out the sound of his step. He moved forward again, carefully avoiding that particular floorboard, and soon the basement stairs loomed to his left. Pressing on, he came to a corner, saw yet another door, this one partially open. Light poured through the crack. The sound of a kettle rattling and steaming. He edged toward it. Were those steps he heard? Was Rawlins right there in the kitchen? With surprise as his only advantage, he paused and calculated every movement.

He moved to the open doorway, toward the light. There was the refrigerator. The sink. Several mugs on the counter. And the kettle, heaving with steam. Yes, and the other hallway, the rear one that led to the back door. That was where Jeff now lay, either unconscious or dead. Todd's eyes returned to the counter. A wooden knife holder sat near the stove. Todd just needed to rush over there, grab one of the large knives. A weapon. He pulled back the door a bit more. Peered into the room. Still no sign of Rawlins. He could make it if he rushed, he thought.

But just as he was nudging back the door, he heard the sound of someone clearing his throat behind him. Todd spun around to see a dark figure standing in the lightless hallway. Aiming a gun at Todd, the man couldn't stop himself from laughing.

"Surprise, surprise," whispered a hoarse voice.

Acting on reflex, Todd turned and dove through the door into the bright kitchen. He desperately felt along the wall, hit a switch that blackened the lights, and dove to the floor, which probably saved his life. A second later there was a gunshot, and a bullet went whizzing somewhere over him, passing out the kitchen window with a clean, hard noise. On his hands and knees, Todd slid across the floor and then clambered around the corner of the stove.

"Good try, sport," called the voice from the doorway of the kitchen. "Come out, come out, wherever you are."

As the tea kettle continued to scream on the large gas flame, Todd's mind scrambled for his next move. His hand sensed something on the floor, and in the faint light he saw a dropped spoon. With shaking fingers he picked it up, then hurled it toward the other side of the room, where it hit the counter with a distinct clatter. The other man leapt from the doorway and fired twice. Todd sprang up, grabbed the boiling teapot from the stove top, and hurled it at his assailant, who screamed as the scorching pot smashed into his shoulder. Todd then dove to a counter and groped for a thick meat cleaver, which he took from the knife block.

But when he turned back, he saw the gun whirling in his direction.

Todd hurled himself toward another doorway as a bullet ricocheted off the refrigerator, then another appliance, and finally into a wall. Rushing frantically, Todd tore past the back door, where he tripped over a bag of charcoal. He stumbled, nearly fell, and his left foot landed squarely on a plastic container of lighter fluid, which burst, spraying its contents across the back hall and down the basement stairs. Todd scrambled through the slick puddle, jumping over Jeff's lifeless body. As steps rushed in from behind, Todd shoved on, reaching another door, which he yanked open. Suddenly he found himself in a dark bathroom, a long narrow space with a toilet and a huge old claw-foot tub. Meat cleaver in hand, he slammed the door shut behind himself and fumbled unsuccessfully with the lock.

"Oh, you're dead now!" called the voice, racing after him like a ghost. "No mercy from me—I'm going to make sure this hurts!"

Todd spun around and raced blindly through the small room. At the other end was yet another door, a line of light seeping beneath it and up one side. That had to be the dining room. As he groped in the dark for the knob, however, he hit something soft yet firm. A shoulder. In response, a flaccid hand flopped across Todd's leg, and he jumped back in fright. A body crumbled into him, and Todd grabbed it as it fell to the floor. He knew it wasn't Jeff, and as Todd fumbled to catch the body his hands ran awkwardly through short, thick hair, then lumbered over a broad, muscular back. A familiar scent hit his nose.

"Shit!" muttered Todd.

The door behind him was kicked open, and a dark figure said, "Don't worry, your pal's not dead yet—"

A light switched on. In his arms Todd held Steve Rawlins, a line of blood curling around the back of his neck.

"—but he will be soon," continued the man from the doorway. "You're going to shoot him with this gun and then . . ."

Todd turned around, saw Michael's brother-in-law standing there, the pistol aimed at him, and gasped, "Rick."

"Then I'm going to kill you," smiled the balding man, "and everyone will assume you killed the others too. Won't that be a tidy ending to all this?"

38

At first she wasn't sure.

Janice hung up the car phone and then climbed out of the Cherokee, not wanting to believe what she'd just heard. Had that merely been a car backfiring? She looked toward the highway. No, 35W was too far away. The sound had been much closer. It had to have been a gunshot from within Jeff's house.

She broke into a run, charging across the empty lot toward the large house, where lights were burning in several downstairs windows. Only seconds later she heard it again, a loud, harsh noise. Definitely a gun, definitely fired somewhere in the house.

"Oh, shit, Todd."

She'd seen him go in, disappearing through the front door. So now what? Had he been gunned down? Was he lying dead?

Janice rushed up to the dark brown garage, hesitated. Much as she wanted to, it didn't make any sense to go charging into the house. If she could do anything, it was from out here. She started to move around the garbage can, then bumped into something. A large green box. The recycling bin, packed full of bottles and cans.

And again. A blasting, explosive sound.

Janice flinched, hurried up behind the fuel oil tank, stood there trying to make sense of this. What the hell was going on in there? She stared at the bay window—the dining room, she presumed—but couldn't see any activity through the thin window coverings. She heard music blaring and thumping away. But where were they?

She rushed around the side of the house, toward the rear, but couldn't see anyone or anything. Damn it, she thought, turning around. What could she do? Ring the front doorbell and run? If nothing else, the odd surprise of it might derail or at least slow whatever was now happening.

Suddenly a light blinked on in a rear window. Standing on her toes, she saw a bathtub, a mirror on the opposite wall. Moving to the side, she saw Todd, bent over and holding something. Or rather someone. A body. Her mind exploding with fear, Janice couldn't discern what had happened, just who had been shot.

Then she saw Todd turn around and look back, the fear crudely evident on his face. Janice slipped to the end of the oil tank, peered at the far end of the room. She saw the gun, now trained directly on Todd. At first she couldn't see the figure holding the weapon, but then he stepped through the doorway, moved in a bit. Oh, God, thought Janice, her heart stopping as she recognized Rick.

Everything was clear, yet nothing was. Regardless, Janice saw the gun in Rick's hand and knew she had only a precious few seconds at most. But how? She spun around, scanned the ground, and her eyes fixed on a handful of bricks stacked up alongside the garage.

39

"Life is nothing but smoke and mirrors," said Rick, holding the pistol steady on Todd.

"It was you?" asked Todd, his voice faint as he sank against the claw-foot tub, Rawlins awkwardly in his arms. "You killed Michael?"

"He figured out what was going on."

"The others too?"

"You're not listening, Toddy-boy. Like I said, life is nothing but smoke and mirrors." Rick smiled, ran one hand over his balding head. "I gave investors a product and a reasonable return on their investment. Similarly, I'm now going to give the law a gay murderer. As they say, case closed. I'll go back to my darling wife and back to my successful business."

"But . . . but what about . . ." Unable to finish his thought, he looked down at Rawlins. "You mean he—"

"He's just a good cop, that's all. Michael apparently said something to Jeff and presumably Rawlins about the account. An unfortunate turn of events that I'm about to correct."

Todd's hand tightened on the handle of the cleaver, and he lifted it slightly. "You bastard."

"Put down the knife, Todd, before I blow your fucking head off."

"I can't believe you killed your own brother-in-law."

"Drop the knife." Rick turned the gun on the other man. "Or maybe I'll shoot Rawlins first. Say, in the stomach. Or—ouch—the crotch."

Reluctantly, Todd lowered the large knife to the floor.

"That's good," said Rick. "I'm sorry about all this, I really am, but it was either Michael or I lose my wife and almost a million bucks. Plus my business, of course. And getting rid of Michael worked. Quite beautifully, actually. I still have my money, and now I've got my wife back too. What in the hell would you have done?"

"Michael was . . . was your friend."

"That's what I thought too, until he came to me and confronted me with what he'd found. We had lunch and he threatened to go to both Maggie and the police."

"About your business?"

"Don't you get it? I poured my heart and soul into that company, as you well know. I helped create and market some of the best software out there. But I almost went under, which was when I had to bring in outside investors. They gave me money, of course, but they also took part of my company. So as far as I'm concerned, I've just been skimming off the cream of the profit and repaying myself money that's mine. My bookkeeper's keeping some for himself too, of course. He's put in his time."

"You asshole."

"I liked Michael, I really did, and everything would have been fine if he hadn't gone snooping around. But I suppose you can blame that on his sister, my dear, money-hungry wife. You'd never think she was a gold digger, would you? So sweet-looking and all." Rick shook his head. "But she's not so sweet. Hell, no. A couple of months ago she went to

Michael before she even told me, her husband, that she wanted a divorce. I mean, is that sick or what? I thought we'd patched things up long ago, that our marriage was good again, but, no, she goes to him and tells him this is it, end of the line. And then she tells him how worried she is about a settlement on account of my business being a little up and down. My finances were such a secret, she said, so couldn't he just take a look at some of my papers and tell her what she might ask for? Next that sneaky bitch goes out and photocopies a bunch of my bank statements, the post office box number I was using for the phony billing, and hands them all to her brother, the accountant!''

"So none of this had to do with being gay or—"

"Hell, no. I could give a fuck about all that. Michael once said queers are society's scapegoat, so that's where I got the idea. I made it look like it was a gay thing so that the cops would look in the other direction. Like I said, smoke and mirrors. You got caught up in it quite by accident, which worked entirely to my advantage. You're the suspect, not me. And in the end everyone's going to think that you, Todd Mills, Emmy Award–winning reporter, were nothing more than another twisted fag, a psychopath homo killer who killed his lover, plus an anonymous young man, and then Jeff and Rawlins here. They'll believe it, of course, and they'll look no further.''

A volcano of fear and panic welled up in Todd. All his life he'd been consumed with the fear of who he was. And obsessed with what people thought of him. The very suggestion that he might be portrayed as yet another lie, a worse one than he had ever imagined, fused with his grief and fury over Michael's death, and in turn sent a crazed shot of adrenaline rushing through his body. He'd hidden for so long, denied not only his internal strength but his integrity as well. But no longer, and never again.

"No!'' he shouted.

Crazed, he shoved the still-unconscious Rawlins to the

floor, then lunged for the meat cleaver. All he could envision was attacking the very man who'd caused all this.

"Stop it, Todd!" shouted Rick, waving the pistol wildly. "Get back!"

Suddenly the bathroom window exploded as an enormous object shattered the glass and came flying into the small room. Rick jumped back, shielding himself as shards of glass and a brick crashed into the tub, and in that instant Todd grabbed the meat cleaver from the floor. Desperately, Todd hurled the knife at Rick's right hand, and the cleaver bit deeply into one of Rick's fingers. As blood poured from a gaping wound, Rick screamed out and dropped the gun. Todd in turn lunged for the pistol, but Rick kicked it with his foot, which in turn sent the gun spinning deep beneath the claw-foot bathtub. His hand dripping profusely with blood, Rick ducked out of the bathroom.

Through the broken window, Janice shouted, "Todd! Todd, are you all right?"

Todd yelled, "I'm going after Rick!"

First, though, he pressed himself to the floor and stretched as far as he could beneath the tub. Realizing he'd never reach the gun, he left the unconscious Rawlins and rushed out of the room after Rick. Todd charged past Jeff—who still lay motionless in the back hall—past the back door and the bag of spilled charcoal, and into the kitchen. Rick stood at the sink, clutching his hand and wrapping a towel around the bloody wound.

"You faggot bastard!" shouted Rick.

Not wasting a moment, Rick grabbed a wine bottle from the counter and hurled it. Todd ducked and the bottle crashed into pieces behind him. Desperate to stop Todd, even delay him for a moment, Rick yanked the toaster from the wall and threw it.

"It's over, Rick!" shouted Todd as he dodged the small appliance.

"Like hell!"

"Janice is outside. You're going to have to kill her too."

"Fuck you!"

"She's called the authorities."

His face red with frenzy, Rick grabbed a simple roll of paper towels and threw it at Todd as hard as he could, then continued on, lunging for the knives that were placed so carefully in a block of wood. The paper towels merely glanced off Todd, ricocheting off his shoulder and onto the stove, where they landed on the still-flaming burner.

"You're not getting away with this!" Todd yelled as he grabbed a frying pan from a rack and lunged toward Rick.

Behind Todd, the paper towels caught fire, tumbled off the stove, and rolled toward the back door, where the broad puddle of spilled lighter fluid burst into flames. Almost simultaneously, a rich blue fire snaked across the floor and down the basement stairs, where recycled newspapers, a straw broom, a can of turpentine, and a variety of other items were stashed. In seconds a cloud of black smoke came eagerly to life and started billowing upward.

Rick grabbed a long, arching knife in his left hand and awkwardly took a swipe. Todd held out the frying pan, blocked the blade. Rick danced to the left, took another slash, missed completely. Todd saw the crazed glaze in Rick's eyes, knew he was more dangerous, more desperate than ever. And when Rick came diving at him again, Todd ducked and fell back against the refrigerator. Rick's blade came slashing at him again, and this time Todd swung the pan and caught Rick on the knuckles.

There was a loud rumbling, and Todd glanced at the now fiery doorway to the basement. A moment later there was a second explosion, this one larger and causing the entire house to rock. Suddenly there was a sharp screeching noise, and the two old gas fixtures in the kitchen exploded. Blue flames nearly two feet tall erupted, and Todd knew at once that the gas lines were on fire.

Todd seized the moment, swinging the frying pan as hard

as he could and smashing Rick on his wounded right hand. Rick screamed in pain, dropped the knife, and clutched himself. The next instant he kicked at Todd, then turned and darted out of the kitchen, through the back hall and toward the front of the house. Todd started after him, hesitated, glanced back at the flames. Shielding his face, Todd rushed through the smoke now pouring out of the basement and found Jeff still in a heap on the floor. Grabbing Jeff by the shoulders, Todd started dragging him toward the bathroom, which Janice had entered via the other door.

"I've got Rawlins!" she shouted as she wrapped an arm around the dazed man and helped him to his feet. "Rick ran upstairs!"

The old gas fixtures in the dining and living rooms were spewing flames as well, and Todd dragged Jeff after Janice and Rawlins, all of them hurrying toward the front door. Rich black smoke started pumping out of the heating grates in the floor. This entire hulking, bone-dry structure was going to be consumed within minutes.

Finally dragging Jeff onto the porch, Todd looked out and saw the flashing lights of the Channel 7 van in the front yard. Determined to give them the truth, Todd left Jeff there and turned back into the house.

"Todd!" shouted Janice after him. "No!"

But he paid her no attention, running through the front hall and bounding up the steps two at a time. Upstairs he started down the second-floor hall, already thick with smoke. Just ahead of him another gas fixture was spewing flames, this one scorching and burning the flowered wallpaper, and he ducked his head as the smoke bit at his eyes.

Suddenly a figure leapt out of a room toward a set of stairs leading upward. The attic. Shit, thought Todd. The door slammed shut and seconds later Todd grabbed for the handle. But it was locked. He pulled and twisted as hard as he could, but it didn't budge.

"Rick!" shouted Todd. "Rick!"

Todd tugged to no avail on the locked attic door. He desperately opened the next door, and a cannon of smoke and flames burst out, blasting Todd in the face. It was the back stairs, entirely engulfed in flames, and Todd stumbled back, coughed and gagged for air.

"Rick!" he shouted one last time.

But there was no answer.

Todd groped for the wall. The smoke was so thick he could barely see. His eyes burned and blurred. The stairs, where were they? Ahead. Yes, he told himself, right up there. And finally the wall gave way and he was there, right at the top of the staircase. He glanced back, saw the billowing smoke and the bristling flames. Todd wiped the smoke from his eyes and stumbled downward.

A voice yelled, "Todd!"

Janice was rushing up, grabbing him by the arm. Leading him on. Through the entry. Out the front door. Onto the porch. Into the night. Todd paused, coughed deeply and painfully, then turned back into the house.

"Come on, doll," coaxed Janice.

"But . . . but Rick . . ."

"Both the police and the fire department are on the way."

"He's in the attic."

"They'll do what they can."

Todd turned and glanced across the front yard. Jeff was sitting on the sidewalk, his head bent forward, rubbing his neck. Rawlins was standing next to a tree, his hand over his eyes. And then, as Janice helped him down the front steps, Todd saw two people rushing toward him. One of them was holding a microphone in her hand. The other was aiming a large video camera at him.

"Todd!" called Cindy Wilson. "Todd, can we have a few words? What happened inside?"

He looked at her, then at Mark Buchanan. Of course he'd given Janice their number, told her to call the station. Of course he'd wanted this disaster captured on videotape. But now that they were here, what was he to say, how was he to put it?

"Todd, any comment for the CrimeEye?"

He coughed, cleared his throat. He wanted to tell Cindy and all of Channel 7 to go to hell. And yet he wanted to show them and every viewer the truth.

"Is this live?" he asked.

She looked at her watch, and replied, "No, but the ten o'clock news comes on in about four minutes."

"Okay, okay . . ." he said, his mind struggling to switch gears. "Call the station and tell them this is going to be their lead story. Then get Mark over to the garage. He can get a good shot of the whole house from there. Then get me a rag or something so I can clean up. You can—"

"Forget it, Todd," Cindy said bluntly. "This is my story and I'm going to be doing the interviewing. You're not taking this one from me, got it? Now, you either let me ask you some questions or I'll proceed without you. Which is it?"

Todd looked away, stared up at the burning house. No corner of his life had escaped untouched, had it?

"Okay." He turned back to her. "But Channel Seven has been making me look like shit, and I won't take it."

"Fair enough." She turned to Mark and said, "I want you to set up by the garage. We're going to do this one live. And ask the station to give me the lead spot."

"No, don't ask them, tell them. Insist. Make it clear you're the best they've got."

"Right. Tell them we have to have the lead." She glanced at the burning house. "Tell them we got the hottest thing yet."

Todd then turned away from her, walking across the grass. So what was he going to say? Was this his chance to publicly lambaste Channel 7? To curse them for portraying him so negatively, for making it seem he was guilty before proven innocent, all in the name of ratings? Or was this his chance to stand on a soapbox and lecture Channel 7 and all of their viewers on how his morality was defined not by his sexuality, but his deeds? Or Michael, should he tell them how much he loved him, how deeply he would miss and mourn him? All of the above, realized Todd. He'd work it all in. As well as his resignation. Yes, that too.

Something shattered behind him, and Todd turned. The dining room window crumbled to bits, and flames began pouring out, licking the side of the house. He stared up at the third floor, thought for a moment he saw Rick in one of the front windows. No, perhaps not. In any case, it was too late. Even though he heard sirens approaching, they'd never be able to save him. God, no. The entire house was a goner.

Before and after. In the closet. And out. Nothing, Todd knew, would ever be the same again. Why, he wondered with a melancholic yet huge sense of relief, had it taken him so damn long?

"I was afraid they'd take me off the case," said a voice behind him.

Todd turned, saw Rawlins standing there, and didn't know what to say.

"I saw Michael down at the bar after your fight. And then I got up the gall to stop by his place later on. I wanted . . . I wanted to . . . well, I wanted him to dump you so that he and I could . . ." Rawlins shook his head, looked away. "I thought it would be great, the two of us back together again, but Michael wouldn't hear of it. He said thanks, but he already had a Mr. Wonderful."

"Michael said that? After what I did?" Todd shook his head in disbelief.

"Well, maybe he didn't call you Mr. Wonderful."

"Unfortunately, I rather doubt it."

"And then when he was killed and Jeff told me what Michael had found out about Rick, well, I wasn't going to let go of it. I had to find the proof. The department would have pulled me from the case if they'd known Michael was such a close friend."

"And you were. In the end you were the best kind of friend to him."

"Thanks."

Across the yard, Cindy Wilson shouted, "Todd, we're almost live!"

"Okay," he called back.

Todd turned, started to go. But then Rawlins caught him by the arm.

"Wait . . ." Rawlins glanced at the ground. "You remember what I said about my first lover being the best?"

"Sure."

Rawlins shook his head, looked away with a shy grin. "Well, actually, my last one was pretty special."

"Are you saying . . ."

"Shit, you been playing dumb so long that you got it down to an art."

Todd managed a small laugh. "Okay, so maybe we need to talk."

"Todd!" shouted Cindy. "Thirty seconds!"

Rawlins quickly asked, "What are you going to say?"

Todd shrugged. "The truth—that Cindy Wilson is really a male chauvinist pig in drag. Determined, I might add, to take my place at the feed trough."

As Todd started toward Channel 7's camera, he heard a ghostly voice, the one that had chided him about finding room in his heart to love himself, the one that had urged him to let go of the fear, the self-hate, that gentle, wise voice that had lectured him on how others would perccive him, saying, "Just remember, people are going to take their cues from you."